INGRID PITT

ANNUL DOMINI:
THE JESUS FACTOR

avalard™
Avalard Publishing

An Avalard Original

Published by Avalard Publishing
Annadorn, Co. Down, UK

1st Edition
Published simultaneously in
hardback and eBook March 2012

www.avalardpublishing.com

ISBN: 978-1-908566-16-4 (Hardback)
ISBN: 978-1-908566-18-8 (eBook)

avalard™

We hope you enjoy this book.
Please visit the Ingrid Pitt Archive at www.ingridpitt.net

Foreword
by Tony Rudlin

Ingrid Pitt came late to writing but once she had the bug it was difficult to stop her. It all started in Argentina. We were there to shoot a film called *El Ultimo Enemigo.* Unfortunately we had hardly started when there was a revolution and we found ourselves hustled off to Uruguay out of harm's way. After a month or so we got word that we could return to Buenos Aires. This Buenos Aires was very different from the one we had left. A military Junta was in charge – and its influence even stretched to the film industry. And their largesse didn't stretch to a film about a woman overthrowing a Military Junta. So it was back to *quadro uno.*

We decided to write a script about a young Welsh girl who inherits a large Estancia in Patagonia. Ingrid, when she had told her mother that she wanted to be an actress, had agreed to take a secretarial course as a fall-back position. So we started by me scribbling on pieces of paper and Ingrid transforming it into something readable. The partnership worked well and it soon became obvious that Ingrid had a bent for writing.

At first it tended to be me doing the writing and Ingrid shoving her pencil in when she thought she could do better. My experience in writing was strictly journalistic – Ingrid wanted more passion. This caused a few problems at first but it soon became obvious that she was capable of producing something readable on her own. Without any agreement or planning Ingrid gradually took over the role of writer and I became a sort of editor and advisor. Advice was often ignored.

About this time we formed a Theatre Touring Company, TRIP, (**T**ony **R**udlin **I**ngrid **P**itt). There was no doubt what our roles were. While Ingrid was away on tour she spent the day churning out manuscripts on her little blue portable Olivetti. At home in Richmond I decided to have the carpets cleaned. When the bed was moved I found a box of typewritten pages marked CUCKOO RUN. When I read it I was hugely impressed. It was much too long, about a quarter of a million words. Too many for a publishers to take on from an unpublished author. I cut it down to a more manageable 100,000 words and the next time I went up to town dropped it off at the offices of Futura. A couple of weeks later I got a call from the editor, Margery Chapman. She liked *Cuckoo Run* and wanted to publish it. Ingrid was appearing in the theatre at Cleethorpes. When I rang her and told her the good news she went berserk and raced up the pier in the pouring rain to tell everybody she was now a published author.

KATARINA, about the Treblinka Concentration Camp, was published by Methuen who also printed THE PERONS, a *faction* about the President of Argentina, Juan Domingo Peron and his beautiful wife, Evita. About this time Ingrid was approached by Batsford to write a number of factual books based on horror and the supernatural. Bedside Companions for VAMPIRE LOVERS and GHOSTS were followed by MURDER, TORTURE AND DEPRAVITY. For a while these became a bit of an obsession and the books she had written while on tour were packed away. She later wrote her autobiography, LIFE'S A SCREAM and a book about Hammer, commissioned by Hammer, about her time with the company called THE HAMMER XPERIENCE. She then turned her hand to life as a journalist and columnist. At one time she was writing for six magazines simultaneously as well as fielding guest pieces in many newspapers and lifestyle magazines. The rigours of book writing no longer appealed and she preferred the quick turnover that the press offered.

The books lay, getting more faded and tattered as time went by, in a filing cabinet After Ingrid died and I was packing up to move to Hastings I came across them.. Some of the pages were almost unreadable. I thought I owed it to Ingrid to restore them and see what could be done with them. I bought an OCR thingy and laboriously restored the manuscripts to a readable form. ANNUL DOMINI, DRACULA WHO....?, PIGEON TANGO (a follow-up to *Cuckoo Run*), HISAKO SAN and a follow up to *The Perons* called THE CHAUFFEUR are now all ready for publication and hopefully due to hit the shelves in the next couple of years.

Tony Rudlin
Hastings, March 2012

Chapter 1

The angry sound of flies woke him. Without moving he listened to their drill-like buzz and tried to orientate himself.

It wasn't easy.

The dream had been too vivid. Even now there seemed to be a confused blurring of the edges between reality and fantasy. He knew it would be all right when he made the final effort to wake but for the moment he was content to stay in the twilight zone.

If it wasn't for those damn flies!

Again he fought the intrusion of his nightmare. The flies frightened him. He raised an uncoordinated hand and brushed his face. The movement caused a frenzy of infuriated buzzing. He let his hand fall onto his face. Slowly it dawned on him that it didn't feel right... Under his fingers he could feel rank, coarse textured hair. His hand traced the outline of his chin. Instead of the firm, clean shaven jaw he expected, he felt a thick bushy beard.

It was wrong!

He was aware of the nightmare state returning but he was unable to do anything about it. Distorted thoughts pushed his reasoning brain further and further back and a grey, mindless box shut off his responses. Robin felt that if he couldn't get his eyes open he would lose his personality. He was aware that the thought was ludicrous but his ability to think rationally seemed to be going from him.

Even more worrying was the blank wall that shut off his past. He was operating on distinct, separate levels with all lines of communication between them severed. Robin Firth struggled to bring the erring facets of his mind together. He knew who he was but the actual facts of his existence seemed to be just eluding his panicking mind. And then there was the deeper level. The one he felt he had the least control over - the physical mind; control of his body.

There was a pressure growing in his head. The clarity of his reasoning ego was being gradually distorted by his feverish search for existence. Robin fought back. His control over his inner mind grew. He tried to make sense out of his present situation; to identify himself.

Suddenly he knew with startling clarity that it wasn't a dream. It was something to do with...

No good, whatever it was eluded him, so he concentrated on getting a response from his body. With an effort he opened his eyes. He was lying on his back. For a moment he was blinded by the sun, but a slight movement of his head shaded his eyes. Robin stared in bewilderment at the rough canvas flapping gently a few inches above his face. There was something terribly wrong.

Why couldn't he concentrate?

Why did the canvas look so familiar yet at the same time utterly alien? He turned his head. He seemed to be lying on a sand floor in a crudely made tent. Again he had the sense of familiarity - the feeling that things were as they should be. Amazed he felt a gurgling laugh push through his teeth and hammer at the shrinking borders of his lucidity.

"Haddaq happy! Haddaq home!"

His brain tried to cope. Robin fought the urge to laugh. His fevered brain throbbed. His hand came up to massage his temples.

And the control he fought to maintain snapped.

The dark, claw-like hand, with its long filthy nails, on the end of the hairy arm, was not his.

With a scream Robin pushed himself to his feet demolishing the low lean-to of canvas and sticks. As he looked down at the filthy rags draping his emaciated body he felt another personality take over his mind. A gibbering, unreasoning personality that held onto its distorted brain pattern by reaffirming its name.

"Haddaq frightened! Haddaq frightened!"

The words beat at Robin's reason. Disjointed images appeared in the brain that Robin shared with the strengthening Haddaq.

It was totally confusing.

To Haddaq the images were normal, unremarkable, but to the Robin overlay they were totally alien. Robin stood in the centre of a collection of small buildings made from mud and thatched with palm fronds. Directly in front of him was an artesian well around which a number of small, black clad women sat nursing children and gossiping. The scene was familiar but Robin was sure he had never seen it before. He staggered forward. Against his will a gabble of unintelligible words flowed, unchecked, from his lips.

"Haddaq want water."

His body jerked forward and stumbled towards the well.

The women looked up as he approached but seemed unperturbed by his sudden appearance. As he tried to get to the well one of the women pushed him to one side and without breaking off her conversation with one of her companions, thrust a bowl of water in his hand. Gratefully Robin slopped the water into his mouth.

The water calmed him. He felt stronger. No longer so menaced by the Haddaq side of his brain. With difficulty he placed the bowl back on the side of the well and turned to thank the woman who had given him the water.

His tongue was unresponsive.

"Haddaq... Haddaq..." was all he seemed to be able to manage.

Annoyed at the interruption of her conversation, the woman pushed him roughly in the chest causing him to stagger and fall against the side of the well. As he looked down into the water the battered remnants of his reason fled.

Reflected in the still water was a face from hell.

Long matted hair joined the beard and spread in a wild tangle over rag-clad shoulders. Mad eyes burned out of a filthy, sore-covered face and were a matched pair for the loose, distorted mouth, dribbling saliva.

A wild scream tore from his throat and he blundered back into the women. His torment amused them and they beat at him until he was forced to run. The excitement had awoken the dogs and they left the shade to rush to the attack.

Again the scene was familiar to Robin, and yet something he was sure he had never encountered before.

The Haddaq personality was strong now. Robin was just a distant observer. He watched as Haddaq fought off the dogs, listened to the repetitive babble that poured from the loose lips in a meaningless stream. Saw the children, drawn by the noise, appear in the little square and pick up stones and throw them with cruel accuracy at the stumbling man.

"Haddaq hurt! Haddaq run away..." The dull mind assured itself and the body went into a halting run.

The children pursued him to the edge of the village and then went back to their work. The incident of the village madman a welcome break in the heavy tasks they had to perform.

It was a long time before the disappearance of the tormenting children was noticed. As the body tired, the Haddaq personality appeared to subside and Robin became stronger. He was still confused and floating in a sea of darkness but it was reassuring to feel that he was no longer subservient to the monster that tried to control his body.

Exhausted and on the borders of unconsciousness he sank down onto the stony sand by the side of the road. As he lay panting, images flitted across his mind. Tall, hard buildings glinting like polished gold in the sun. Vehicles running in never ending convoys between high walls and everywhere people dressed in sparse utilitarian clothes. Robin seemed to be riding in one of the vehicles. It was familiar and natural but somehow distant and unconnected. He saw himself sitting high in the air overlooking a strange city. The phantoms frightened him. In spite of their familiarity he was unable to associate them with anything stable or relevant. Again he seemed to be back in the midst of the fast moving vehicles. Faces loomed at him and disappeared. Noise crashed into his head and tried to pull it apart. Comforting darkness crowded in and Robin gratefully let it purge his tormented mind.

A voice spoke to him out of the blackness.

He understood what it said but when he concentrated the words were strange and alien. It was like hearing a foreign language and getting an instant translation.

"That's better. Try to drink some more."

Gratefully he let the cool water fill his throat. He opened his eyes and looked at the bearded man holding the bowl. Robin was calmer now. He was still no nearer awareness of his position, but there was no longer the uncontrolled Haddaq intruding on his thoughts. There was a reason for being where he was. At the moment it was obscured but it would come back.

Robin smiled at his benefactor and tried to speak. Panic came back as the thick tongue refused to pronounce the words he tried to say. Concentrating on the words brought back their alien sound. It was confusing. He seemed to think in one language but wanted to speak in another, unknown, but overwhelmingly familiar. The man hunkered down beside him could see the distress and the rising excitement. Soothingly he patted the wetted end of his long woollen galabia against Robin's temple.

"Calm yourself, son. You are all right now. Just lie there for a few moments and gather your strength. You've been lying in the sun too long but you'll be all right."

Weakly Robin nodded and let the older man help him sit up.

"My name is Isaac. I'm from Galilee. Who are you?"

The word *Galilee* exploded in Robin's mind and echoed louder and louder.

"Galilee!"

It was important. There was some connection. It meant something to him, but his schizophrenic mind wouldn't supply the answer. Isaac watched him, unsure of what to do. The tattered figure he had found by the roadside looked like one of the tramps that wandered the desert, but it was unusual to find them out in the open during the midday heat. Their instinct for survival in the arid wastelands made them too cunning. He offered the bowl of water again but the man seemed to be having a fit. Froth had formed at the corners of his mouth and his lips writhed as if he were trying to say something but only a meaningless, guttural whine came out.

Isaac inched away, frightened that his act of charity had been towards a man in the throes of rabies. Pushing the bowl aside Robin stumbled to his feet and looked around. On the narrow footpath wandering through the low foothills stood Isaac's team of mules laden with merchandise. Beside each of the mules stood a black-robed woman. Robin was aware of their wide, dark eyes staring at him from the security of their jashmaks.

It was all as it should be. Why then could he not understand it? Vague shapes and sounds echoed in his mind.

Pushing aside the kneeling Isaac he staggered up the slope to the caravan of mules. The women watched him approach with the first flicker of fear in their eyes. Robin ran his hands over the coarse hide of the nearest mule and then felt his own rough clothes and unkempt beard. He turned to look at Isaac watching him from the side of the road. The need to communicate was like a burning brand in his head. His eyes bulged and his breathing almost stopped. With a super-human effort he sought control of his thick tongue.

"Robin! My…name is...Robin!"

He forced the words out one by one, aware that his alter-ego had awoken and was trying to destroy his rigid control. He felt the maniacal laughter building inside him. Robin wanted to scream and shout the one name that he knew he must not utter or he would lose the modicum of control he had managed to gain.

"Haddaq. Haddaq. Haddaq!"

The name beat at his bones and tried to escape from his tightly clenched teeth. Robin could feel the sheer mindless strength of the word squeezing sanity from his thoughts.

Beside the road grew a stunted iron thorn tree with hard, inch-long spikes like nails jutting from the branches. Deliberately Robin concentrated on raising his hand. The pain as the thorns bit deep into the flesh of his palm sanitized his thoughts and drove the babbling Haddaq back. Robin let the pain swell and cauterise his brain. He saw Isaac running towards him and tried to smile reassuringly but he felt weak and tired. He sank to his knees and let therapeutic tears wash over his burned face.

Again the mysterious figures that he knew so well, flooded in. Through the shadows of the hard, tall world he seemed to inhabit in another life he could see Isaac help one of the women pull the thorns from his palms and wrap his hands in bandages. He wanted to tell them not to worry, that those hands had nothing to do with him. They were Haddaq's hands. The thought of Haddaq called him from the dark recesses where he skulked. Before Robin could put up a defence Haddaq smashed into his mind. Mercifully Robin felt the darkness rush in and swamp both of them.

Chapter 2

The Eastern looks of the young Johannes had been used to advantage.

Dressed from the slop-chest furnished by the booty from recent raids, Johannes ventured into Landan.

He was readily accepted as a minor Islam official so long as he kept his mouth shut and out of situations where he might be uncovered.

He was able to move about with comparative freedom. Within a year his quick wit and nimble brain had supplied him with a good understanding of Arabic and he could become more adventurous in his search for intelligence. Just to make sure that his accent was not penetrated to expose him as a Briton, he developed a disguising lisp. The need for any such ploy had long vanished, but the lisp remained.

Johannes could have gone on making a passable living as a small-time trader and part-time spy if it hadn't been for the devastating effect the firearms, now introduced to most branches of the Pict Police, had on the forces of the Underground.

Johannes was ordered to get up-to-date information on the construction of the weapons and the formula for making the powder. The Britons figured that with their greater inventiveness and pressure, they could soon outstrip the conservative Arabs and the less aggressively minded Chinese.

It was a new concept of spying as far as Johannes was concerned. So far, he had been a non-directional listening post. If information came his way, he passed it on. If it didn't, he didn't go out of his way to track it down.

His attempt had been clumsy.

Nobody without special qualifications had access to the innermost part of the city.

So Johannes tried to bribe an Arab technician.

A meeting had been set up for the men to meet some dissidents who wanted to contact the local rebels.

Natural caution had stopped him rushing in without a certain amount of circumspection.

Johannes suggested the fenland on the outskirts of the city on an island bounded by the river Temases. That way he would be able to see who approached and make his getaway by boat if he didn't like the set up.

The meeting had been agreed for midday. Johannes arrived before dawn and selected an observation post where he could command the approach from upstream as well as the marshy land to the east. Across the river was the south bank with dense forest coming right to the edge.

The day before he had moored and hidden a boat on the island opposite the trees. If he thought there was any danger he intended to row across the river and disappear into the forest.

It was a warm day and Johannes had a job staying awake through the long morning. As the sun rose higher he told himself that his caution was a waste of time and he let his concentration wane.

He jerked into sudden alertness when he heard his name called. Alarmed, he flattened into the bracken and tried to locate the sound.

From his right he heard a twig snap and the rustle of ferns as someone forced their way through.

"Johannes!"

The call came again. It was close at hand but in spite of the open nature of the ground he couldn't see who was calling.

He cursed himself.

If anyone could get that close without him seeing them it was obvious that he had been asleep. It meant that a whole army could be concealed out there and because of his stupidity he wouldn't know.

Again there was a movement and his name called cautiously.

Whoever it was out there didn't want to be seen.

Johannes thought about it. It sounded all right. Whoever had come to meet him would have reservations about it also. It gave him confidence to feel that his contact was so careful.

He drew in a breath to let the hidden men know where he was when the sharp, warning snap of a dry fern breaking underfoot froze him into immobility.

It was from the other direction to that he had identified as the hiding place of his contact.

He sank down again and listened. A partridge clattered into the air and flew low across the fern in indignant fear. Down by the waters' edge a brace of moorhens ran in blind panic across the sluggishly flowing river.

Fear pressed down on Johannes. He felt trapped.

He had seen nothing that confirmed his feeling, but his long years on the periphery of violence had built in an alarm system that he had learned to ignore at his peril.

He watched a low flying chevron of ducks approach the island. Without warning they separated into two phalanxes as they spotted danger below their intended flight path.

Johannes made up his mind. He needed to be away. He gave up the idea of the boat to take him across to the south bank. Somehow he had to get to the north bank by fording it in one of the shallows.

He eased in the direction that felt safe. Two hours later he had moved about a hundred yards and was exhausted. In the open terrain he was a target as soon as he raised his head. But he couldn't go on.

He had just decided to lie up and wait for nightfall when he heard a noise.

He raised his head and looked to where his boat had been hidden. The discovery of the boat had told them that their quarry hadn't been altogether happy with the arrangements for the meeting and his non-cooperation in showing himself meant that he knew they were there.

They abandoned their plan to take him by stealth.

A whistle shrilled in the still afternoon air and fifty men, like Jason's dragon teeth, grew from the island bracken.

Johannes stared open-mouthed.

The nearest man was only twenty or so yards from his resting place. He had come the short distance he had maneuvered on pure luck.

Again he cursed himself with futile fury for having dozed off and let himself be surrounded and blocked from his escape route.

Frightened that a movement might attract the searchers, he slowly sank back to the damp earth. A second whistle pierced the air and he heard the men move off in the direction of the boat. He hugged the ground closer, frightened that men behind him might, inadvertently, discover his refuge.

Although a couple passed within a few yards of him he was unseen.

When he felt it was safe, he took another look.

The men had spread out and were moving in line abreast across the island. He recognised them instantly as a local division of the Pict Police by their polished leather tunics and black and red tartan kilts. On their brass reinforced berets they had the black scarf, worn turban-like as a gesture to their employers, of the dreaded Mosque Special Police.

Johannes felt sick with fear.

In their hands he could expect no quarter.

Innocent or guilty, nobody ever survived unscathed a visit to their headquarters in the old Roman fortress on the banks of the river below the old bridge.

And they were moving towards him in a chain that couldn't be breached.

If he waited until they got nearer he would have less of a head start.

Johannes drew a couple of deep breaths, more in an effort to cool his racing heart than to fill his lungs, and broke cover.

Instantly he heard a yell taken up by others along the advancing line. Bent double to present as small a target as possible for their firearms, he snatched a look behind.

Still strung out, so that he could not double back and outflank them in an attempt to reach his boat, the Police were now trotting after him.

He had intended to pace himself so that he would not be exhausted before having to face the river but the sight of the implacable line behind him drove caution out and replaced it with blind panic.

In sight of the river, he realised that all was lost.

Lined up along the riverbank, cutting off any chance of escape, was another patrol of kilted Police.

It hit him that this was more than an exercise put on to trap an over inquisitive trader. Somehow they had learned of his links with the British guerrillas and wanted him alive.

In desperation he veered to the right.

As he did, he saw one of the men raise a long firearm and sight it on his fleeing form. Before he could duck, he saw the weapon buck in the man's hand, a flash at the end of the barrel and something hit him with tremendous force in the side of the head, cart-wheeling him forward into the scrub.

As he lost consciousness he hoped he would die before the Pict Police could get to him.

Chapter 3

The hard metallic blue of the sky, resting on the sharply defined caps of the mountain range, gave notice of the coming summer. In the valley the eddying air currents, conjured up by the changing temperatures of the late afternoon, tore with nagging fingers at the nervous palms and indifferent olive trees. The bright, shadowless light lent uneasiness to the desert scene, and robbed distance of dimension. Even the small strips of cultivated earth, shouldering jealously at the narrow trough of water bringing irrigation to the valley floor, were bleached of colour and looked dead and sour.

Under a tall olive tree, supporting and shading the front of the tavern, a long rough table divided two bench seats. On one side of the table sat a man who would stand out in any company. From his confident manner it was obvious that he was used to getting his way and would not take kindly to being thwarted. The natural hued woollen galabia took on a style and grandeur from the tough, well-proportioned body beneath it. Above average height with long black hair framing a strong, weathered face, his wide-spaced, hooded eyes looked cynically at the three men facing him. James picked unconcernedly at a plate of dried dates and let his companions work out their grievances. He was aware of a number of other men spread out around the area and especially of the two that had quietly manoeuvred to stand behind him. The crude tactics of the man opposite didn't bother him. Aliph was a petty criminal that political expediency had promoted to leader of a group of reckless outlaws that had preyed for years on the unguarded, agricultural communities of the valley. Civil unrest in the cities and growing resentment of the heavy Roman hand hardly reached out as far as this. The farmer's problems were more basic. Keeping a constant water supply to the crops and making sure that the circling crows didn't get their harvest kept them isolated from more sophisticated worries. Ignorance was no defence and the growing conflict of interest between the Hebrew ruling classes and their military masters, the Romans, reached out into the isolated communities and brought a growing unease and distrust of strangers. The unrest had one beneficial result. Searching out the outlaws worked against the Romans. Gradually the hard, resourceful criminals deserted the easy pickings of the plains and banded together in uneasy squadrons in the inhospitable mountains. Regular clashes with the policing Roman patrols resulted in a satisfying number of victories for the bandits and soon they were regarded as genuine patriots waging guerrilla warfare against the invaders. From there it was an easy step to bracket them with the ancient warrior sect of the Zealots. The glamour of popular respect, for a time, changed the nature of the outlaws. They began to see themselves as the last heroes.

James saw the possibilities in the ragged groups and fed their egos with stories of the riches to be won and the fame of defeating the Romans and driving them from the land.

For a year Aliph and his band of desperados waited for the call to arms in their cold, inhospitable caves, gradually becoming disillusioned with the diverging polemic. Now they wanted action and James could see that it was not going to be possible to keep them fettered much longer.

This was a shame because the situation had changed in the last twelve months. It had become less vital to mount an open attack on the military governors. Rome's rule was weakening. Trouble throughout the empire had escalated in the wake of the explosion following Julius Caesar's murder and Rome had found it expedient to devolve power to local Tetrarchs.

So successful had the policy been that the latest Jewish 'King', Herod Antipas, by pledging unequivocal support for Tiberius Caesar, had strengthened the role of the Jews in the running of the country. Reduction in the number of Legions and less frequent communication with the Roman sponsored trade routes all contributed to a reduction of pressure. Now it seemed that a policy of friendship and understanding was likely to bring better results than graffiti and a well-honed knife across the windpipe.

But how did you sell laurel-branch philosophy to a mob of uneducated, mountain men whose ideas of glory hardly rose above stripping the merchants of their gold and raping any women with a drop of warm blood in their veins that chanced their way.

It wasn't easy, James acknowledged.

Aliph's job was even more hazardous. If he was going to go along with the new line he had to sell it to his cutthroats and they weren't famed for their charity.

James spat a date-pip forcefully into the sand some distance from the table and gave the wiry little man an avuncular smile.

"I don't want an argument, friend," he said in a quiet, agreeable tone. "You have got to make your men understand. There is to be no revolution for the moment. If things don't work out right then we will think again. For the moment we want you to hold off. If you try anything on your own you will fail. The Romans will cut you to pieces. You will get no support from either the villagers or the other guerrillas. You have to understand..."

James was cut short by Aliph slamming both hands with an echoing crash on the table. James didn't so much as blink. Before he could continue Aliph thrust his face close to his.

"Understand? What is there to understand? The last time you came through here with your brother you promised that if we banded together and waited your call to action we would be able to destroy the Romans and seize their property and gold. We have kept our side of the bargain! We have sat patiently in the hills training and waiting for your signal to go into action." Aliph jumped excitedly up from the table and shouted at James, thudding his fist in the palm of his hand for emphasis.

"Nothing! Messages saying 'hold on, wait a bit longer.' 'Wait until the weather's colder', 'wait until the weather's warmer.' Wait! Wait! Wait! The only thing that has kept my Zealots together is the stories of the great leader who is going to sweep everything before him. Well - where is he? Show him to me! Show him to me or I join forces with Seph and lay every village between here and Jerusalem waste. That's not a threat, that's a solemn promise and you can tell Jesus just that!" Aliph again slammed his hands on the table and leaned aggressively towards the seated James.

The expression on James's face didn't change as he swept Aliph's hands off the table and the guerrilla leader, off balance, tottered towards him. James gripped him by the throat and stood up. It was obvious from the ease with which he held the writhing bandit that he was abnormally strong. He gave Aliph a couple of shakes and then held him at a distance, the steel band of his fingers encircling his victim's windpipe, squashing any resistance.

"Listen to me carefully, little man," James said in a low, agreeable voice. "You just do as you are told. The first show of anything unscheduled and I will personally lead the Romans to you. Do you understand?" James looked expectantly at Aliph but he was almost unconscious.

The big man was aware that the other men were closing in menacingly. He shrugged and let go of Aliph's throat. Gasping the guerrilla sank to his knees and stayed there until he had regained control of himself. Solicitously James bent and helped the panting man to his feet.

"Come on - we shouldn't be arguing. I think we understand each other now. It was a good thing to clear the air. Now - another bottle of wine? Landlord!"

James, still smiling, returned to take his seat. His way was blocked by one of Aliph's men. In his hand a long dagger aimed at James's stomach. The big man's smile didn't falter. He gripped the bandit's wrist and squeezed. Grunting with pain his hand slowly opened and James took the knife and without appearing to aim, hurled the blade with tremendous force into the bole of the olive tree five yards away. It drove in up to the hilt bringing a gasp of awe from the tough mountain men. James released the man's wrist and sat down.

"Now come on. No more business. Let's all have a drink. After all, we are all friends here."

Slowly the men came back and sat down at the table and allowed James to refill their wooden goblets with the strong red wine.

Chapter 4

The room is tall and filled with boxes that wink and flare with light. The air is heavy with a dense acrid smell that seems an extension of the crackle and buzz that makes a low-key cacophony of sound to underscore the scene. Men in short white robes move purposefully amongst the lights, occasionally touching the boxes with gentle respect. It was a familiar scene. Robin tried to adjust to it. First he concentrated on the lighted cabinets. Tried to remember their purpose. The more he probed his mind for information the less distinct the picture became. He shifted his focus to the men. Again their function eluded him. It was as if only his peripheral vision were working. So long as he did not try to make sense of what was going on he had an overall awareness. An awareness of himself - of his purpose and his situation.

But it didn't help him much.

As soon as he tried to go beyond the general picture, to concentrate on any particular aspect, his mind wandered and he was unable to make sense of what was happening. What was even more alarming was the terrible feeling of menace that came from within - the glowering presence of the unstable Haddaq pushing and nudging on the borders of sanity, ready to rip Robin's last vestige of lucidity from its uneasy resting place.

Robin felt hands lift him and place him in a sitting position in the soft sand. Reluctantly he forced his eyes open and peered around. He was back in the village again. The man Isaac stood over him looking down with a puzzled expression on his face. Behind him Robin could see the villagers huddled together in groups talking and giggling. The arrival of the merchant with his team of mules and women was novel enough to cause excitement. That he should bring back their fool and treat him with all the respect that would be accorded a sane man was something to marvel at.

In the familiar surroundings Haddaq suddenly reared up with renewed strength. Before Robin had a chance to suppress the gurgling laughter the mad man wrenched back his mind.

"Haddaq! Haddaq!"

The word twisted from his tongue and forced Robin back into the depths from where he could see events only through the distorted mind of his host body. Panic hit Robin then. His sense of purpose, his knowledge that he was there in the mind of another person, out of his own time, for a specific reason, had acted as a bulwark against all the ego-sapping attacks to his sanity he had sustained since he first become aware of his paradoxical position. But the ease with which the deviant mind of Haddaq thrust him aside and almost crushed the spark of his personality beyond recall, frightened him. Dimly he was aware of a voice calling him. As the light of his personality flickered on the edge of extinction he heard his name:

"Robin!"

It echoed and grew. It was like a life belt. He inflated the word in his mind, cherished it, gave it substance and then buried his ego-flame solidly in its depth.

Gradually feeling returned. He was aware of the pain in his palms and he remembered the hard spikes of the Iron-thorn tree. Angrily he took charge of the fevered, skittering thoughts that Haddaq had started and still pushed perilously at the shaky walls of Robin's mind. He stopped the subconscious whine filling the back of his throat and straightened up the weak, sore covered body. Like a drunk he opened his eyes and stared unblinkingly into the compassionate eyes of the man bending solicitously over him with a bowl of water. Desperately he formed the word that had become the symbol of his salvation:

"Robin!"

The word was thick and guttural but understandable. Isaac nodded.

"Robin! Come on Robin, drink some water. It will make you feel better."

Shakily, Robin held the bowl to his lips and drank deeply. His eyes roved over the villagers. They were silent now, sensing that something beyond the ordinary was happening.

Suddenly the fear of the familiar yet totally alien surroundings was back and he started to shake. Aghast, he heard again the keening in his throat and felt his control start to slip. Isaac acted quickly. He wasn't sure exactly what was happening but he knew that the weak, filthy man wandering on the borders of insanity was more than he seemed. Isaac had listened to the babble of words that flowed unchecked from Robin's lips as they carried him into the village. Isaac hadn't understood most of what he said but enough of the sense came through to convince him that Robin was no ordinary madman. Even the name that he clung to was strange and not one that Haddaq, isolated in the small desert village and in the distorted vagaries of his damaged brain, was likely to have heard or been able to invent.

But the one word that had quickened Isaac's interest was one he had not expected to hear in this part of the country let alone on the lips of the village idiot: *Jesus.*

Robin had mentioned the name several times but more Isaac couldn't understand. And he felt it was important that he should understand. A traveller like Isaac heard many tales and was privy to many plans and ambitions. As a merchant he had access to sources denied less mobile citizens. The merchant carried messages from village to village and was entrusted with secrets that the Roman commander would have given heavy gold to know. For years now

Isaac had heard the tales of the Messiah. It was an oft repeated theme used as a threat by the Rabbis when they felt their control was slipping. When the Messiah came he was going to smash the might of Rome and restore sovereignty to the Jews - to the pious Jews of course; he wasn't going to have anything to do with the sinners.

Recently Messiah fever had increased. Although nobody actually came out in the open and proclaim him there seemed to be a general feeling that 'The King of the Jews' had already arrived and was about to swing into action. Isaac watched the religious fever grow.

John started it all. A wild violent man he came in from the desert and started baptizing people and telling them that God had fulfilled his promise and sent them a King. It caused a lot of trouble and in the end John was arrested. But not before he had set a fire that was being fanned into flame by Jesus and his followers.

Isaac's inquiring mind wanted to know more.

As Robin stiffened, and the obscene whine rose in his throat, the merchant slapped him across the face. The blow wasn't hard, but had enough sting to remind the jumbled brain to stay in touch. It was a dangerous move. Before Isaac could get to his feet he felt hard hands grasp his arms and pull him backwards. Off-balance, he sprawled in the sand. Crouched menacingly around him were half a dozen men attracted from the fields by the excitement. They had arrived just in time to witness Isaac striking Haddaq and that was enough to prod them into protective action.

Quickly Isaac sprung to his feet and waited for the attack. He was a full head taller than the tallest villager and years of good eating and strenuous living had packed his frame with hard muscle. It was appreciated by the villagers. Now that the initial thoughtless fury of their attack had deserted them, they looked at each other uneasily and wished that they could get out of the confrontation without a fight.

Their salvation arrived on the scene in the form of a short bustling black clad figure with shoulder length, greasy hair covered by a round black skull cap. His robe was shabby and faded with thick mud on the hem where he had been working in the field. Isaac watched him take up a defiant stance in front of the villagers and smiled to himself. He knew the type well. Every village had one. They were as obligatory as the fool. The fool gave the people a standard of superiority and the other a mediator with God and the outside world.

Isaac bowed towards the little man.

"Good day, Rabbi. I seem to be causing some trouble. That was not my intention. I assure you."

The Rabbi was mollified by Isaac's careful respect and swung angrily around to the men now grouped submissively behind him.

"What is going on here?" he demanded.

The men looked sheepishly at each other but said nothing. Without asking a second time the Rabbi grabbed the hair of the nearest man and twisted it, forcing him to his knees.

"Answer me! What have you been up to?"

Gasping, the man tried to answer but the Rabbi was shaking his head so hard he couldn't get the words out.

Isaac intervened.

"I think it was probably my fault, Rabbi. You see, I struck Haddaq and these men came to his defence," he explained.

The Rabbi let go of his victim's hair and turned slowly towards Isaac. The fury on his face had changed to genuine amazement. He looked at the figure of Haddaq leaning against the wall of the well and then at the merchant.

"You hit Haddaq?" he said.

Isaac nodded culpability.

"You hit Haddaq..." the Rabbi repeated unbelievingly to himself.

Pulling himself together he squared up to Isaac.

"It is not permitted to strike Haddaq. He has been touched by the hand of God."

Isaac nodded humble repentance.

Touched by the hand of God - the euphemism for madness; the protection that stopped corporal persecution of the poor madman, but did nothing positive about his well-being. If he starved to death that was put down to Yahweh, if he was animal enough to scrape together food to keep himself alive, then he was allowed to stay in the village.

Isaac again bowed respectfully to the village Rabbi. In Jerusalem he employed a dozen men of greater intellect as clerks but he acknowledged he was on the Rabbi's home territory and nothing was to be gained by antagonising him.

"Forgive me, Rabbi. I could not know. I found him in the foothills and thought he was a traveller overcome by sickness. He seemed to be deranged by the sun so I brought him here." Isaac explained patiently.

The Rabbi nodded forgiveness and brusquely turned to the gathered villagers and drove them back to their labours. Isaac crouched down in front of Robin and looked into his face.

"Robin?"

Intelligence crept slowly into the staring eyes. Isaac looked carefully around. He didn't want the Rabbi to know of the miraculous forces that were stirring in the weak body of Haddaq.

"Robin. Listen to me. Do you want me to take you away from here?" Anxiously he waited for the answer.

Slowly and with great effort the shaggy head moved up and down.

"Good!" Isaac said and pushed himself to his feet.

When the Rabbi returned Isaac introduced himself and invited him to dine at his table. The Rabbi accepted with alacrity. Chances of dining at the fabled table of one of the Prince Merchants of the desert came his way rarely. In fact, this was the first time.

With a gesture Isaac set his women and boys scurrying about erecting his tent and starting a fire. He put his arm around the Rabbi's shoulder and walked with him through the village.

"Now Rabbi, tell me about this Haddaq. He interests me."

Suspiciously the Rabbi shot a covert glance at the big merchant.

"Haddaq sir? You are interested in the madman?"

Isaac nodded.

"Yes. You see, I am also a physician and I am making a study of the insane. You will have noticed that madmen usually have physical defects as well as mental problems."

The Rabbi cut in.

"Those are where the hand of Yahweh has touched them," he answered Isaac solemnly.

The big man suppressed the joke that God must be a little heavy handed. It obviously wouldn't go down well with the poorly educated priest.

"Of course," he agreed. "That is just the point. In the case of Haddaq there does not seem to be the actual mark of God. Of course he has the thickening of the tongue and the protruding eyes. His co-ordination is bad and he seems to have trouble with his left leg but all these symptoms could be brought on by physical disability."

He didn't add that if the villagers had been more diligent in feeding the poor man a lot of his trouble might have been overcome.

The Rabbi didn't answer. He was overwhelmed by the conversation of the stranger and found words hard to conjure up. Isaac turned and walked back towards the well. The Rabbi quickly followed.

The tent was now erected and the women were busily carrying the carpets and cushions inside.

"I would like to study Haddaq further. With your permission I would like to take him back to Jerusalem with me where I can consult with other physicians and Elders of the Temple who know a lot about his sort of thing."

It was too much for the Rabbi to take. Half an hour earlier he was standing up to his knees in mud in an irrigation ditch and now he was discussing matters of great substance that involved the highest orders of the great Temple of Judaism. He tried to say something, to make some mark on the tremendous event. Dozens of thoughts chased through his mind but he couldn't stop one of them long enough to articulate its content.

Isaac helped him.

"Of course I will pay for his services." Dumbly the Rabbi nodded acceptance. "Good." Isaac clapped him energetically on the back. "Now we must eat."

He led the Rabbi into the tent and sat him on a cushion.

"If you will just excuse me a moment. There are a few chores I must attend to." He clapped his hands and one of the women came in.

"Look after our guest," he told her and left.

Outside the tent he summoned two of his mule drivers and led them to the well. Gently he picked up the body of Haddaq and took him behind the tent and laid him on a paillasse. While Isaac entertained the Rabbi his servants gently stripped and bathed the frail, sick body that housed the fluttering light from the future.

Chapter 5

Robin Firth stood in the transmitter room of the electronics complex on the Isle of Dogs and tried to reassure himself. It wasn't easy. He had a feeling that if word got out that he had spent millions of pounds on equipment that he was assured would send his thoughts back in time he would become the laughing stock of the commercial world. He had been laughed at before and had the satisfaction of seeing the hilarity drain away in shame faced apology. Trouble was that this time he wasn't a hundred percent convinced that he hadn't bought the electronic equivalent of the alchemist's stone. Every day he came to the transmitter room and stared at the dials that betrayed the vast drain of power from the massive transformers. It was pointless and he was aware of the sniggering that went on behind his back but he couldn't help it.

He had been set up as the prize pigeon of the millennium, and a minute part of his brain pattern was being held in place two thousand years in the past!

If it had found a receptive host, and the thought-module still contained his instruction, then there should be some indication of change happening very soon.

So far there was no sign of it. Afghanistan was still as bloody as ever. Islam and Judah still stood toe to toe delivering slaughter at close range and the African situation had flared into a cynical inter-tribal massacre.

Ten days had passed since Robin sat in the transmission cubicle with the conical, hair-drier type transmitter pulled over his head. It was all over before he had adjusted his clothing. He felt nothing and there was no sense of occasion. Mayer placed the cowl over Robin's head, pressed a button and took the cowl off again.

Robin hung around for an hour after that, trying to impress himself with what was being done, but the off-hand way the scientists treated the transmitter finally depressed him and he left.

It was tacitly agreed to leave the transmitter on for a month. They would then turn it off and see what happened. Robin secretly hoped that he would get not only the thought-module back but be aware of all that had happened in the thirty days. He didn't speak to Mayer or Sanderstead about his hopes but he could not control the urge he continually felt to return to the transmitter.

The puzzle that occupied his thoughts was the baffling aspect of a change in history and how it would act on the present time. What would happen if his thought-module found a home in the mind of Pontius Pilate or maybe Herod? Would their whole attitude to Jesus change? And, equally important from his point of view, would he be aware of it. If history changed, wouldn't it become a fact that had been there for all time and was therefore indiscernible by anyone in the twenty-first century? Maybe changes had already taken place? Become a fact that he had lived with all his life but which had been motivated by him in another time continuum.

Robin Firth was, is and always will be a pragmatist, he assured himself. He lived by the code that what he wanted to do, what could be done, he did. He didn't ask questions just got the target in his sights and wham!

So what was he doing hanging around a machine which to him was little more than a mass of LED lights and a tangle of cables? He had little idea of the purpose of anything in the room. He had been spun a tale and somehow had cast all his usual questions and caveats aside to embrace an idea that sounded at best a little far- fetched - at worst a con-trick that relied on his gullibility to succeed.

And he had fallen for it!

He paced the space between the wall and the transmitter, his steps getting shorter and quicker the more he thought of how he had been made a fool. How he had sat there and let a couple of scheming boffins pull a con trick that even the most ingenuous entrepreneur would have seen through in an instant.

Time!

Travel in Time!

You only had to think of it for a moment to realise it was impossible.

The old conundrum about crossing a space by halving it and never getting to the other side was okay for kids and simpletons, but what was he doing falling for it?

He picked up a telephone and hit the keys. Before he could get through he crashed the handset back into its cradle.

He stood glowering at the transmitter that he had imagined carried all his hopes. Gradually he calmed down. What did he know? What did Mayer and Sanderstead know? They had more or less confessed that what they were doing was experimental. They had even tried to talk him out of his obsession with travelling back to the time of Jesus. So what was he expected to do now? He hadn't been sold a pup. He had broken into the kennel and stolen it. Crying was for babies and unrequited virgins.

The dialectic cudgelled Robin's tired brain to a virtual pulp without resolving anything. He gave the dials another searching look, dug his hands deep into his trouser pockets and walked from the room.

Chapter 6

The dying sun shot out a sliver of golden light across the gently heaving amber of the Sea of Galilee before sinking into the depthless horizon. James stood for a second to watch the solar finale and then, as the glow left the water, tucked his galabia into his waistbelt, settled his pack more comfortably on his back and set off once more along the smooth, wet border of the lake. He was tired but far from exhausted and could carry on walking for hours if necessary but his destination was only a mile or two ahead.

A dark, square shape stood out against the light background of sand. It was only a few yards from the water's edge surrounded by the smaller shapes of beached boats. From poles fishing nets hung, a shimmering haze in the silver light of the rising moon. About thirty yards from the building James stopped. He looked carefully around before putting his fingers in his mouth and giving off a high-pitched whistle.

He waited.

Slowly a crack of light appeared in the black slab. It widened into a thin oblong and then was divided as a head thrust out. A low answering whistle gave James the all-clear and he swiftly covered the distance to the shelter of the wooden boathouse. The interior was lit by a couple of guttering tallow lamps, the rag wick smoking acridly into the heavy air. Peter slammed the door shut behind James and they clasped each other in a friendly bear hug. Beside Peter, James looked small. The big fisherman with his fierce, leonine head and barn-door shoulders seemed to fill the workshop.

"James - it's good to see you." Peter roared, his dark tanned face split by a white smile. "We've been wondering what had happened to you."

James looked at him sharply. He sensed a rebuke. "You know where I've been," he said flatly.

Peter nodded and picked up a wineskin from the bottom of the upturned boat that filled the centre of the workshop.

"Sure I know where you've been. That's the trouble; everyone knows where you've been. Every day there is another new story. Sometimes I wonder what you need the rest of us for." Peter's voice had risen plaintively as he spoke.

James shrugged angrily. "Someone had to go!" he snapped.

Peter spurted a long jet of wine into his mouth and wiped his chin with the back of his hand.

"Sure, someone had to go. But you forget the danger you put us in. The Temple police have been sniffing around for days. They want to take you in for questioning. You know what that means." Peter handed the skin to James but he pushed it aside.

"No. I don't know what it means - tell me." James said, hard and menacing.

Peter lifted his shoulders and spread his hands placatingly. James frightened him at times.

"Well, it means that they will be looking for your contacts. If they know you are here it could cause trouble for me." Peter avoided his visitor's eyes and took another swig from his bottle.

Pursing his lips James regarded Peter through hooded, cynical eyes. Peter had been one of the first. He had gone along with the plans and been a great help in making converts to their policy. He thrived on the power and importance but now that the time for unequivocal action was approaching he was showing dangerous signs of weakness.

James looked around the shed. Business was evidently good. That was always a problem with revolutionaries. Give them a hard time and plenty to whine about and they kissed your arse and pleaded undying servitude. But once they lost the fear of starvation they were looking for the easier cop-out.

James nodded and gave Peter a flat smile.

"Of course, we wouldn't want to upset your business. Now you are a folk hero it would spoil your image to be dragged in with a load of rough necked dissidents, wouldn't it?" James's face hardened. He spread his arms wide and announced: "Business as usual. Peter the Fisherman - friend of the people, leader, guide and mentor, tends his boats and gives comfort to the poor. As long as it doesn't harm his trading potential, of course! What's the matter with you? Losing your nerve?"

Stung by James's sarcasm Peter moved menacingly towards the smaller man. Unmoved by the threat of Peter's proximity James took the wineskin and casually spurted wine into his mouth. Peter slapped the wineskin aside.

"Me? Me?" he roared, struggling against his anger to get the words out. "Me? Lose my nerve? You forget it's me that stays here and takes the risks while you flit about all over the country. It's me that has to run your errands and keep the people primed. And for what? You are still no nearer taking over the country than you were two years ago." Peter drew a deep breath, almost a sob.

"And who is going to be blamed if it all falls to pieces? Not you and your weedy little runt of a brother, that's for sure. All he ever does is send messages and stir up trouble." Peter ran out of wind and dragged to a halt.

James looked at him with wide-eyed innocence.

"Trouble? Is that how you see it now?" He looped a leg over a saw-horse and settled back comfortably against the wall.

"Whatever happened to the big campaign? I seem to remember you making a speech about how you were going to walk through the fires of hell to make a better world. I thought it was fine rhetorical crap at the time but you had all your fans leaping up and down and thumping their chests, promising to walk with you, so I accepted it."

Peter tried to protest but keeping his voice soft and friendly, James rode straight on.

"I also remember the next morning, when your headache wore off, you spent the rest of the day hiding in case the Sanhedrin spies had also been thumping their chests in the crowd and reported back."

James's sarcasm prodded Peter into action. With his face close to James's he snarled, "Who do you think you're talking to? Who? Be careful, little man. Just remember it's me the people follow around here. If you want my co-operation you had better try being a bit more respectful."

James gave a short laugh and picked up the wine-sack. "Bravo! I'm sure you frighten the hell out of the shopkeepers and shepherds. Just keep doing it."

James slowly got up and walked across to lean on the upturned boat.

"But keep the big talk for your pillow. It has to take it - I don't!"

Peter, stung by James's continual needling, stepped forward, his fist raised. James didn't move. He looked at the transfixed fisherman towering over him and smiled broadly.

"Come on - forget it," he said, and watched the anger fade from the big man.

"You've heard about John?" he asked, changing the subject.

Peter nodded glumly.

"Had a couple of his men here last week, wanted to know if there was anything we could do."

"And?" James prompted.

Peter shrugged.

"What could I do?" he made the question a challenge.

James smiled sympathetically. "Nothing I guess. Anyway, he's dead now."

They stood in silence for a moment remembering the wild man, James's cousin, who had done so much for their cause only to be the victim of Herod's vacillation.

James pushed the sombre thought aside.

"Where are the others? Has Jesus got here yet? And did you get a message to my mother to meet us in Jerusalem?"

Peter nodded and took another swig of wine.

"Good," James commended him. "We have to move now. We can't keep the Zealots in the hills much longer. They want to rob and rape a bit and they feel that piety could get in the way. Everybody wants to follow a Messiah who can hand out material advantages. Love is harder. But Love it is and on Sunday week we carry the palms into Jerusalem and see what happens."

A flicker of anger crossed James's face as Peter nodded uncertainly and took another long pull at the wine.

"And you, my dear Peter, are you still the rock on which our movement is to be founded?" James asked slowly.

As Peter tried to think of an answer James reached out and took the wine-skin from his hand.

"Or is our strength in your wine-skin?" he said disdainfully.

Again Peter was stung into action and gripped James's arm.

"Okay James, you're the clever one but I'm warning you. Lay off or you'll get more trouble than you can handle." he growled belligerently.

Without a sign of fear James gently broke Peter's grip on his arm and walked a few paces away.

"I think you are forgetting something," James told him in a mock-sorrowful voice.

"You only function because I pull your strings. Jesus does the thinking and I attend to the practicalities."

James picked up his pack and moved back to stand in front of Peter.

"And I need you like a whore needs a catamite. The ignorant peasants want a leader to be bigger and prettier than they are. Stand you beside Jesus and from ten paces there's no contest." James moved even closer to Peter and stared hard into his eyes.

"But the man is in the eyes. And do you know what I see in your eyes?" James looped the string of his pack over his shoulder, pushed Peter disdainfully aside and walked to the door.

"I see fear. Fear submerged in wine. I recruited you for your size, like a dog or a camel. Don't make the mistake of thinking you have a brain or I will have to teach you a lesson." James opened the door but made no move to go through as Peter started towards him.

"You'll be told when and where you are wanted. In the meantime, lay off the wine." He turned abruptly and disappeared into the night leaving Peter open mouthed. The big fisherman shut the door with a crash and picked up the wineskin and defiantly directed a spurt of the red liquid into his mouth.

Chapter 7

Skeins of dark cloud tugged at the rim of the golden orb and distorted the symmetry of the edge. The scene was familiar to Robin as a recurring dream. Gradually the glow was suffocated as the darkness crowded in. Colour appeared gradually and, with indiscernible slowness, moved into a pattern at once familiar and alien. As it came together, grouping, blending and distorting its outlines, figures writhed in dissolving agony and were replaced by even more exotic shapes and hues. The colours began to shrink and fade, expelled, banished by a thick, horizontal bar of black. In either direction it stretched forever, never fading or diminishing. A bulge appeared on the upper and lower side. As it bisected the black horizon it initiated fear and evil, and a physical tactile menace. The crossed bands expanded and enveloped everything. The darkness was more than the simple absence of light. It was a tangible nothingness. The antithesis of light and life. Despair and terror sucking life and hope from the very structure of being. And yet there was still something there - something that seemed to strain to be seen. A presence in the void that was at once less than the void and more than the universe.

Robin wanted to see.

He felt the awaking of Haddaq - his darker self. For once he wasn't afraid. Even the primitive Haddaq was awed by the gathering colossus in the spaceless infinity. Shadows gathered together and took form. But instead of dark shadows they pulsed with a calm inner light that cast no reflection. Images crowded dizzily into Robin's mind. Images not of the hot, primitive world of agony and confusion. A place where he understood, and was aware; where no dark drape curtained off memory and clouded action.

Through the jumble of memory the dark cross shone out. Robin needed it. It was the answer. Desperately he reached out with arms that knew no restriction but as far as he reached it was not enough. The cross of darkness eluded his straining fingers.

"Jesus..." he sobbed. "Jesus!"

Sweating and confused, Robin jerked into a sitting position. He felt his newly acquired knowledge draining from him even as he tried to formulate in his mind the answers to all the questions that had dazed him since consciousness first came to him in the fly infested hovel more than two weeks earlier.

Robin's cries brought Isaac running. He was used to the ramblings and terror of his guest now and was on hand to comfort and reassure him when his nightmare became particularly bad.

Isaac's interest in Robin grew daily. He was still no nearer knowing the devils that drove the tortured man but was determined to unlock the store of knowledge that was bursting to free itself from the confused confines of Haddaq's body. As Isaac held the bowl of cool water to his lips Robin smiled gratefully at his friend. He was the only constant in Robin's tenuous grasp on rationality. Isaac gently took the bowl away and pulled the coarse, goat-hair rug up to cover the trembling body.

In the time Robin had been with Isaac the shambling, sore covered body of the village idiot, Haddaq, had responded to good food and kind treatment. Frequent bathing and liberal application of soothing balms and lotions dried up all but the most persistent festers. Plentiful, high protein food strengthened the weak body. But it was in the mind that most progress had been made. Since their first meeting when the feverish gibberish produced by the struggling entities of Robin and Haddaq to control the body conjured thoughts outside local knowledge, the merchant kept careful notes.

They did not add up to something that he could understand but by patiently feeding the gleanings of Robin's unconscious ramblings back to him, a pattern began to emerge. Somewhere in Robin's mind was the key. If it could just unlock the gates of memory they would know everything. Instead they daily sat and tried to piece together the random jigsaw of impressions and words that alighted, feather-like, in Robin's mind and could only be taken by the gentlest touch.

Language was one of the problems. Although Robin had access to the word store of the uneducated Haddaq, it was barely enough to cover the basic requirements of day to day life. That was one handicap. Even worse was the inability to explain concepts because there were just no words available in the language to convey them. So far what had been won from the miserly purse of Robin's memory was that he was from another place.

The 'wheres' or 'hows' weren't known.

He had an overriding sense of mission but what it was - wasn't known. From the recurrence of the name *Jesus* in his more fevered moments it probably had something to do with the Nazarene although that was by no means certain as the name *Jesus* was almost as popular a name as Isaac in that region.

Isaac's assumption that the Robin phenomena had something to do with the rabble rousing Rabbi, Jesus the Nazarene, was based on nothing more substantial than the coincidence of finding Robin shortly after coming under the influence of the new, humanitarian, teaching.

Another factor that came over loud and clear was the need for haste. Isaac fed Robin's receptive mind with what he knew of Jesus. He plucked responsive chords. Particularly when he told him that Jesus was expected in Jerusalem for the Passover.

While Robin rested and tried to strengthen the emaciated host-body of the simpleton Haddaq, Isaac made inquiries. From his quiet oasis, surrounded by groves of citrus fruits at Sumaria, he sent out his servants to gather the latest news. Rumour had it that both the Romans and the Jews were making more of the agitator than he merited. The Jews saw it as an excuse to worry the Romans into granting more power to the priesthood to control the dissident Rabbis and the Romans looked on it as an excuse to unsheath the sword and make a few political adjustments. But come what may, Jesus was scheduled to make a big entry into Jerusalem in two weeks' time and the graffiti was proclaiming him, amongst other equally grandiose titles, *King of Kings!*

Chapter 8

Pilate reined in the sweating white Arab he had been riding for the last four hours and gave the thick stone walls of the Antonia Fortress, Herod's present to the Roman invaders, a sour look. It wasn't the place he wanted to be but ceremony demanded it. He threw the reins to a groom and eased creakily out of the saddle. A centurion sprinted forward and saluted. Pilate waved a dismissive hand and signalled to the Tribune, Tavian Aleppi, who was his local Commander to join him. Tavian was the complete opposite of his superior. Pontius Pilate was fifty, heavily built with a humorous, almost handsome face while Tavian was little more than half his age and tended towards southern peninsular looks - tall, a hard, fierce face and dark skinned. They were old friends and easy with each other.

"How's it going?" Pontius asked of nothing in particular.

Tavian looked around as if trying to see the building from the view point of the newly arrived Prefectus.

"Quiet enough," he ventured.

Pilate gave him a cynical look.

"What does that mean?" Pilate asked. "Is there something you are keeping in store for me? Local uprising? Envoy from Tiberius telling me he's made me a Senator?"

Tavian shrugged good humouredly.

"What did you expect? Bandits with hoods over their heads blowing raspberries? It's when everything's quiet you've got to be most careful."

Pilate stopped and looked him over thoughtfully.

"Right! Out with it. What are you not telling me?"

Tavian glanced around at the household staff, still standing, heads bowed, honouring the great man who was to be their master for the next few weeks. Pilate was a careful man and wasn't happy about the loyalty of some of the staff members. Rome was a long way away and inevitably military personnel had engaged in relationships with some of the natives. He was also very aware that many of the local staff were in the pay of malcontents who would love to be able to make problems for the ruling elite.

Tavian linked his arm through Pilates and drew him towards the entrance. Pilate looked at him enquiringly.

"Well?" he asked, his good mood under threat.

"Nothing specific. Just rumours." Tavian told him.

"Rumours?"

"There have been reports of bandits gathering in the mountains. It is said that they are part of a movement to take over Jerusalem."

Pilate laughed out loud.

"And you are worried?" he asked incredulously. "Send in a couple of cohorts. That should defuse the situation. The men are looking for a bit of bloodletting. Soldiers need a fight to break up the dice games."

Tavian nodded agreement.

"I agree. Problem is that real intelligence is hard to find. I've had reports that there are thousands of them, a lot of them ex-soldiers, looking for some pay-back. Other reports say there are just a few dozen who are gathered to rob the Jews when they leave the city after the festival?"

"And your solution?" Pilate asked, his good temper returning.

"Wait and see. I can't see the Jews putting together an army that can do us a lot of harm but I would like to be ready and put any insurgency down as quickly as we can. We could blunder around in the mountains for weeks without finding their hideouts. As soon as they move down from the hills we will be waiting for them."

Pilate laughed and put an arm around Tavian's shoulder.

"Problem solved."

He turned to survey the household staff standing attentively on each side of the main entrance to the domestic quarters of the military post.

"Who have we here?" he asked.

An elderly man in a long hessian tunic, a dark shawl draped around his shoulders, hair cut short and bobbed in the Roman manner, stepped forward.

"Welcome, Praefectus, I am Marcus Albinus, the steward of your household. Welcome to Jerusalem," he said in a calm voice that lacked enthusiasm.

Pilate frowned.

"Albinus? What happened to Quintus?"

Albinus drew in a breath to relate the sorry story of his predecessor who had been returned to Rome in disgrace after being caught negotiating deals that were not in the interest of the Roman authorities. Before he could speak Pilate waved him to silence.

Albinus felt his temper flare but long years of being a 'yes' man had helped him to school any signs of irritation.

Indiscretion had cut him off from his well-connected Patrician family to eke out a less than satisfactory life at the beck and call of any jumped up military appointee that turned up in Jerusalem and he resented it. Not enough to throw in the position and take his chances in the outside world but it coloured his attitude. Pilate recognised the breed and returned the coldness with disdain. Pilate was from a plebian family and was well used to being marginalised by those whose birth conferred high status upon them. He no longer cared what they thought. He was now the master of all he surveyed with the backing of Rome and had the power to do what he liked with anybody who mistakenly tried to take advantage of his usually relaxed attitude to life.

"Our quarters are ready?" he asked abruptly, not caring to enquire what had happened to the steward who had looked after the residence for as long as he had been the Procurator.

Albinus made an ingratiating bow.

"Of course, my Lord," He managed to force out through a rictus smile.

Pilate looked at Tavian.

"Right, stand down the army. I need a bath."

He turned abruptly and walked through the door.

Tavian gave the escorting cavalry the order to dismiss and followed Pilate into the house.

Albinus sharpened up his attitude when he realised that Pilate wasn't someone to mess with and was now hot on his heels explaining how well he had done his job taking over in the most trying circumstances and soldiering on so that Praefectus Pilate would have no extra worries. He worked hard at selling himself, assuring Pilate that he considered it a rare pleasure to work for such a famous and charismatic person as Pontius Pilate.

Tavian followed them through the inner courtyard with its bowers of flowers and a fountain that drained into a paved fishpond used as a larder as well as decoration. Under the vines of the shading ambulatory they walked between rows of Roman nobility immortalised in stone by new-wave artists keen to express themselves wherever money was available. At the end was the large, airy room set aside for the Governor.

"Caiaphas, the High Priest, sent word to say he would be here later this afternoon," Albinus said, praying that he would stumble on a subject with which he could ingratiate himself with the new arrival.

Pilate stopped and gave him a look that convinced him that he hadn't picked the right subject yet.

"You can tell the High Priest that I will decide when I will see him and it definitely won't be today. Now, get some food and fill the biggest bath in the place. I'll call you when I need you."

He turned abruptly away and walked into his quarters. Albinus looked at Tavian hoping for sympathy but the soldier wasn't in the sympathy business and strode straight past him.

The cool, beautifully aspected room didn't work any magic on the overheated Governor. Two young body-servants ran forward with drinks that he waved irritably aside while he struggled to undo the clasps on his breastplate. Mistakenly they tried to help and were roughly cursed for their trouble. Pilate ripped off the strangling cuirass and slung it across the room. Underneath was a sweat soaked undershirt caked with sand.

It followed the breastplate.

"I swear that bloody sand's made of powdered glass," he said as he divested himself of his kilt.

Diplomatically, Tavian kept quiet.

"Where's that bath?" Pilate demanded of one of the boys, and followed him from the room. Tavian trailed after him.

The bathroom was big and well attended. Without a word Pilate flopped into the cool water and floated face down until he needed to breathe then turned on his back and grinned at Tavian.

"What you waiting for, Tav?"

Tavian let the boys help him off with his uniform then plunged gratefully into the pool.

"Might as well enjoy it, I'm here for a couple of weeks whatever happens."

Pilate pulled himself out of the pool and accepted a towel from one of the attendants. Tavian followed.

"Will the Lady Claudia be joining you?" he asked, although he had already guessed the answer.

"Gone to Rome, lucky cow." Pilate gave a short, ugly laugh. "She's always going to Rome."

He pulled himself together and accepted a goblet of orange juice from one of the staff. At the door he stopped and looked back at Tavian.

"And get me one who speaks Latin this time. I can't make love in Hebrew."

Chapter 9

The attic room was low-ceilinged and stuffy. In the winter it was used as a hayloft for the more valuable animals that wintered in the living quarters below. Now it was spring and the lambs, goats and fowl were allowed to fend for themselves in the open. The lower level of the two-storey house built of sun-dried bricks, held together by a greenwood structure, was partly below ground level. This had an insulating effect that cooled the savage summer sun and retained body heat in the winter. The upper storey was therefore no more than four feet above ground level.

James had chosen it as a meeting place because it was on the outskirts of the village and its situation on top of a small hill made it a good lookout post to see who was approaching. Not that the men lying around asleep or chatting in a desultory manner to each other seemed particularly worried by the thought of hostile assault.

The sun had cleared the mountains and was casting shadows in the well when Matthew woke. He ran a dry tongue around his parched mouth without producing much saliva. He still had a splitting headache, brought on by the wine two nights before and the total absence of exercise since. He heaved up onto his elbows and looked around. The rest were either asleep or disinterested. Cautiously he rose to his feet and stood swaying while he fought off the dizziness the unaccustomed exertion brought.

Outside he relieved himself. Then he swallowed a lubricating draught of water in the shade by the door, fallen drops glistening in jewel-bright globules on the porous clay surface. Matthew poured some water onto the corner of his galabia and wiped some of the dust and dirt from his face. He delayed going back inside although he had instructions to keep outside visits to a minimum and short. He sunk down on his heels in the cool shade of the wall and shut his eyes. He was almost asleep when he heard a slight sound. Frightened he jumped up, fists clenched, ready to fight. Instead his face split into a relieved smile.

"Judas, you shit! What are you trying to do, give me a heart attack?" He laughed.

Judas stood looking at Matthew. He wrinkled his nose.

"You've been sleeping with the pigs?" he asked, straight-faced.

Matthew put a comforting arm around Judas and drew him to the side of the house where the crude, uncured wood steps gave access to the loft.

"You shouldn't talk about our friends like that, Judas my boy, you might offend the pigs."

Both laughed loudly.

They had a lot in common although they were years apart in age. Matthew was a middle-aged man in his thirties, with a long pepper and salt beard, thinning hair and a sun-wrinkled face. He was still big and powerful but the time he spent poring over manuscripts and painstakingly composing poetry was beginning to bow his well-muscled shoulders and produce a myopic, birdlike set to his head.

Judas, in contrast, was straight with long smooth athletic limbs and supple, slim-waisted body. He was scarcely sixteen and still wore the short shift, a Roman influence, of the adolescent. His black, tightly curled hair and clean, unbearded face, had the quality of the beautiful Greek statues that had proliferated in the gardens of the wealthier, cosmopolitan Jews to the fury of the Priests. Optimism and wellbeing shone from his warm, brown eyes rimmed with thick, black lashes. People were drawn to him by his open face and the latent strength of his developing body.

"Anyway, what are you doing here? I thought you were working for Nicodemus in Jerusalem?"

Judas gave him a sour look.

"He thought a spell on the road might do me some good. I've been on the road with the tax collectors for the last week. Not a happy time. We're heading back to the Temple tomorrow," Judas explained.

Matthew drew him into the room where the others waited.

Sun blinded, Judas peered around the gloomy attic. All the occupants were awake now but a general air of apathy had settled over them like a thick blanket. Matthew edged the boy aside and looked around at his sullen companions.

"Not exactly what you would expect of God's revolutionary army, is it?" Matthew said, in a low-pitched aside to Judas.

He raised his voice.

"Okay. Listen everybody! We have to make a decision. James is four days overdue and we have heard nothing from him," he said.

His words held the attention of the rest. They sat up and showed interest.

"There is always the chance that James has been arrested. In that case the best thing we can do is disperse for a while and await new orders."

There was a general murmur of assent. Matthew continued.

"I will stay here. When I know anything more I will get in touch and arrange a new meeting. Any questions?"

The men looked at each other.

Thomas got to his feet and started to roll his possessions in his blanket. He was as tall as the others but of slighter build with high, narrow shoulders. Like the others his hair was shoulder-length and now, just awakened from sleep, tied back into a queue. A savage looking hawk-nose gave his eyes an unnatural intensity that riveted an audience, daring them to be inattentive. In the company he kept he was still a striking figure. Only a slight pout when he spoke and a habit of sneering at statements that he didn't agree with whole-heartedly, betrayed any weakness. He spoke without looking up.

"What about Jerusalem? Is that still on?" Thomas asked.

Matthew thought for a moment.

"I should think so. That part of our plan stands whatever happens."

Thomas gave a sardonic snort.

"Even if James has been taken?"

Before Matthew could answer the door behind him opened. All eyes swung to the silhouette filling the small opening, black against the white light of the sun.

"Don't worry. James is back," a cool voice assured the questioner.

"James!" Matthew exclaimed and rushed forward to clasp hands.

"We thought you had been arrested."

James laughed and playfully swung a fist at Matthew's head.

"I see. Ready to take over were you? Well - hard luck. I'm here now."

He let his pack fall to the floor and looked around at the others. They were all on their feet now. The low ceiling made them stoop and it heightened their attitudes of attention to their leader. He smiled broadly at them as his eyes became more accustomed to the light. Judas was still standing beside Matthew, eyes shining in frank hero worship. James saw him and stretched out an arm and looped it familiarly over the youth's shoulder.

"Judas, you young devil, what are you doing here? I thought you were in Jerusalem!" He roared in high good humour.

Judas opened his mouth to explain but James wasn't interested. He walked forward and stood in the middle of the room and inspected the men one by one. Slowly he shook his head. The humour fled from his face. It was a discomforting habit of James that threw people who met him into confusion.

"You lot are supposed to be examples. When you were taken on you were to keep yourselves clean and tidy. Look at you now."

He spoke in a menacing voice that had them all nervously straightening their clothes and trying to repair the damage of three days boredom in a hayloft.

James swung around to Matthew.

"I want this lot cleaned up and ready to leave in ten minutes."

James picked up his pack and strode angrily to the door. He looked back at Judas. "And you, boy, get back to Nicodemus. I want you to stay close to the Temple for the next ten days. If you hear anything of interest you know how to contact me."

James waited while Judas sidled past him, for once his friendly smile extinguished, and then gave another disparaging look at the slowly preparing men.

"I'll wait outside. If you could manage to get yourselves ready before nightfall I would be grateful." He looked at Matthew. "I want to speak to you - outside."

Without another word he left.

Matthew followed.

James perched himself on a pile of cut firewood and watched the lithe figure of Judas walk down the hill towards the village. Just before he went out of sight the boy turned and waved a hesitant hand. James reply was full and friendly. Even at the distance the renewed smile on the face of Judas was apparent. James turned back to Matthew who hunkered down beside him in the shade.

"What do you think, Matt?" James asked shortly. Matthew looked up, puzzled by the question.

"About what?"

James nodded towards the loft as he untied the leather thongs on his sandals to ease his feet.

"Our friends up there. Are they going to carry through and do as they are told?" he asked.

Matthew frowned.

"I think you are a bit hard on them. It's not easy sitting around in a dung-hill like this, not knowing what is happening, your nerves get jumpy."

James nodded understanding and examined the sole of his sandal for wear. Neither spoke for a few minutes.

Matthew broke the silence.

"We still march into Jerusalem for the Passover?"

James gave an amused chuckle.

"March? Not march, Matthew. That's for soldiers. We walk calmly through the gates and then see what happens."

Matthew digested the information and frowned.

"We're going to look idiots if no-one takes any notice of us," he ventured.

Again James laughed.

"Don't worry, that's all taken care of. Our supporters will line the route and make sure our progress is noticed," he reassured the older man.

Both looked up as the first of the men came out of the door and lowered himself carefully down the rough steps. James gave a slow, sarcastic hand clap.

"Bravo, James son of the famous Zebedee. Did you manage to wake brother John or does he want to rest some more?"

James's question was answered by a broad, slightly podgy, face appearing in the doorway and smiling self-consciously down at him.

"Morning John," James said good-humouredly as the vast bulk carefully negotiated the steps.

John swung his pack on his back and beamed sweatily at James.

"Good job you turned up at last. Much more of that date syrup and my stomach would have revolted." He stopped and looked around. "Is there any food anywhere?"

He moved towards the door into the farmer's part of the building but was stopped by Matthew telling him the outcome of an earlier exploration. John shrugged resignedly and contented himself with a swig of water before stretching out in the shade.

Next out was the lanky Thomas. He said nothing and spent a good deal of time trying to clean up his face while James watched him, fascinated by the meticulous care he took with his hair and beard.

James was getting restless. He wanted to get away. There were only ten days left for them to make the long journey to Jerusalem. If they arrived late the whole point would be lost. Irritated by the slowness of the others he went to the doorway and banged an irritated tattoo on the wooden frame.

"Come on! Come on! We have to get moving!"

He picked up his pack and without a backward glance strode off down the hill. Matthew fell into step beside him and they were half-way down the hill before the dozing John, his brother James and the preening Thomas gathered their possessions and followed.

From the loft, Simon, Bartholomew and Taddeus scrambled after them, anxious not to incur the leaders' mounting anger. The remaining three of the band of twelve: Andrew, Quiet James and Philip were already in Jerusalem spreading cheer and a little gold to make sure that nothing went wrong when the rest arrived. Peter was due to meet them that evening.

Chapter 10

Isaac watched his guest pick at the remains of a chicken bone and came to a decision. So far he had countered all suggestions that a meeting should be arranged with Jesus with the argument that until Robin could remember exactly why he wanted to meet the leader it would be a waste of time. The real reason was that the Haddaq body was so debilitated that Isaac doubted that it had the strength to undertake the strenuous journey to Jerusalem. Good food and rest had worked wonders and there was now really no reason why they shouldn't make a start. Although Haddaq's body was getting stronger and more co-ordinated under the discipline of Robin's dominance, Isaac was worried that the strain on the poverty weakened body and Haddaq's untrained mind might be too much. Isaac smiled reassuringly at Robin as he put the chicken bone in one of the shallow earthenware dishes and washed the grease from his fingers.

"I have received an invitation from an old friend of mine who lives near Jerusalem. I sent him a letter about you and he is anxious to talk to you. He spent some time in Canaan in his youth and knows the people well. His name is Joseph. He comes from Arimathea."

Isaac watched Robin's face as he said the name. Names meant a lot to the man imprisoned in the alien brain. Isaac was disappointed. Robin frowned and stared at his fingers, trying to place the name.

"You've heard of him?" Isaac prompted.

Slowly Robin shook his head and replied in the careful, halting voice he used to control the untutored Haddaq tongue.

"No! Or....I don't know. I had a feeling of sadness when you mentioned the name - that's all," he told Isaac.

The old man nodded understanding.

"Joseph is a benefactor of the Temple and a lay-member of the Sanhedrin. He made his money steering a precarious course between the Romans and the orthodox Jews. Not an easy task. He is still one of the main traders with Rome but now he takes a greater interest in his own people. He lives in Jericho now. It's on the way to Jerusalem. If anyone can help you - he can."

Robin sat and looked at his host for a few moments and then thoughtfully nodded. "You are right. Whatever or whoever I am, I don't feel that I can keep control for much longer. There is too much frenzy, too many conflicts and contradictions in my mind. Sometimes I feel Haddaq is very near, waiting to take permanent control. I'm not sure of anything."

Suddenly Robin dropped his head into his hands. Isaac heard a sob but made no move. With an effort of will Robin controlled himself and sat up.

"I appreciate your help, Isaac. I can't think what would have happened if you hadn't come along when you did," he said with simple sincerity.

Isaac shrugged off the gratitude with a smile.

"You have provided me with more interest than a merchant travelling the road usually gets. It's God's will, I suppose."

Robin suddenly got up and walked across the small room and pushed aside the dried reed shutters to look out at the cool courtyard surrounding the house.

"I don't know who I am. I don't know what I am doing here. I am not even sure that I am sane," he said softly.

Savagely he beat his clenched fists against the rough plastered walls and swung around to Isaac.

"All I know is that I *MUST* see Jesus and it must be soon!"

Robin spoke with a savage intensity, his newly disciplined tongue barely controlling his enunciation.

Isaac gave a placatory nod.

"We leave tomorrow. Joseph will fix everything. Don't worry. I promise you we'll be in Jerusalem before the Passover."

Robin came back to the table and picked up a stem of grapes.

"Before Jesus reaches Jerusalem? I don't know how I know but there is no doubt in my mind that Jesus must be stopped!"

Sweat stood out on Robin's pockmarked forehead. Pulling himself together with an effort he carefully supervised the inept Haddaq fingers as they picked grapes from the bunch.

Isaac clapped his hands. Instantly two serving boys entered and started clearing the table. They were about twelve, dark skinned and scrupulously depilated. They wore short tunics with the blue boxed edge of the Canaanites. Roman influence in dress had not touched the older generations but the wealthier houses followed the fashion for house servants. Overseeing the two boys was the Major Domo. He had been with Isaac's parents and looked on the merchant as a son. Now he was well over forty and Isaac only kept the old man on for sentimental reasons. In deference to his age and long service he was allowed to wear a white galabia.

"We will be leaving tomorrow morning at day break. Get everything prepared. We will not be taking any merchandise, just a few presents. I will pick those out myself and let you have them."

The Major Domo bowed gravely.

"Yes sir. Will six pack animals be enough do you think?"

Isaac waved his hand in dismissal.

"Yes. Yes. I leave it to you."

Again the Major Domo bowed and then smoothly withdrew.

Within minutes the house was a hive of bustling figures preparing the packs for the animals and servants that would accompany their master and his strange friend to Jerusalem.

As Robin lay awake on his wool-pack through the long night he could hear the murmur of voices and the whisper of bare feet preparing for their departure. A little before dawn he finally fell asleep and returned to his strange but comforting world of tall buildings, crystal carriages that run without apparent energy and gigantic flying machines. The wondrous world of his other self was only spoiled by the sense of disaster, hatred and blood that went with it.

Chapter 11

James dropped back and let the others file past him. It was already getting dark and their destination was still at least a couple of miles away. The dark didn't matter. Even the hardiest footpad would think twice about taking on twelve of the biggest men they had ever seen in one group. The problem was that the path they were following wasn't the most well-defined in the world and it would be easy to spend an uncomfortable night wandering around looking for the village they knew was ahead.

Then there was Jesus.

The long journey had taken a terrible toll on his meagre store of energy and he was having trouble keeping up. It was the necessity of walking to a pace he could manage that had made them so late.

Jesus saw James waiting for him and made an effort to straighten up and fan some energy into his halting stride. James wasn't fooled. In the fading light he was able to see the dark circles under his brother's eyes and hear the rasp of his breath as his tortured lungs sucked in air.

"Not much farther now!" James said encouragingly.

Jesus managed a strained smile.

"No problem. I'm getting my second wind...," he said as forcefully as he could.

James gently took the canvas bag Jesus was carrying over his shoulder and put his hand under his elbow. Jesus was grateful for

James's concern but hated being a burden. He gently pulled away from James and tried a reassuring smile.

"I'm okay. I just need a good meal and a night's sleep and I'll be as right as rain."

His words were belied by a hacking cough that left him bent-over and breathless. James put his arm around him and was distressed to see the trickle of blood leaking from the corner of his mouth.

"Don't give me that," he said roughly.

He looked after the others who were ploughing on without looking back.

"Peter!" James called.

The towering figure at the front of the party stopped and looked back.

"Come here a minute," James ordered.

Peter looked as if he might be considering refusing but ambled slowly back.

"Carry Jesus," James said curtly.

Peter looked annoyed.

Before he could cause a problem Jesus put his hand on James's arm.

"It's all right. I can make it. You go on. I'll get there in my own time," he said.

Peter changed his mind.

It was an opportunity to show how big and strong he was and Jesus had given him the excuse to ignore James and take on the task on his own terms. Without a word he picked up the lightweight body and walked stoically off in the direction of the rest of the group.

James stood and watched his departing back for a few moments.

Peter was becoming a problem. His commitment to the cause was great when things were going well. When something untoward happened he panicked. Not in an overt way but he became very negative. Physically he was brave enough. What was suspect was his mental resilience. He was afraid of failure - afraid of being afraid. If Jesus had been big and strong Peter might have been able to overcome his misgivings and be more supportive. As it was he couldn't overcome the gap in reality between what Jesus promised and what he was. All Peter saw was the weak, dying man. Not the spirit, not the intelligence locked in the fragile frame. James humped the packs on his back and followed into the gathering darkness.

Chapter 12

In the shadow, out of the bright sunlight, the rocks radiated a grey coldness that syphoned the warmth from the marrow of his bones. Aliph edged a couple of feet to the right to get back into the sun. At that altitude the sunlight was more of a psychological warmth than a corporeal comfort. From his perch the guerrilla leader had an uninterrupted panorama of the terrain in front of him and to each side. The vista was as boring as his existence in the isolation of the mountains.

Aliph was trained in one of the native cohorts of the Roman legion. It hadn't suited him. The discipline he could stand, he became so hardened to the lash of the Roman centurion that he could, with a minimum of movement, misdirect it to fall onto the least sensitive areas of his tough skin. What he couldn't stand was the food. Canaan wasn't exactly renowned for its cuisine but every stew-pot had at least a memory of a piece of lamb or goat locked in its ferrous depth, which was more than could be said for the whole Roman army. Meat was considered a luxury that was beyond the common soldier. The stomach that the Roman legionaries marched on was tightly packed with untainted corn mush and purifying dried fruit eked out by what could be liberated from the local peasantry and traders.

Aliph carried a shield for four muscle building years. His hatred of the Romans began to outstrip his natural yen for other people's property. It was his fever for the latter that brought about the circumstances that gave him a chance to do something about the former.

He was out on a patrol when they came across a tent in one of the small rocky passes that surrounded a minor cataract on the lower reaches of the Jordan. Aliph's twelve men patrol had been out of touch with the main group for a couple of days and food was running low. Their intention was to merely appropriate some food and pass on. The chance of some easy pickings was too much for Aliph. He made an excuse to be the last to leave the encampment and then laid the hilt of his sword across the back of the merchant's head and helped himself to some of the goodies lying around. Unfortunately the trader had friends in high places and Aliph was promptly arrested as soon as he rejoined his Legion. On the way to confinement in the Roman penal garrison at Capernaum, Aliph managed to slip his chain and disappear into the desert.

His shrewdness and lethal dexterity soon put him at the head of a gang of outlaws preying on the smaller villages. Ambition made use of his military training and within a year he had a partly trained band of cutthroats around him that held a region from Jerusalem to Bethlehem in a grip of nervous terror.

His recruitment by James was easy. Aliph wanted to be more than just a brigand skulking in the foothills. He had a grander goal. Everywhere there was talk of insurrection. The weakening Latin hand was allowing fermenting pots of patriotism to test the lids. Progressive disinterest from successive Governors produced the atmosphere for dissention and riots. The more obvious troublemakers, when identified, could expect a nocturnal visit from a centurion. In spite of the savage new law that ordained death by crucifixion, nailed to a wooden beam either with a cross-bar or singly in the vertical position, the sense of freedom abroad in the land was enough to assure a ready flow of candidates for the painful and humiliating execution.

Aliph had officiated at quite a number of crucifixions. Now, a prime candidate for the starring role himself, he was anxious to find a way out. He had watched men die. Sometimes it took a couple of days unless a friendly soldier was willing to smash a shinbone or pierce a vital organ with his spear. James's promise of an overwhelming campaign, coordinated throughout Judaea and the Galilees, with the ennobling aspect of a religious leader to ensure victory, suited Aliph. It solved all his problems. It got him down from the mountain, gave him martial respectability in the new order and, coincidentally, gave him a chance to loot a fortune in keeping with his new status. But he felt it was all beginning to go wrong.

Aliph could understand James. The Nazarene was big and had a toughness and temper that made him a man among men. Like an animal, the guerrilla leader was willing to back off in a confrontation that did not challenge his leadership or had a doubtful outcome. James was a random factor that Aliph wasn't prepared to test.

Yet!

But the time was coming when he might have to take on James - and his band of mercenaries. The big man made no secret of the fact that the General directing operations, the eagerly awaited Right Arm of God, was his brother Jesus. The fraternal connection didn't impress Aliph but he wondered what sort of man the leader must be to control such a man as James.

Natural curiosity made the bandit chief risk detection to see his promised Messiah. Jesus was staying in one of the fisherman's houses on the shores of the Sea of Galilee. Regular early evening philosophy sessions gave Aliph the chance to get in close. Keeping to the lengthening shadows he hid in a tree growing beside the garden wall when Jesus met his followers. It was a shattering experience for the intensely physical guerrilla.

His disappointment spilled out onto his followers. Like himself they were outcasts, living on the edge of bloody extinction. Their leader's sudden loss of confidence spread amongst the bandits like a debilitating head cold. Their common cause, the excitement at the prospect of a campaign that was to bring them respectability and wealth, began to fade.

Desertions were only a minor problem. The bandits were not exactly loved by the hard working communities in the valleys and could expect short shrift from them if they were taken. Aliph's problems were in the camp. A hundred or so men hiding out amongst the rifts and crags and their growing sense of betrayal produced blood.

The situation hadn't been helped by the attitude of a neighbouring bandit gang led by an escaped Roman slave - Seph.

Seph was a giant black man from the fabled country to the south. He was picked up as a child by an Arab slave trader and sold as a houseboy to a Roman senator. Life was good and the young boy, nurtured on rich, plentiful food, outgrew all the other children to become an imposing black colossus by the time he was sixteen. The bored Roman matriarchs, their husbands continually either away on business, war or pleasure in the wide variety of clubs that provided hedonistic delights through the gamut of simple hot baths and even hotter massages to magical rites with vestal virgins and cherubic choirboys, found employment for the bulging muscles and virile stamina.

Within a short time Seph acquired a small fortune from gifts pressed on him by grateful dowagers.

Seph was happy and contented. But he became too self-assured and aggressive. His Roman masters were happy that their wives had found worthwhile entertainment and would have preferred to continue to turn a blind eye to the sexual exploits of the slave if he had let them. Unfortunately, in his arrogance, he forgot that the Latin's wife was above suspicion, whatever she did, but the daughter was the source of all purity and light.

Especially in the conservative household of Petias Polimite, an ex-banker with high senatorial ambitions once the stigma of trade had been exorcised from his address. Seph had been obliging the embryo senator's wife for a couple of months when he met her sixteen year old daughter, Dontius.

Dontius had watched the visiting black comforter with interest. She even watched, fascinated, through the drapes over the window of her mother's dayroom, as the accomplished stud drove her usually refined and fragile mother over the borders of delirium into a land where she was a screaming, ravening beast. The prospect of an encounter with the ebony superman made her sick with anticipation.

The next time he left her mother's room Dontius pulled him with an excess of ardour and a lack of subtlety, into her nursery and fell on him with a fury sustained by lithe muscles and a natural talent for acrobatic manoeuvres.

Seph responded splendidly.

He was still responding splendidly when he was seized by four Roman guards and dragged, screaming and fighting, to the main square and whipped with the metal tipped cat o' nine tails until he was little more than a bloody, flayed-flesh mass, lying inert on the cobbles without even the energy to groan for the loss of his right eye, picked cleanly from the socket, by one of the iron tips.

The incident caused a good deal of trouble for the outraged apprentice politician. Seph's owner pressed for damages and Petias was forced to pay the full market price of a prime Nubian slave in spite of the damaged state of the goods. He managed to recover a few *denarii* by selling Seph to a galley owner who was willing to take a chance on the muscular stud recovering and being fit enough to pull an oar. The seaman was lucky and Seph found himself behind an oar providing the motive power for trade on the Mare Internum sea routes.

Seph was one of the few slaves to get away when the galley drifted ashore during a storm and broke up on a rock shelf. He didn't wait around to see if there were any other survivors. He hadn't done a lot of running as a fettered oarsman but he soon learned the technique and by the first light of the following day had put a comfortable distance between himself and the flotsam that had been his home. Elevation to brigandry was a matter of natural selectivity.

As a branded slave he couldn't risk living in a town, his size made him too conspicuous. The scourge that had robbed him of an eye had also cut his face to shreds. A sight of the terrible mutilation was enough to make hardened men shudder and even prostitutes charge double.

He still had his strength and with this he whipped together a band of a hundred or so outlaws and became one of the most feared bandits on the coast.

News of gathering unrest and a chance to provoke a bloody clash with the Roman masters drew him, with his gang, like a magnet to the hills outside Jerusalem.

Aliph and Seph had lived in uneasy truce for over a year, united by the promise of a victorious uprising. Jesus's message of *Love* dropped into their uneasy union by the forceful James, did not help.

Aliph was dragged from his morbid thoughts by the sound of a skittering pebble.

His hand dropped to his sword.

Assassination was an ugly word that was a recurring theme in his mind lately. His hand stayed near the sword's hilt when he saw that his visitor was the man who was occupying his thoughts.

Seph!

The Negro went down on his hunches in front of his bandit colleague and pushed back the hood of his thick woollen galabia.

Aliph wished he wouldn't.

He still couldn't look at the mushed flesh, torn eye socket and yellow exposed bone without feeling an uneasy constriction of the stomach.

"I'm going down to Jerusalem. Travellers are coming from all over the provinces for the Passover. I mean to profit by their devotion." Seph broke the silence at last in his soft, light voice with the musical Latin accent.

Aliph shrugged his shoulders and said nothing.

"Are you coming with me?" Seph asked.

Aliph stood up and walked to the edge of the ledge on which they sat. It gave him the excuse to get away from the gargoyle face. He gestured towards the men below.

"I don't know. Something's got to be done. I don't know how long I can keep that lot together unless we get some action."

Seph smiled.

"So you come with me. Together we could pull the town apart," the Nubian said encouragingly.

Aliph again shrugged.

"Not that easy, friend. There is at least a cohort of troops there and they are expecting trouble."

"You were willing to march if the Nazarene ordered it. There was still a cohort then. So what's changed?" Seph demanded fiercely.

Aliph swung around.

"The Nazarene commands respect. We would have the town on our side. If we move by ourselves, we will be fighting the Jews as well. That's the difference."

Seph spat provocatively on the rock between Aliph's sandaled feet. It was a provocative insult but Aliph was too good a tactician to be angered into a fight without an advantage. He stared into Seph's good eye with an assurance he didn't feel.

"You are making a mistake if you think you can take Jerusalem. I want nothing of that. But you are right about the need for action. We will move down with you and take cover in the hills around the city. I'll try and get a message through to James and tell him that we are not prepared to wait any longer. He must either give the signal to co-ordinate the revolution or he can forget any help from us. If he still refuses to go ahead with our plans it's every man for himself. Do you agree?"

Aliph sat down on the rock and waited for the giant Negro to reply.

Seph nodded his head thoughtfully.

"I agree to that. But you might as well get this into your head now. I don't have any responsibility towards the Nazarenes. They're your pigeons. We march tomorrow but I do what I consider best."

Aliph nodded agreement and watched as the mutilated man walked down the rocky path. He wished events would occasionally work out the way he planned. The prospect of an easy life as a rich, respected member of a prosperous community policed by Aliph and his friends, seemed to be fading. Fate was leading him by the nose to a confrontation he neither wanted nor was sure he could win.

The sun was low on the horizon and heatless. He picked up his heavy cloak and followed the path Seph had taken a little earlier. A fire blazed in the shelter of the rocks as the men prepared a meal.

Their chief surveyed the scene for a few minutes. The glimmer of military discipline that he had been able to impart to the unruly mob was being rapidly eroded by the patina of inactivity. If he didn't give them a direction for their energy he would soon be unable to control them.

He shook himself.

It was time to act!

As Aliph made his way to the fire he saw one of his more able lieutenants sitting honing his heavy bronze sword.

"Barabbas!" he roared. "Get your gear together. You're leaving for Jerusalem immediately."

Chapter 13

A small crowd standing outside a largish house, surrounded by a split-wood fence that enclosed a number of olive trees sheltering a tiled veranda, looked up with interest as James led his group into the village. Peter brought up the rear, still carrying Jesus. James waved a friendly hand in greeting. An elderly man returned the greeting and appeared willing to talk.

"Evening. What's happening?" James asked.

The old man nodded towards the house.

"The Mayor's dead. We're waiting for the Rabbi to arrive," he explained.

James looked around, suspecting there was an opportunity for exploitation.

"Rabbi? You haven't got a Rabbi?" he asked.

A woman heard James's question and came over.

"He's in to the next village. We've sent a boy but I don't suppose he will be back before the morning," she said.

James looked covertly towards where Jesus, still semi-supported by Peter, was watching what was going on.

"You're in luck," James told the woman, "We have a Rabbi with us. Perhaps you'd like him to sing Kaddish?"

The man and woman exchanged glances and shrugged.

"You'd better ask Martha," the woman said and turned away.

"The Mayor's sister," the old man offered before he also lost interest.

James went back to Jesus.

The rest he had been able to get over the last couple of miles had helped. He looked better although there was still a deathly pallor to his features and his limp was more pronounced.

"The mayor's dead and the Rabbi's gone missing. D'you feel up to offering your services?" James asked Jesus.

Jesus nodded.

"Right. I'll see the lady of the house. You try to clean up a bit. I'll be right back." James gave Jesus a long speculative look then pushed his way through the crowd and into the house.

On a table, smoky tallow candles at the head and foot, lay the body of a middle-aged man. Slumped on the floor, her head resting against the edge of the table, a black-clad, elderly woman sobbed helplessly into a fold in her head-scarf. Sitting around the room were a number of neighbours, all expressing their grief in a low-pitched keening.

James stood in the door and took in the scene before stopping beside the woman on the floor and taking her hand.

"I'm here to help you in your sorrow, Martha," he said in a gentle voice, correctly guessing her identity.

The woman looked up and tried to speak but couldn't make it.

James patted her hand sympathetically.

"I've brought the Rabbi. He will comfort you in your sorrow," he assured her.

She closed her eyes and James took that as acceptance of his offer.

"I'll get him," he said, and eased his way out of the room.

Jesus limped towards him as he came out of the house.

"I've spoken to the dead man's sister. She's given the go-ahead." He put his arm around Jesus's shoulder and led him towards the house.

"What d'you expect us to do," Peter asked belligerently.

James turned to him.

"Surely you don't need a nurse?" he said sarcastically. "There must be dozens around here who would like to look after a big lad like you."

He turned to the old woman he spoke to earlier.

"What about you, Mother? Can you give my friend here something to eat and lodgings for the night?" he asked.

The woman looked Peter over and nodded.

"There you are. Fixed up - no problem. The rest of you be ready to leave at dawn - right?" James said tersely.

The others nodded agreement and looked the crowd over for other perspective hosts.

James led Jesus through the garden and into the house.

The scene was the same as before in the room of the wake. James put out his hand and gently helped the grieving sister to her feet.

"This is the Rabbi I told you about. Jesus."

Jesus held out his hands and the woman clung to them. She looked into the dark, pockmarked face of the Rabbi but all she saw was the large, sympathetic eyes which radiated a comfort that, while not diminishing the pain of her bereavement, made her feel that she was not alone.

"I'm sorry for your pain," Jesus said slowly. "But he has gone to a better place and is in the care of Yahweh, the Father of All Things." Jesus turned to the body on the table. "What is his name?" he asked.

"Lazarus," Martha sobbed.

"When did he die?" Jesus probed gently, not sure why he asked the question.

The woman controlled her sobs and touched the hand of her late brother.

"Four days ago," she said.

Jesus looked at James in surprise.

"Four days?" he said sharply.

"The Rabbi left last week. We didn't want to bury him until he returned."

The thought of the burial hit her and she sank once more to the floor in a welter of tears.

Jesus touched the cheek of the dead man, then leaned forward and sniffed. James watched, surprised by Jesus's actions. Jesus picked up one of Lazarus's hands and flexed the fingers. He frowned and again felt the flesh around the face of the corpse.

"What is it?" James asked quietly.

Jesus shook his head.

"I don't know. I would have thought...," he knelt down beside the sobbing woman.

"I'm sorry but....how did he die? Was he ill or did he just collapse?" he asked.

One of the women standing by the wall answered for the distressed widow.

"She found him sitting in a chair," the woman volunteered. Jesus stood and went to her.

"Who are you?" he asked.

"Mary. I'm his younger sister. I live here," she claimed.

Jesus nodded.

"I'm sorry to bother you at a painful time like this but....was he ill?"

Mary shook her head.

"Not really. He had a bit of trouble with his bladder and was always thirsty but we put it down to his age."

Jesus nodded and turned to Martha. Before he could speak James grabbed his arm and moved him away to a secluded corner.

"What is it?" James demanded once more.

Jesus shook his head, undecidedly.

"They say he's been dead four days. I would have thought... I'd like to examine him more thoroughly," he said.

James sprang into action immediately.

He asked Martha if there was somewhere the Rabbi could be alone with the deceased. Martha was surprised by the request.

"The Rabbi likes to be alone with the departed so that he can recommend his spirit to Yahweh," he said quickly.

Martha looked up at Jesus, hesitated for a moment, then nodded consent. Mary helped Martha to her feet and opened the door to a small back room.

James picked up the body of Lazarus and carried him through. Jesus followed. James laid out the body on the table, then eased the mourners out of the room and shut the door.

"What now?" James asked.

Not sure if they weren't, in some way, making fools of themselves, but aware that his brother rarely embarked on any enterprise without justification.

Jesus stood over the body and expertly ran his hands over the pliant limbs. He pulled back the man's eyelid and looked long and hard into the pupil. Jesus stepped back and shook his head.

"Give me your knife," he said.

Without hesitation James handed him his ram-horn handled blade. Jesus turned Lazarus's arm over and ran the knife edge down the inside of his forearm. The cut was not deep but it instantly began to ooze blood.

"What the...?" James stepped back - not sure of what he was witnessing. "He's not dead?"

"Some sort of a fit, I would guess. I've seen something like it before. I must tell his sisters."

Jesus turned to the door but James held out a restraining hand.

"Hold it. You say he's not dead?" he asked.

"Not at the moment but if something isn't done soon he will be," Jesus assured him. "Right. Let's think this through before you go out there and raise everyone's hopes."

He turned back to the body and laid his hand on the bare arm.

"If he's not dead, how do we wake him?" James asked.

Jesus went and stood on the other side.

"I would think it's a matter of getting the blood flowing again. Three days is a long time. Maybe it's too late but it's worth a try," he said slowly.

James clapped his hands together, sensing an advantage but not sure how it would work out.

"What do we do?" he asked simply.

"We need to raise his temperature," Jesus said, and started to strip off the blankets covering Lazarus.

"See if you can get some hot water."

While James explained that the Rabbi wanted to personally wash the body of Lazarus and organised hot water, Jesus massaged the flaccid limbs. By the time James returned with the water, Jesus was exhausted. It worried James that Jesus had so little stamina but he hadn't time to be solicitous. Jesus rested in the corner while James washed the body with the hot water and applied the hot cloths to the cold limbs of Lazarus. When he had done all he could he hunkered down in front of Jesus and shook him awake. Jesus allowed James to pull him to his feet.

"That's the best I can do. The water's getting cold," James told him. Jesus nodded and once again examined Lazarus's eyes.

"Get him into a sitting position," Jesus ordered and James complied. "We have to try to get him breathing and the blood circulating. I'll hold his legs, you push him forward until his head's between his knees, then pull him back until he's laid out flat. Just keep doing it rhythmically and we should get a result," Jesus instructed.

In the flickering light of the oil lamp the bizarre operation of bringing the dead man back to life was more reminiscent of a torture scene from a Roman dungeon than a technique to restore life.

A number of times James was tempted to quit but Jesus assured him that their strenuous efforts were beginning to have results. A couple of times inquisitive mourners tried to enter and were only just thwarted in the attempt. James hated to think what Lazarus's friends would make of the macabre gymnastics they were making him perform in an effort to resuscitate him.

Even Jesus was beginning to lose faith when a slight twitch of an eyelid gave them renewed hope. Slowly Lazarus began to breathe. Irregularly at first but then he gave a deep, dramatic sigh and his breath came regularly without the aid of James strenuous efforts. Jesus instructed James to wrap him up again and went back to massaging the limbs. With another dramatic sigh Lazarus woke up and looked around, puzzled by his surroundings and the strangers at his side. Jesus gave him a reassuring smile and laid a comforting hand on his shoulder.

"Don't worry. You've been ill. You're all right now. Just rest," he told him soothingly.

The words and Jesus's presence had a calming effect and Lazarus closed his eyes and relaxed.

Jesus went to the door.

"I'll tell his sisters."

Once again James stopped him.

"In a minute. Let's make sure he's going to be all right first," he suggested.

Jesus looked at the sleeping Lazarus and smiled.

"He'll pull through," he promised.

Still James wasn't ready to announce what had happened. He knew the tales of miracles his simple countrymen were spreading about the new Rabbi who was coming to Jerusalem to claim his birthright. James was responsible for a lot of them although he was constantly surprised by other miracles that were being claimed on behalf of Jesus. Their present little drama, properly presented, had all the earmarks of a gift. He didn't want to spoil it by rushing in before he had a chance to use it to its maximum effect.

"Rest a while. There's no need to rush into anything," James told him.

Jesus realised James was up to his old tricks, trying to exploit the situation to their advantage but he was too tired to argue. Without a word he slid down in the corner and rested his head on his knees. He didn't know how long he had slept when he was awakened by a scuffle at the door.

James was resting with his back against the door when someone tried to enter. He wasn't having that. It would spoil the spectacular entry he had planned while Jesus dozed.

"Not now!" Jesus heard his brother say tersely.

He pushed himself to his feet.

"Open the door. I'm Rabbi Esau. What are you doing in there? I demand entry," a stern voice bellowed from behind the closed door.

Jesus checked Lazarus.

As he bent over him the resuscitated man's eyes opened.

Jesus smiled at him.

"How are you?" he asked.

"Could I have a drink?" the man asked.

"Open this door - at once. Do you hear? At once!" Rabbi Esau was getting impatient and the chair braced against the door to keep it closed wasn't going to hold much longer.

James nodded to Lazarus.

"D'you think you can walk?" he asked.

Lazarus answered by swinging his legs over the side of the table and bracing his feet on the floor. He pushed himself erect, wobbled and sat abruptly down again.

"He needs to rest," Jesus intervened.

"I'll be all right," Lazarus assured him and tried again.

This time he managed to stay on his feet, although he needed the support of James's steadying hand.

Someone, probably the furious Rabbi Esau, was making a determined assault on the door.

"Lean on Jesus," James said curtly.

Jesus gave James a wry look. The thought of someone needing to lean on him seemed amusing, but he let Lazarus transfer his weight from James to him.

James strode swiftly across to the door and took the chair away. The black-clad Rabbi almost fell into the room. James wanted a bigger audience for the unveiling of his miracle than the religious teacher. He caught the smaller man, turned him around so that his back was to Jesus, and the newly re-vitalised Lazarus, and stepped into the room beyond. He went straight to Martha and Mary and clasped them in his arms.

"Jesus has intervened with the Father Yahweh!" he told her solemnly, then turned her around as Lazarus, supported by the exhausted Jesus, inched slowly into the room.

Chapter 14

Naomi urged Robin's donkey past the stack of dried corn stalks piled high in a wind nagged heap beside the road. The hot, greasy wind from the desert, as predictably punctual as a Roman taxman, abraded patience into a hard, self-flagellating cynicism. Robin was spared external pressures. His constant battle to survive in the rapidly deteriorating brain of his host, Haddaq, his mounting compulsion to find the wandering Jesus, the perpetual struggle to grasp and relate the frighteningly vivid but impossibly transient pictures in his mind and the fear for his sanity, were proof against the vilest meteorological conditions.

The outskirts of Jericho struck a responsive chord. There was something about the way the people moved, how they walked swiftly and purposefully along the narrow streets. Robin looked at the strange, tight packed buildings decked with laundry and pots of straggling plants. He tried to read some significance into the self-conscious importance of the crowding houses. Why they seemed more familiar to him than the drab, utilitarianism of country life? Like most thoughts he tried to pursue, the solution remained a frustrating enigma eluding his grasp.

Robin saw Isaac stop his mount, swing a leg over its rump and dismount. One of the black-clad women dashed forward to control the animal as he gestured for Robin to join him. They had stopped outside a high, blank wall, well maintained and painted in smoothing layers of yellow lime. The wall stretched in either direction for a considerable distance and was not flanked or over-looked by any of the other houses on the suburban street.

Set into the wall was a sturdy, solid timber door. It was a symbol of opulence that could not but impress anyone passing. In the centre of the door was another indication of the wealth and standing of the owner: a heavy iron door-knocker in the shape of a bunch of grapes. Iron had a smelting value only fractionally less than silver in the thieves-kitchen that had developed over the centuries outside the city gates. No one ever considered touching the valuable adornment on that particular door.

The owner was Joseph of Arimathea.

Joseph was a member of the fraternity that lived off the cupidity of those who considered themselves his betters. He was a pirate. A man who operated with, through, on, above or under, whoever was likely to make a profitable deal for him. Contradictorily he was a kindly man. A *bon viveur;* a thoughtful host who would do anything to make his guest happy. His friends were legion and his enemies a host. Only the smartest and most ruthless could survive in the vortex of violence, envy and greed that he occupied. It was a tribute to his superiority that he was able to do it with a grace and charisma that brought him admirers in all walks of life.

Isaac grasped the metal grapes and banged vigorously on the door.

His small train of donkeys had attracted a group of street urchins who hung around in the hope of some easy pickings. The authority with which Isaac pounded on the sacred door convinced them that there were easier marks in distant parts of the city, marks who did not pound on the door of the notorious Joseph. As Robin joined Isaac, the old man smiled reassuringly at him.

"Not much longer now. My friend will be able to help, if anyone can."

Robin smiled faintly back but could think of no reply for his helpful benefactor. A small metal grill above the knocker flipped open and an eye glared through.

"Who is it?" a discouraging voice demanded.

Isaac moved around so that he could be seen through the hole.

"Isaac from Galilee. Your master is expecting me."

Instantly there was the dry rasp of bolts being drawn and the heavy door swung open and a short, fat man in a brown robe bowed to them.

"Greeting, gentlemen! I am Goth the Gaul, body-servant to my Lord Joseph. Please, enter"" he said in a halting, accented voice.

Isaac looked back at the animals and his servants. Goth the Gaul forestalled any request.

"Do not worry, sir. Your chattels will be safeguarded. I will send a man to direct them to the gate at the rear of the estate," he assured Isaac smoothly and gave as deep a bow as his pot-belly would allow.

Isaac put his arm around Robin's shoulder and drew him through the gate. The servant bolted the door and then squeezed past them with an apologetic smile and led them towards the house. Within the walled garden the oppressive afternoon wind was banished. There was a dense humidity to the air that fused with the subtle odours of the plants and flowers to make an invigorating, almost sensual, concoction. It was like stepping into another world. The close-grown fruit trees, aromatic herbs, trained vines and bright flowers had nothing to do with the dust and heat of the desert trail or the sleazy dinginess of the city streets. As they approached the house through the avenue of sheltering grapevines, Robin, for the first time, felt a sense of peace. The darting, trilling birds and the low throb of busy insects was a soothing symphony.

Joseph's house was large and single storeyed. Like everything else that came within his domain it was immaculate and comfortable. Around the wall of the building the roof extended outwards to form a cool sheltered terrace. Using underground ducts, a lesson learned from his friends in the Roman army, he had piped water from the surrounding hills into a number of high-level cisterns about the grounds. These, combined with the natural spring and well water that was his reason for buying the site originally, gave him an abundant supply of crystal clear water which he fed through a series of fountains and waterfalls. The splash and ripple of the cool water made Joseph's garden a paradise after the arid world beyond the walls. To Joseph it represented his power; his ability to bend even beauty and the natural elements to his bidding. Even the winter cold he had conquered in his private world. Rome's finest engineers installed a hypocaust that not only heated his house and gave him constant hot water in his bath but assured a steady soil temperature in his garden on the coldest day.

Isaac, a man of social standing in his own community, was constantly impressed by the splendid lifestyle of his old friend. Isaac - the only son of a wealthy land owner; and Joseph - the youngest of the large family of one of the Royal stewards. Joseph's father had little time for his family, spending most of the day at the court of Herod. As Joseph, the baby of the family, became just another mouth to feed he lost his sheltered position in life and had to fend for himself. The easy, women dominated life of Isaac's family became his home. Joseph's father's, disgrace at the hands of the unpredictable Herod and his subsequent poverty when his honours were stripped from him, produced in the adolescent Joseph a determination to secure a place in the world that he could control and not be subject to the whim of others. Isaac's father helped him to get started. Against the advice of his advisors the old man outfitted a caravan with top quality merchandise and gave Joseph a list of contacts throughout the country.

Within a year young Joseph of Arimathea paid back the loan, plus a handsome profit, which he insisted was his benefactor's right, and laid the foundation for an expanding and highly profitable business. Within five years he was running goods into every port in the Mare

Internum and beyond. Later he even invested in the tin mines of the tenuous colony that Rome established in the backwoods Britannia. His first visit to the wild settlement was his last.

Ordinary trade, the clairvoyant need of supply on demand, the often betrayed trust by unscrupulous dealers, soon convinced Joseph that he was still too vulnerable for his liking so he sought a little insurance. It wasn't long before the word got around that underhand dealings with Joseph meant a visit from a party of his insurance men. Which meant at least a few days in bed nursing bruises, and at the worse the destruction of business or the more final alternative - death!

For added security Joseph helped a Roman senator, teetering on the borders of bankruptcy, with the grisly business of slashed wrists in a hot bath the only escape, buy off his creditors and continue his degenerate life for a while longer. The price was citizenship; the seal that granted the owner seigniorial powers throughout the colonies.

Isaac was a privileged friend. While the caravans of other market competitors were constantly the object of attack from Joseph's armed trade advisors, they knew better than to interfer with the friend of their employer.

As Isaac and Robin stepped onto the shady terrace Joseph burst from the house. Without a word he wrapped his arms around his friend. Robin had a chance to look him over. After the stories Isaac had told him of his piratical background Robin expected someone more fearsome than the medium built, balding man in the thin, blue bordered toga in front of him.

Joseph let go his affectionate hold on Isaac and turned to Robin and grasped his hands.

"Welcome to Jericho. My house is your house for as long as you wish to stay." His frank, sensitive face reinforced his words.

Thrown off balance by the serenity of the hidden garden Robin had difficulty in mastering his tongue. Concern showed in his host's face as, with a covert glance at Isaac, he took Robin by the arm and gently guided him into the house.

"Calm yourself. You are tired. Have a rest first and then a bath. You'll feel better for it," he said reassuringly. "Then we can have a long talk about your problems. Isaac's letter was fascinating but tantalisingly short on detail."

Joseph led him to a cool, airy room with limed walls and a smooth, clean floor tiled in the Roman manner. The wide bed with a gossamer fine net over it to keep out the flies had also made the long journey from the Italian peninsular to the city of Jerusalem on the ubiquitous caravans of Joseph.

Joseph helped Robin get under the net and promised to send one of the servant women with fresh clothes when he woke. On the borders of sleep Robin heard the deep voice of Joseph order a servant to keep him cool with a fan as he slept.

For once his sleep was not harassed by inexplicable dreams or threats from the submerged Haddaq ego and he awoke refreshed and more relaxed than he could remember. As soon as he moved one of the black clad women pulled back the netting and handed him a cool bowl of water with a small sprig of mint floating on top. Gratefully Robin sat up in bed and drank. Darkness had fallen while he slept and he had developed an appetite. The woman appeared by the side of the bed again with a neatly folded garment. From the blue border Robin correctly surmised that it was a toga thoughtfully supplied by his host. He smiled at the woman and handed her the empty bowl. Her dark eyes, highlighted by her black yashmak, sparkled a friendly greeting. Suddenly Robin wanted to know her name. Since he first met Isaac the woman had attended Robin constantly and silently. She never seemed to sleep and was abnormally susceptible to his thoughts.

"Thank you. Tell me, what is your name?" he asked in his carefully controlled manner.

The woman stepped back quickly, as if insulted by the inquiry. Impulsively Robin gripped her hand. She made no attempt to shake him off.

"Don't be frightened, please. I just want to know what I should call you," he pleaded.

The woman ducked her head in assent.

"I am not frightened. My name is Naomi. I am the daughter of Isaac." Her voice was young and fresh and Robin realised that she was little more than a child.

"Thank you, Naomi," he said solemnly.

She moved back to give him room to get off the bed.

"My Lord Joseph told me to take you to the bath," she said gravely.

Robin got up and followed her along the corridor and across an open terrace in a long building separated from the main house by an encircling patio. As he walked through the door he stopped, amazed. Most of the centre of the room was taken up by a polished marble bath. The deep, clear water dimpled and swirled as the circulating current of warm water filtered in through ducts in the floor heated by the hot chamber below ground level. On the paved surround were several low couches set beside tables laden with fruit and sweetmeats. Bath-servants hastily put away their dice as Robin entered and came around the pool to meet him. He let them strip him and then slipped gratefully into the warm pool and allowed the sensual currents to flow around his unaccustomed body.

While the attendant worked on Haddaq's underdeveloped muscles Robin's mind floated clear and peace came to him for the first time.

Isaac and Joseph arrived to collect him as he was wrapping the obstinate toga around his body with the help of Naomi. Isaac had also succumbed to the Roman influence and looked perfectly at ease in the flowing garment. Both of the older men roared with laughter at Robin's clumsy attempts to stop the toga unwinding and falling to the floor. At last the robe hung to everybody's satisfaction and Joseph led his guests out onto one of the small courtyards where a table was laid for supper. Before taking his place at the low table the host made sure they were comfortably cushioned and able to reach the food with ease. Throughout the meal Isaac and Joseph reminisced about past events and mutual friends, carefully explaining their stories to Robin so that he would not feel like an intruder. As they finished eating Joseph brought the conversation around to the reason for their visit. Whilst Robin slept Isaac had brought Joseph up to date. Joseph was amazed by his friend's story but trusted him and did not go into a long interrogation to find the basis for Isaac's obvious belief that his protege was something more than the village madman that he appeared to be. Joseph had seen too many wonders in his journeys through the east to doubt that there was more to life than the obvious.

There was another point of interest for him that he hadn't bothered to explain to his old partner. When he heard of the growing support that the Nazarene Jesus was getting in the north, he sent one of his agents to report on what was going on. The area around Nazareth had a particular interest for him. When he began to establish trade routes, it was there that he set up one of his first warehouses. He remembered those times with nostalgia tinged with sentimentality for what might have been. His man had mingled with the people and listened to the stories they told of the Messiah who was going to banish the Romans with a word, a prophet who was able to make blind men see and lame men walk, a mystical man of marvellous birth in whose blood the heroes of the testaments rejoiced.

Joseph sent out an invitation to Jesus to meet with him and discuss whether he had a future.

James came instead.

There was instant rapport between the two men. Both recognised in the other mutual qualities of ruthlessness and superior intellect.

James realised that the entrepreneur was not a man to try and hoodwink. He told him about the philosophies of his brother and how he was able to exploit them. Joseph was impressed with his masterstroke of providing Jesus with a bodyguard of the biggest and most intelligent men he could find. The two men talked the night away and in the dawn made a pact. Joseph would provide funds and contacts for the desert Rabbi and his band in exchange for a high Government position when they finally ousted the foreign administrators.

The following night they discussed tactics.

It was patently obvious that while Jesus stayed in the desert his following was going to be a rabble of nomads with little or no influence on the military might of Rome. Jesus had to take Jerusalem!

Once the Judeans had their own city to defend they could be relied upon to join the rebellion in large numbers. What Joseph hadn't liked was James's plan to unleash the hordes of outlaws in the mountains. His kindred spirit told him that once the bandits took power they would be uncontrollable.

And that would be bad for business.

Joseph advised James that he would only go along with him if he could guarantee a bloodless coup. A popular rising that would isolate the Roman administration and make them vulnerable to pressure from the more tractable forces at the command of the revolutionaries. James could see the sense of the older man's plans on an academic level although he had reservations about the neutrality of the military administration in a confrontation with the Jewish hierarchy if it should become unavoidable.

But it wasn't a point to argue at that time. If they didn't press on their support would decline and his plans would come to nothing. James finally agreed and aborted the plan for guerrilla support. So far Joseph was satisfied with the way his plans were working out. The unexpected appearance of the village idiot with thoughts and information that should have been beyond his feeble intellect threatened a danger that Joseph was not prepared to dismiss without investigation.

He looked at the shrivelled figure on the opposite side of the table.

"Isaac has told me what he knows. It seems you want to meet the Nazarene Rabbi, Jesus?" Joseph opened the serious discussion with deceptive disinterest.

Robin snatched a look at Isaac and ducked his head nervously in acknowledgement.

"But you don't know why?" Joseph added.

Again Robin silently agreed. Joseph clucked his tongue on his front teeth and shook his head doubtfully.

"It could be difficult. Jesus is never alone and his bodyguards need a reason to grant an audience to anybody he doesn't know," he said, as if talking to himself. Robin looked at Isaac for support and was encouraged by an imperceptible nod.

"I just know it is vitally important that I meet him when he arrives in Jerusalem. In my head there is the reason but I just can't find it. Everything is mixed up. I know I do not belong here but I don't know how I know or where it is I feel I come from....At night I have strange dreams in which I seem to understand many things which I forget when I wake up. But their memory persists although I can't understand them." He paused and looked at his host.

The old man nodded understandingly.

"There seems to be two sides in my brain. A dark, uncontrolled personality called Haddaq who is trying to get rid of the Robin side of my brain. Most of the time I am Robin, but a Robin with only the memories of Haddaq - and a jumble of nonsense in my mind. Except for the Jesus factor. That stays there all the time. I know I have to be in Jerusalem when Jesus arrives. What I shall do then I don't know but I am certain that when the time comes, I will know!" Robin slumped back onto the cushions, exhausted by the intensity of his speech.

The two men looked at each other without speaking. Joseph took an orange and began to peel it as he considered what to do.

He came to a decision.

"Very well. I will help you. I have a friend who has recently got a position at the temple for a young man who, I believe, is one of the intimates of Jesus. If I can convince Nicodemus that it is crucial for you to meet Jesus he will get his young friend to arrange the meeting." He smiled at Robin confidently.

Relief brought tears to the tortured man's eyes and impulsively he reached across the table and gripped his benefactor's hand.

"Thank you. Thank you sir! I'm sure you won't regret it," he promised fervently.

Joseph patted his hand and prepared to go to bed. He had no way of knowing the reaction his next, innocent words would produce.

"Don't thank me. I'm just the man in the middle. If it works out you will have to thank Judas," he said.

JUDAS!

In Robin's brain the word swelled and echoed crushing the restraint that held his personality stable. Haddaq stirred and reached for the body's motive centres. Robin reared to his feet and crashed down across the laden table sending the silver dishes and earthenware bowls skidding across the floor. He felt cold, cramping convulsions squeeze the walls of his stomach in a rhythmic counterpoint to the throbbing pain in his head: *Ju - das! JU - DAS! JUUU - DAS!!*

The febrile madness of Haddaq snatched at the word, tore at it with mind warping glee. The word became a babbling tangle of bestial sounds torn from the imprisoned tongue of the deranged man.

Chapter 15

Robin's vigil in the transmitter room had become a compulsion. Every moment he could spare he sat in the overheated room staring at the uncommunicative dials. It didn't matter that he was becoming a figure of fun. He knew something that no one else did. Whatever the scientific opinion might be he now was certain that he was getting feedback from his memory implant in the past. It was not strong enough to give him impressions or allow him the comfort of insight into what was happening. But when he sat in front of the transmitter he could feel a definite empathy with the host of his thought-module held back in time by the vast current feeding the transmitter.

Tonight the vibrations were exceptionally strong. He wanted an explanation!

Robin Firth picked up the telephone on the desk beside the transmitter console and dialled his secretary.

"Get me Sanderstead and Mayer. I want them here – immediately," he ordered.

His secretary objected.

"They are both at the Edinburgh conference…"

Before she could finish Firth cut in.

"I don't care where they are. I want them here immediately. Do you understand? Tell them to drop everything. Send the Lear to pick them up. I want them here in the morning!"

Without waiting for an answer he slammed the handset down and returned to his favourite seat. Through the long night he sat unmoved, transfixed by the sense of drama being enacted over the centuries and held by the unseen, unfelt power of the transmitter. He thought about the possible inaccuracies of the machine. Even about the possibility of the whole thing being nothing more than a trick played on him by his bored mind. He quickly discarded that thought. Whatever was happening, it was no trick.

Sanderstead and Mayer found him sitting mesmerised by the dial that showed that the transmission was still taking place at the elapsed time. Sanderstead had to touch him before he became aware of their presence. Neither was very amused at being forced to leave a conference, which was partly in their honour, to return to the laboratory at the whim of a layman who had been overcome by his own demons of grandeur.

Firth got up stiffly and without a word led them into the more comfortable outer office. He poured himself a coffee from the glass Cona pot simmering on the electric plate and stretched out in an armchair with his feet on the low, glass-topped table in front of him. Mayer took a seat by the wall as far away as possible. His head resting on his hand and his crossed legs spoke louder than words his disapproval of the 'breakfast' meeting. Sanderstead was equally upset but tried not to show it. He perched himself on the front edge of the low armchair facing Robin as if he had only dropped in for a moment and needed to get away.

Robin sipped his lukewarm coffee and looked them over.

Neither seemed to be in the mood to give much credence to what he was about to tell them. It was unscientific and not covered by an equation, therefore it couldn't happen.

Only it had!

Robin placed his cup and saucer on the table and addressed himself to Sanderstead.

"I'm sorry to call you in like this, Korky, but I have something to say that is important and can't wait." Robin Firth paused to gather his thoughts. "Something is happening that I don't understand. It may sound crazy to you but I want you to approach it with an open mind."

Mayer shifted in his seat. He was still trying to give an appearance of total disinterest but Firth could tell that he was listening. Korky frowned and looked at the door leading into the transmitter room.

"To do with the transmitter?"

Slowly Robin nodded.

"Not directly. At least it isn't something that is being produced by the transmitter itself. For several days now I have had a feeling that I am getting a reaction, a sort of subliminal communication. It is hard to describe. It has nothing to do with actual images or thoughts that I can either understand or direct. I just know that when I sit in front of the transmitter I communicate." Firth looked at Sanderstead but before the big man could make any comment Mayer pushed himself to his feet and walked to the door.

"Impossible! You are hypnotising yourself. Now, if that is all, I've got to get back to Edinburgh!" Mayer spoke in a cold, insulting voice.

Sanderstead flushed red and made a placating gesture with his hand.

Firth's face went hard.

"I do mind! Sit down and listen to what I have to say. I'll tell you when you can leave."

For a second Mayer looked ready to rebel but he caught a signal from Sanderstead and suddenly remembered the generous salary and support they received from the Firth Foundation. To get control of a similar set-up might not be so easy, especially if Firth refused to let them publicise their space/time regressor. With bad grace he returned to his seat and studiously examined the stitching on the instep of his patent leather shoes.

Robin Firth poured another cup of black coffee and let them wait. It was pointless antagonising the two scientists. He could order them to find an answer to the phenomena that he was experiencing but if they weren't convinced that the phenomena existed he didn't think they would come up with a satisfying answer.

"All right, I know that what I am suggesting seems fanciful - to say the least. At first I felt the same way. But now I am convinced! Last night the....er....vibrations were particularly strong." He saw that he had used the wrong word.

Vibes had been a hippy concept in the sixties and had connotations of drug taking and flower power. He held up his hand.

"Okay, okay. So you are not convinced. Well I'm sorry but you have got to hear me out." Robin thought for a while before continuing.

"Let us suppose, for the sake of argument and to please me, that what I say is correct. That somehow I am getting feedback from my thought-module in the past. This would pre-suppose the possibility of two-way transmission - right?"

Sanderstead nodded reluctantly but Mayer still appeared to be ignoring the issue.

"In that case it would open a whole new dimension to what you have achieved. It would mean that the possibility existed for monitoring any period in history."

Firth let the new concept sink in. He carefully avoided looking at Mayer but was certain that he had his attention now. Mayer wasn't going to be subverted that easily.

"That's if you ARE getting feed-back!"

Firth nodded.

"I'm willing to grant the possibility that I'm fooling myself," he agreed. "But what if I'm not? What if there is some way of monitoring the past? You said yourself that there was no practical application for the transmitter. You only went along with my suggestion to transmit my thought module back to the time of Christ because there was no way else you were going to get the sort of money you needed to perfect your machine. Isn't it worth a shot?

Have you ever even seriously considered the theory that we could develop a direct link with the past?"

Robin Firth had said enough.

Mayer, on his feet now, looked with unseeing eyes at his partner. Sanderstead, totally oblivious to everything, had unconsciously taken a computer from his pocket and was playing absentmindedly with the buttons. Firth let them get well and truly hooked before attempting to reel them in. When he finished his third cup of coffee he stood up.

"Right, gentlemen. There are still seven days left before we terminate transmission. I want an in-depth report in simple language before then. In addition to the physical possibilities of direct communication I also want to know what will be the physical results if we attempt to engineer events in the past. What will be the actual effects on the present day?

"You said originally that a comparatively minor historical change could not only completely alter present day conditions but would be unnoticed now because it would become a part of our alternative history. What I want to know now is the possibility of accurately forecasting the consequence of change on the development of history."

Robin Firth walked around the desk and stood between the two scientists, a faint smile on his lips. Now he was satisfied that he had given them something to think about he felt tired.

"Well gentlemen. Thank you once again for your attention. Let me have a report as soon as you can. In the meantime I intend to stay here until we have made a decision about what we should do with the present transmission."

Mayer waved vaguely at him but Sanderstead was already deep in mental calculations trying to find a premise that would support the thesis that the space/time regressor was duo-directional!

Chapter 16

As consciousness returned, Cassio found himself lying on a stone floor in a small, unfurnished cell. Cautiously he moved his head and looked around.

It was a weird sensation.

He was about to try and stand when he heard footsteps approaching. From the sound he imagined a dark, damp passage carved out of living rock.

Behind him a door crashed open and he could sense someone standing there. He left his eyes open but pretended to be unconscious. Feet in heavy, steel tipped boots passed noisily within inches of his staring eyes. He felt strong hands grab his arms and legs. The floor canted crazily and he was carried out of the cell. The passage lived up to his imagination except that it was darker and damper than he had guessed. Face downward he could only judge his progress by the floor. He was carried up a long flight of stone steps that got dryer the higher they went. Suddenly he was in a room with polished wooden flooring, flooded by bright sunlight. They pressed through a doorway and he was thrown carelessly onto a table.

Still he managed to disguise the pain as his face hit the metal surface.

Under his head he could see a shallow channel. He nearly revealed his state of consciousness as he realised what it was.

A blood channel - the sort that was cut into the surface of a mortuary table - where *post mortems* were carried out.

His mind cringed.

Did his captors intend to dissect him alive?

He saw the red and green plaid kilt of the MacGregor come into the limited scan of his eyes and identified it with the Pict police.

Someone else entered the room.

"Is this the man?" demanded a harsh, unseen voice.

"Yes, *Effendi*," the man beside him answered with servile respect.

"Well, turn him over so that I can see him, you fool," the voice snapped.

Cassio was rolled over roughly so that he was now staring at the ceiling. A hard, dark grey-bearded face, framed by the black drapes of a burnoose, came into vision and stared down into his eyes.

Decision replaced suspicion and he turned away.

"Put him in with tomorrow's executions. Death by amputation and beheading. He won't be regaining consciousness so put him in with today's amputates and carry out the sentence in one go."

"Yes, *Effendi*," the guard acknowledged, fearful respect in his voice.

Cassio was picked up again and carried on the return journey down the steep steps that led to the cells. Instead of taking him back to the lower cell where he had originally been held he was taken along a long corridor. At the end was a heavy, iron studded door. The man leading the bearers threw open the door and gestured for them to throw Cassio in.

They swung him backwards and forwards a couple of times, and on "three" threw Cassio's helpless body though the door. Cassio was aware of the cartwheeling stone ceiling and the steep steps but had no way of controlling the flight of his body. He heard rather than felt the snap of his leg at his flailing body hit the steps. He bounced into the air, his head smashed against the side wall and he lost consciousness before he hit the floor of the cell, breaking his collarbone and several ribs.

Chapter 17

Spiny camel-thorn bushes crowded close to the narrow path, worn smooth and hard by centuries of use. It wandered with aimless authority through the sparse, grey vegetation, coming out of the dull distorting heat haze and disappearing into the uncertain horizon. The persistent wind that heralded the coming of darkness and the cooling of the upper layers of air, blew straight into the small band of men moving slowly in the direction of Bethany. The breeze moulded their galabias to their sweating bodies and tangled their hair and beards in tight knots.

In Bethany only the dogs were awake and they greeted the travellers with their usual ferocious cacophony of aggressive yapping and frightened whining. The noise caused few curious faces to appear in the open apertures of the crude dwelling houses but the group ignored them and strode on through the jumble of buildings until they came to a larger structure on the other side. In years gone by it had been the home of a man who owned most of the fields around the village. As he got old and tired he sold off parts of his farm until only the main buildings and stock pens remained. Situated as it was on two of the main routes from the north to Jerusalem it attracted the attention of Joseph and he bought the old man out. Now it was used as a warehouse and staging post for caravans that had the blessing of the powerful trading boss. James was told that he could use it until he was ready for the final push into Jerusalem two miles away.

As they approached, a man, alerted by the dogs, detached himself from the shadows and came towards them. He was small and bowlegged with a large bald head canted sideways as if his scrawny neck was unable to support the weight. In spite of the night chill he was dressed in only a short, coarse linen shirt covered by a stiff leather apron. In contrast to his grotesque figure his voice was deep and assured.

"Good evening gentlemen. Welcome to the Bethany trading post. Do I have the honour of addressing the party of Jesus the Nazarene?" he inquired.

James stepped past Peter and gave the little man a short formal bow.

"Good evening. I am James, the brother of Jesus." He gave a brief nod to Jesus.

"I'm afraid Jesus is not well. I would be obliged if you could direct us to our quarters so that we can look after him."

"Of course. Please follow me." The man turned and hobbled towards the dark buildings.

James fell in beside him.

"What is your name?" James asked.

"Ganod, Sir," the man replied.

"Have you any messages for me, Ganod? Either from the city or from Lord Joseph?"

The man led them around the back of the buildings and indicated a small door before replying.

"Mary Magdalene was here earlier today. She was hoping to see you. She left a message. Everything is going according to plan. If she can make it she will be back tomorrow," Ganod told him.

James grimaced.

The thought of Mary's meddling in their affairs was something he could do without. Their close relationship irked James but Jesus refused to terminate his friendship with the girl. Now she was butting in at a time when the relationship of the Rabbi Jesus could seriously be compromised by the scandal of his association with a notorious courtesan like Mary Magdalene.

James followed Ganod into the house.

The interior was a single room with thick tree trunks supporting the plaited palm frond roof. Originally it was the main hall of the house but its more recent history had been as a grain store. The acrid tang of last years' crop was still strong in the air. In the centre of the room a small fire burned on a hearthstone and glowed smokily in the gloom, relieved only by the guttering rush torch in a clamp on one of the supports. Around the room were a number of straw paillasses for the men to sleep on. At the far side of the fire a crude table with benches was ready for a meal. Ganod touched Jesus's arm and pointed to an area just inside the door that was partitioned off from the rest of the room. Jesus tried to thank him but the effort was too much and he sunk back on the soft straw, his breath laboured and uneven. James knelt down beside him and gently wrapped blankets around him while Ganod held a flaring torch.

James sat back on his heels and listened to his brother's rasping breath. For once he felt indecisive.

In three days' time he had to enter the city. It wasn't a long journey, less than two miles, in fact. That was the reason they had chosen this place. They were close enough to be kept well informed but wouldn't cause too much comment in a place that was used to itinerant travellers and traders resting up before making the final stage to the town. But as near as they were, it wouldn't make a lot of difference if Jesus were so sick that he couldn't make the journey. The whole campaign would go badly awry if the cheerleaders turned out waving palms and chanting *'Hail to Jesus'* and the star guest wasn't there. If it were just a matter of postponement for a few days, James would have done it straight away.

But it was more than that.

The Feast of the Passover was the most powerfully emotive festival of the year for the Jews. It was the time of renewing their faith; when the past was forgotten and the future bright. When families got together from all over the country and assured each other that God, who had rescued them from the humiliation of the Egyptians, would shortly deal the Romans a blow from which they would never recover. And with the talk of the Messiah being hotly whispered in every group of Jews from the elders down to the beggars at the gate, it was the ideal time to come onto the market. James wasn't sure that he could support the cause for another year. Especially without Jesus. In all their teaching Jesus was the central character. He was the one with the healing powers, the man with the direct link to God. If Jesus died, or was too sick to carry on, the movement would be dead. There was no provision in the campaign strategy for substituting another candidate.

James straightened up and looked at the little manager.

"Have you got something hot, Ganod? Soup or something?"

Ganod nodded.

"Of course sir. May I suggest you let me look after him while you get some food and have a rest," he said in his calm deep voice.

James nodded his thanks and left the room.

Ganod carefully hung the torch on the wall and went out and got a jug of water.

The men were sitting around the table at the other end of the room. Servants appeared with bowls of hot food and they tucked in with a will to the first square meal they had eaten since they set out on the road two weeks earlier.

With a cloth Ganod gently wiped the perspiration from the sick man's face and made him as comfortable as he could. There was empathy, unspoken but recognised, between the two men. Both were physical misfits. Ganod with his obscenely bowed legs and overlarge, hanging head and Jesus whose weak body with its shrivelled leg and ugly pock-marked face was judged without regard for his intelligence or compassion.

The cool towel on his face revived Jesus.

He looked into the worried eyes staring lopsided at him and smiled his thanks. Ganod held the jug to Jesus's dry cracked lips and encouraged him to swallow.

"'I'll get you some hot soup sir. That will help you get your strength back," he promised.

Jesus tried to refuse but the manager had already gone.

The soup did make him feel better. He was careful not to take too much or provoke a fit of coughing that would exhaust him physically and mentally. Ganod quietly left the room to attend to his other guests.

Jesus sank back into the dark warmth of the thick blankets and slept. Gradually the noise and movement died away in the room outside as the others sought the warmth of their beds. Only James stayed at the table staring, unseeing, at his hands.

The prospect of defeat was one that he could not come to terms with easily. Finally even his morbid thoughts were not able to ward off sleep and his head sank to the table and he drifted off.

Chapter 18

Mary Magdalene lounged back in the silky comfort of her palanquin and tried to get some sleep. It was an impossible hour to be travelling. More appropriate an hour to be going to bed than starting out on a journey. As she sagged back, leaden-limbed, she regretted the instruction she had given the trading post manager to inform her as soon as Jesus arrived. Or at least he could have made provision for her delicate condition. When she arrived home from a party celebrating the birthday of the son of a minor senator, recently sent out to the colonies to get some military experience, the messenger was waiting for her. She tried to go to bed to get a few hours sleep but in the end abandoned the attempt. Jesus's illness worried her. She had seen it develop over the years. Mary was afraid that the ambitious James and the driving need of Jesus to make the world a better place were ultimately going to be more deadly than the consumption that rotted his lungs. Her mind made up she sent her house-matron to stir up her four Ethiopian eunuchs to take her to Bethany.

Mary was one of the most enterprising courtesans in Judaea. Her beauty secured her a large Roman following. There was never a party or concert organised by the military to which she was not invited. In the end she was organising galas and entertainments for the officers and supplying their beds with a steady flow of young girls rescued from the poverty of the shanty towns that had grown up around the walls of Jerusalem.

Mary had met James on one of his first visits to Jerusalem. She was hardly fifteen but already a shrewd adventuress willing to peddle her only commodity, her body, for a share of the wealth that the Jewish merchants extorted from the garrison troops. The tall, athletic James with his sturdy body and calm face attracted her. She let James know it and he used her like he used everyone that came his way. At first she didn't mind. It gave her some satisfaction to pass on anything she heard from her customers. There was even the justifying hint of patriotism in her action. But she didn't fool herself for long. She had seen men drool over her dark beauty since she was eleven. As she became aware of James's cynical exploitation of her she realised that he didn't even like her. His small town mentality, in spite of the liberalising effect of his brother, inhibited him. He preached anarchy but was bound by his conservative background. As her interest in James faded she became aware of Jesus.

He had always been there. Quiet, polite, his large sensitive mouth quirking a good humoured smile when she told her boisterous stories of some of the parties that she and her girls put on. Jesus was able to help her over the breakdown of her plans for his brother James. At first it was a comfort for her to have someone willing to listen to her. In public life her profession demanded that she was constantly life and soul of any gathering she graced. She couldn't afford to have personal problems. Hers were the ears that heard the hopes and fears of others. No one had expressed an interest or offered comfort to the desperately lonely prostitute before. She was either used or despised. Nobody ever offered her friendship.

Except Jesus!

He would sit in the shade of a tree or by the river bank and listen to her for hours, offering advice only when asked and never criticising.

Mary had just drifted off into a state of fantasy when the palanquin was lowered to the ground and she heard a voice with a soft Galilean accent ask where they were going. Quickly checking to make sure that her long hair was in place, she flicked aside the heavy silk drapes. They had been stopped by one of James's men. She had met him before but for the moment she was unable to recall his name.

"Well hello!" she said in a voice pitched for maximum provocative connotation.

The man smiled and ducked a jerky embarrassed bow of welcome.

"How are you, lady?" he asked, afraid to use her name although it was well known to him and provided him with the occasional erotic thought.

Mary suddenly remembered his name.

"Is Jesus around, Philip?" she asked, swinging her legs to the ground and offering him her jewel encrusted hand to help her out.

Blushing with pleasure Philip gallantly pulled her upright. He would have liked to have closer contact with the beautiful and exotic woman but he didn't dare. Mary wrapped herself in a voluminous black cloak as a gesture to the social custom that demanded that women hid themselves from all strangers although in the case of Mary Magdalene the rule was superfluous. Even muffled to the eyes with a full face veil there was still an aura that flooded from her and made her every movement an act of libidinous provocation. Before Philip could gather his wits Ganod came from the house and hurried towards them, his curved legs imparting a rolling gait to his body that swung his head in crazy gyrations on his shoulders. He was still dressed the same as the night before, his shirt and apron spotlessly clean.

"Good morning, Lady Mary," he panted, bowing solemnly from the waist. "I am glad you were able to come. Would you follow me please?"

As they entered the building, Mary unhooked the side of her veil and pushed back the hood of her cloak, freeing her long, black hair, high-lighted with knots of precious stones plated into the ends and across her forehead in a fringe. Ganod watched her frankly, not trying to hide the admiration shining in his eyes. She reached forward impulsively and kissed him on the cheek.

"How are you, dear Ganod? Is everything going well?" she asked.

There were tears in his eyes as he nodded his bloated head. Ganod had been little more than a beggar when Mary had taken pity on him and got him his present job with Joseph.

But it wasn't this that fuelled Ganod's unlimited love for his benefactress. It was the way she treated him. All his life women laughed whenever he tried to talk to them.

Until Mary!

Now he didn't care about what other women thought - or even what the rest of the world thought. It was enough to know that the beautiful Mary Magdalene was his friend. She smiled understandingly and he led the way through to where Jesus was lying in his bed. He was the only one still there. The others had gone down to the river for their morning ablutions. Mary pulled aside the curtain across the door and looked in. She wrinkled her nose as the pungent smell of the sick room hit her.

"Thank you, Ganod. Now, could you get me a bowl of water and some clean towels, please?" she requested.

Ganod smiled eagerly and bowled off on the errand.

Mary pushed back the curtain to let more light in and entered the small room. As her eyes became accustomed to the gloom she could make out the slight figure of Jesus propped up in the corner. He was awake and his large bright eyes were crinkled with amusement at the myopic peering of his lovely visitor. When he saw she had located him he raised a hand in casual greeting.

"Hello. And how is the beautiful Mary today? Still stealing the soldiers blind?" he asked in a detached voice.

Mary pulled off her cloak and threw it on the bed.

"Listen Nazarene; I don't steal from soldiers. They are only too eager to give me what I want. And if they are not, I put it down to shyness and help them out by helping myself." Mary Magdalene spoke with mock indignation, her clenched fists on her hips. Jesus held up his hand in pretended fear.

"Of course. Of course, sorry..."

Mary shrieked with laughter. She looked ravishingly beautiful in the dim light, her nubile body highlighted by the figure hugging silk and damask robe she was wearing.

Jesus held out his arms to her and she ran to him and knelt on the paillasse while they embraced passionately, the exotic courtesan showering her kisses freely on the ill-favoured, pock-marked face of the sick man. She sank back against the wall with him, his thin, stick-like arms around her shoulders, her head resting on his chest.

Ganod came through the door bringing the hot water and towels himself. He never passed up an opportunity to be in Mary's presence or do a service for her. He put the bowl down beside the bed.

"If you want more let me know. Is there anything else I can get you, Lady Mary?" he offered.

Mary shook her head and rewarded him with a dazzling smile.

"Not now. Thank you Ganod. If there is, I'll let you know."

Ganod turned to go but she stopped him.

"Is there any way of getting some more light in here?"

Eager to please, Ganod went across to the wall opposite the doorway and thrust the wooden shutter open.

"Is that enough?" he asked, determined to knock the wall down if it wasn't.

After he had gone Mary pulled back the blankets covering Jesus and held her nose. "You smell worse than a herd of camels," she complained.

Jesus raised his eyebrows apologetically.

"Why is my smell always being compared with the body odour of some poor animal? I just stink," he informed her flatly.

"That you do," she agreed and started to pull off his sweat-stiff galabia. He helped her as best he could, pretending not to notice the look of pain in her eyes as she saw the state of his body. There was not an ounce of fat on his entire body and ugly pustules caused scarlet blemishes on his white skin. Mary bent down and laid her cool hand on the hot swellings on the knee and ankle joint of his lame leg.

Jesus watched her, a suspicious luminosity in his dark eyes. He was highly sensitive about his crippled leg but allowed Mary to examine the damage the long walk had done without embarrassment.

"You're in a hell of a mess," she informed him soberly.

Jesus gave a weak laugh.

"Can I rely on your diagnosis or should I call in a physician for a second opinion?" he joked.

Mary gave him an exasperated look.

"When are you going to take your health seriously? I'm worried about you. If you carry on like this you will kill yourself," she told him in a hard, serious voice.

The concern of his friend sobered Jesus.

"Don't worry about me, my love, I'm not afraid of death. I'm not looking for it and I would like to live forever but, if it must be, there's not a lot I can do about it," he said philosophically. Angrily Mary snatched one of the towels from the bowl of hot water and vented her frustration on savagely wringing out the surplus water.

"What do you mean there is nothing you can do about it? You can stop this trotting about all over the country to satisfy James's delusions of grandeur."

She stopped her gentle mopping of Jesus's body and looked beseechingly into his eyes.

"Please, Jesus, go home. Go back to Nazareth. The air is better there. Rest, eat good food. Do almost anything but stop this wandering around." She was close to tears.

Jesus put his hand behind her head and pulled her close. He kissed her softly on each eyelid.

"Thank you for your concern, Mary, but you know it's impossible. Everything is arranged. James and I have worked hard for this. Especially James. The time is right. After all, we are not teaching anything new. Just a chance to live better, more fulfilled lives." He tried earnestly to convince Mary Magdalene that there were no problems. But she was hard to convince.

With her network of spies she was more aware of the currents eddying through the corridors of power than even the scheming James. She had heard first-hand the anger and opposition that the stories that James was spreading provoked amongst the priests and elders of the Sanhedrin. It was here that any trouble was likely to erupt. The cosmopolitan Romans couldn't even imagine a situation where they couldn't stamp out insurrection with hardly an interruption in their interminable dice games. Even this disinterest could pose a threat.

The priests could not cause civil disturbance without getting the full weight of the Roman administration down on their heads. Regulations had been progressively relaxed over the years and a reasonable, harmonious way of life, steering a prickly path between Jewish religious law and Roman military order, had been found. But the military administrators were sticklers for regulations and would listen to any complaint made by the priests if it appeared to offer a threat to the comfortable truce they had manufactured between them.

What worried Mary especially was the way Jesus was promoted as the leader, the way he was linked with the promised Messiah. The tales of the guerrilla build-up in the surrounding countryside tended to smother the message of Love that was the new policy.

Mary was also suspicious of James's ultimate motive. Why there were only twelve men popularly known as Jesus's students. Why did James keep such a low profile while all the time he stage-managed every aspect of his brother's teachings? Mary didn't make the mistake of trying to point out James's discrepancies. Jesus was too close to his younger brother to allow even Mary to defame him. She could only keep her ears open and hope that if Jesus ran into trouble she would be able to help.

She finished cleaning him up in silence and then wrapped the blankets around him while she washed his hair. Mary made an effort to shake off the morbid thoughts. She patted his hair into place and leaned back to admire her handiwork.

"There you are."

She draped a lock of hair across the bald spot left by his receding hairline.

"That gives you a sort of aesthetic, holy look. Just right for your game, I suppose." She laughed at her own joke.

Mary leaned forward and kissed him on the mouth.

"Thank you." Jesus managed a tired grin. "And what is my game?" he demanded in a bantering tone.

Mary got up and picked up his galabia and held it up in the light.

"The con-game. It's arguable whose profession is the oldest. Yours or mine! Have you got another robe?"

Jesus was thrown off-balance by the unexpected question.

"I don't think so. I like to travel light and a change of clothes is heavy. And it's obviously mine."

Mary stopped in the doorway, not sure what he meant.

"Sorry?" she asked, puzzled.

Jesus smiled happy to have caught the nimble brained Mary off guard.

"The oldest profession. Yours or mine?" he explained. "It must be mine. There had to be someone there urging the first young girl to bargain her body for silver."

Mary nodded, a faint smile playing around her lips. She loved the intimate, frank relationship she had with Jesus and wished she could spend more time with him. "Gallantly spoken, friend, but do you really think that a girl has ever given anything she didn't want to give in the first place? Now rest for a moment, while I raid James' wardrobe and get you something decent to wear. If there is one thing you can be sure of it's a robe for every occasion in James's pack."

Mary left and Jesus snuggled down beneath the blankets. The move, slight as it was, started him coughing. He felt the hot blood tear from his lungs and suffuse his throat. Desperately he tried to calm his vibrating chest. He didn't want Mary to see him like this. Jesus quickly lifted the corner of the paillasse and spat out the blood. He rested on his elbow, frightened to move and chance bringing on another coughing attack.

Mary heard him coughing.

She forced herself to stay in the outer room, sorting through James's clothes. She wanted to save Jesus the embarrassment of having his attack in front of her. When she finally came back into the little room Jesus was calmer although there was an unhealthy flush on his cheeks and his eyes were bulging and feverish. Mary held up the results of her scavenge.

"How's that? It may be a little on the big side but it's good quality, clean and smells as fresh as a morning."

Jesus nodded.

"Thank you. Now, what about you? Tell me what you have been up to since we last met," he asked, not from any real interest but to get away from the dark thoughts of death that were crowding in on him.

Mary sensed his despair. She pulled the clean garment over his head with the tenderness of a young mother.

"You don't want to hear about my wicked life. Besides it's boring. One fat old money-bag is very much like another. They all want to take me away from all this - until they have humped their ten talents worth and then they don't even want to be seen in the same town as me. But it's a living and it beats being ground under by some boring husband who thinks his wife is just an equation of goats and camels."

Mary sat back on the paillasse and snuggled up to Jesus.

"Tell me what's bothering you," she asked softly.

Jesus didn't answer for a few seconds. Mary thought maybe he hadn't heard her question and was about to ask again.

"I'm dying," Jesus grated out in a voice choked with emotion.

Mary felt tears spring to her eyes but she forced her voice to eradicate her tragedian tendencies.

"So what's new?" she joked. "We all are. Did you think you would live forever?" She paused for a second. "Hold on!"

She pushed herself up and looked into his face.

"You're not beginning to believe the stuff James is spreading around, are you?"

Mary's attitude gave Jesus something to hold onto.

He fought off his fear.

"If I did I wouldn't think I was dying - would I?" he said petulantly, playing her sad game. Mary snuggled back on the bed with him.

"Good! Good that you're not being swallowed by your own propaganda, I mean. Not good that you think you're dying," she told him solemnly.

They both laughed.

Jesus moved lower into the bed and pulled Mary closer to him, luxuriating in her soft warmth and fragrant smell. She gently brushed the tip of her fingers across his face in a soothing pattern. They lay like that while they slept.

After an hour Mary awoke and tried to get up without disturbing the sick man but his arm tightened around her and she looked up to see his kind eyes smiling down at her.

"Where do you think you're going?" he asked. "I thought you were staying the night?"

Mary Magdalene shook her head and extricated herself from his arms.

"Sorry my love but it's impossible. There is a big party at the garrison tonight. If I had known you would definitely be here today I could have arranged for someone else to take over. That's your problem, you're unpredictable." She kissed him lingeringly on the lips and then jumped up and struggled into the robe she discarded before lying on the bed with him.

He watched her, enjoying the graceful strength of her supple body. Ready to go she bent down and kissed him once again.

"Good-bye, my love, take care of yourself. Be careful. If there is anything I can do let me know."

Without another word she turned and hurried out of the door.

Jesus listened to the whisper of her sandals as she crossed the big room outside. He heard the murmur of her voice and the melliferous tones of Ganod as he wished her good-bye. Jesus lay and pictured her muscular slaves carrying her in her brightly coloured palanquin back to Jerusalem. With a sob he turned to the wall and let the tears flow down his face.

Chapter 19

James stood uncertainly in the corner of the Court of the Gentiles and watched the bustling scene. He couldn't make up his mind if he should go ahead with his plan or forget it. If Jesus hadn't been so ill there was no way that he would even have contemplated going to the Temple and talking to the High Priest, Joseph Caiaphas. It wasn't that Caiaphas was a particularly awkward man to deal with - at least not under ordinary circumstances. In fact there were times when Caiaphas welcomed visits from the brothers. It did his reputation no harm to be seen patronising young men of exceptional ability.

Caiaphas began to go off the Nazarene brothers when he found that their *laissez faire* interpretations of the scriptures, by inference, brought not only the temple and the priesthood into disrepute but also his authority personally.

He tried to reason with them. Pulled rank. Asked them if they believed they knew better than the combined intellect of the entire Priesthood. Jesus was understanding - even conciliatory. He claimed to be a devout Jew and only seeking a new and valid interpretation of the law. James hadn't been so diplomatic. Not only had he called Caiaphas's position of High Priest into dispute but he had virtually claimed for Jesus a pipeline to God.

The pipeline to God Caiaphas might have forgiven, put it down to the aspiring Rabbi's impetuosity. But there was enough truth in the accusation that his Priesthood was not entirely legal to make him react angrily.

Now James stood in the courtyard and regretted the harsh words he had used. He didn't have Caiaphas down as a forgiving man but his plight was now so desperate that he had to try and forge a bridge between the guardians of the Temple and Jesus or risk being snuffed out like a candle when Jesus failed to perform as expected by his admirers.

The door into the inner Temple opened and Caiaphas, flanked by two black clad acolytes, came into the outer court.

James pretended not to see him. He still couldn't decide what his attitude should be and he felt going to the older man might compromise his position.

Caiaphas saw him and picked his way through the worshippers and traders towards him.

James looked up at the last moment and gave the Priest a wide, relaxed smile.

"Caiaphas!" he said in acknowledgement of his presence.

Caiaphas was not amused at the casual informality of the younger man's greeting but smiled and bowed politely to hide his displeasure. There was no point in reinforcing barriers before he heard what James had to say.

The Priest signalled for the two younger men to leave him, then stood and looked James over thoughtfully. He was surprised to see him. Surprised and gratified. When he asked for the meeting he thought James would turn it down out of hand. Temple security reported that James had raised a considerable force in the mountains. They also reported that the Nazarene's agents in the town had spent a lot of money to ensure a good turnout when Jesus arrived.

What reason could the revolutionary have to come to a meeting with the establishment?

"James." Caiaphas greeted him neutrally. James gestured to the crowded courtyard.

"Business as usual, I see."

It wasn't the most tactful opening but Caiaphas judiciously ignored it.

"How is Jesus?" Caiaphas asked, pre-empting the moment when he would have to declare his hand.

"Fine. Bit tired. He's had a gruelling couple of years. But - he'll be as right as rain tomorrow," James assured him, echoing his brother's words.

Even to his own ears he sounded as if he were plastering over cracks but he hoped the High Priest wouldn't notice.

Caiaphas did notice.

He was used to interpreting what his fellows said from what they didn't say, and James wasn't saying a lot.

But what?

"And your mother?" Caiaphas asked, digging for more unspoken communication that would help him to form an opinion of where they stood - relatively.

"She's in Jerusalem. Staying with Nicodemus. She's as well as can be expected," James replied.

He was also having trouble working out a position.

By coming at Caiapha's request he indicated that he wanted to talk. *Ergo* - there must be some common ground - at least as far as the Priest was concerned. But why didn't he come out with it instead of indulging in social chit-chat?

"Good! Give her my regards," Caiaphas said absent-mindedly.

He breathed deeply and launched into the reason he had suggested the meeting.

"The Romans are not happy," Caiaphas ventured.

"Good," was all that James replied.

Caiaphas tried again.

"It's said that you have an army in the hills, surrounding the city."

"Whoever said that knew what they were talking about," James claimed grandiosely. He liked the way the meeting was going. Caiaphas seemed to be feeling him out from a position of ignorance. All he had to do was stand firm and let the old man think he could call the desert forces down on the city with a wave of his arm and there was a good chance that he could salvage something from the present tenuous situation. Maybe somehow keep the Sanhedrin on the prod long enough to re-muster and try again later in the year. Maybe at Pentecost. By then Jesus should be well enough to do his stuff and the extra couple of months could be used to consolidate their position not only with the guerrillas but also with their followers throughout the country.

Caiaphas stopped by a stone seat built into the wall and gestured for James to sit beside him. The Nazarene would have preferred to have kept walking, it gave a sense of freedom, but he still wasn't looking for a confrontation and sat down on the stone slab.

"The Romans have taken Jesus's claim to be the King of Kings at face value, I'm afraid. They want a retraction. The temporal ruler here is Tiberius Caesar. They want to arrest Jesus when he arrives in the city but I managed to persuade them he was speaking metaphorically." Caiaphas nodded to himself as if to confirm that his interpretation of the Nazarene's motivation was correct.

James shook his head.

"Jesus has never claimed to be the King of Kings. If that's what the people are saying there is nothing we can do about it," he stated trenchantly.

Caiaphas nodded. "And his claims to be the Son of God?" he asked quietly.

Again James shook his head.

"Son of man. That's all he claims. Just like you and me."

Caiaphas drew in a long breath and let it out slowly.

"And he's prepared to swear that in front of the Sanhedrin?" he asked.

James frowned and wiped the palm of his hand on his sleeve.

"The Sanhedrin?" he repeated nervously.

A call to justify themselves in front of the ruling Priesthood always had been a possibility.

Jesus rather relished the idea of explaining himself.

James had a different programme. The two stated accusations, although not put in that way, could cause problems if Caiaphas was able to pull in witnesses who swore to have heard Jesus claim both Kingship and Godship. Factually this would be lying but James had allowed the other disciples to make the claims and hadn't tried to check them. It was dangerous waters. A flat refusal to attend the Sanhedrin meeting would be seen as an admission of guilt.

"Sure. When do you suggest?" he said boldly, trying to grab the moral high ground with a display of frankness and courage.

Caiaphas gave him a long hard look.

He hadn't expected James to give in so easily. He began to worry that the intelligence he had learned about the health of Jesus was false. He quickly reconsidered his position. Basically he wasn't interested in what Jesus said or did. In most matters he was hardly more radical than some of the Sanhedrin council. If he was left alone he might manage to form a splinter group that would attract a few followers. It was unimportant. There were already so many breakaway Jewish sects that another was hardly likely to pull the Temple down around the ears of orthodoxy.

What made Jesus special, what made James special, was that they were a bit more organised than the usual prophet or would-be Messiah. John, the Essene, had been a more typical seer; a bit of an entertainer; striding about naked and half drowning his followers in the River Jordan to save their immortal souls.

Caiaphas looked James over carefully.

The big man pretended to be preoccupied with an argument going on nearby between two traders over the ownership of one of the sacrificial lambs.

"This afternoon would be a good time?" Caiaphas said casually, as if the timing was unimportant.

James looked at him and nodded cautious agreement, then thought again and shook his head.

"Not today, I'm afraid. Jesus won't be coming into the city until tomorrow," he apologised.

"Tomorrow might be too late. If the Romans get to him first there might be problems," Caiaphas warned and hoped that James would stay with his objection.

The last thing the priest wanted was Jesus turning up at the temple before he had a chance to prepare. What he wanted was the maximum embarrassment for the Roman Procurator, Pontius Pilate. Somehow he intended to get Jesus arrested so that the cancellation of his planned rally over the Passover would be seen as an act of Roman aggression. Pilate wasn't the most tactful Prefect the Romans had sent them. He liked his statues and symbols of authority and didn't care that the Temple and the Jewish community as a whole had laws banning images.

And then there was the slur on the Caiaphas name that seizing the temple funds to build the aqueduct had caused.

The Priest didn't intend to forgive or forget that.

"Where will you be staying?" Caiaphas asked innocently.

James grinned at him. He wasn't falling for that.

"Not sure. We'll just wait until we get into town and then make up our minds," he said.

He wasn't expecting Caiaphas to cause any problem on the streets where they undoubtedly had a lot of support but if they could be segregated somewhere it might be a different matter.

Caiaphas nodded acknowledgement of the evasion. It wouldn't be too hard to find the group when the time came. He still needed someone to point the finger and tell the tale but he was sure he could get that.

Caiaphas was happy that James was being so cagey. If he had agreed to bring Jesus in front of the Sanhedrin he would probably have got a reasonably sympathetic hearing. Now he had set himself apart from the Elders of his religion and would have to suffer the consequences.

Satisfied with the morning's work Caiaphas rose to his feet and smiled at James.

"I'm glad we had this chat. Helped to clear the air. I'll try to keep the Romans out of this but it might not be too easy. My regards to Jesus. Yahweh be with you."

Caiaphas turned abruptly and walked back towards the inner temple. The two black clad acolytes fell in beside him and scattered the crowd as they marched across the courtyard.

James watched them go uneasily. He couldn't understand why Caiaphas had asked for the meeting and then so easily been put off - it worried him. He hadn't a lot of time for Caiaphas. He considered him stupid and only holding down his position because of the social position of his family.

James sat, as the High Priest made his way through the hustling dealers, and let his anger grow. It could have all been so easy.

Now?

He pushed aside the thought.

Angrily he swung down and nearly fell over the table of one of the money lenders. Exasperated he kicked out and overturned the table. Coins scattered in all directions. The dealer foolishly tried to grab James. The big man shrugged him off. Another dealer shouted abuse at him. James stuck his hand in his face and pushed him backwards. The man stumbled over another low table and fell across the table next to it. Other dealers jumped up and started shouting at James.

James was now in a black mood. He had controlled his feelings while he spoke to Caiaphas but he could no longer contain his temper. He relished the physical release of taking on the riled men.

Caiaphas was about to enter the anti-chamber when one of his men touched his arm and drew his attention to the riot gathering force in the courtyard.

"Your visitor, James, is causing a bit of a riot, your Honour," he said.

Caiaphas turned and watched James progress.

A satisfied smile touched the corners of his mouth.

"James?" he asked.

"Yes. There he is. By the gate."

Slowly Caiaphas shook his head.

"That is not James. That is his brother Jesus."

His man was about to argue but the Priest gave him a look that told him that now was not the time to have thoughts of his own.

He nodded.

"Of course. Jesus!"

Caiaphas turned and walked into the Temple.

The meeting had turned out better than he expected.

Chapter 20

When James arrived back from Jerusalem he found his brother lying on his bed staring at the ceiling. Philip had told him of Mary's visit. He was annoyed at first but when he saw how much better Jesus looked he was grateful that the busy courtesan had taken the time to visit his brother.

"How was Mary?" he asked.

Jesus smiled at the happy memory of his visitor.

"She's very well. She couldn't wait to see you, she has a big party on tonight." James nodded understanding.

"Perhaps it's just as well. We don't exactly see eye to eye on most things." He looked around.

"Is there anything I can get you?" James noted that Jesus was wearing one of his galabias but didn't mention it.

Jesus shook his head.

"I'm afraid there is nothing you can do for me, James. In fact I'm beginning to think I'm more of a liability than I'm worth." He spoke lightly but there was no doubting the seriousness behind his tone.

James squatted down beside him.

"Don't say that," he pleaded. "You'll be alright. We're nearly there."

Jesus looked at his brother and slowly shook his head.

"You're fooling yourself. I know you mean well, James, even if I don't totally agree with your methods. But we are still far from achieving what we dreamed. And I don't think I'm going to make it." Jesus spoke without a vestige of self-pity.

It was a fact that he wanted his brother to be aware of, to admit so that he could formulate other plans.

James didn't want to hear his own fears being expressed by his brother. Although, on a practical level, Jesus's idealism was a stumbling block, James had too great a respect for his brother's intellect to dismiss his suggestions lightly. Jesus hated to make James unhappy but he wanted to let him know how he felt.

"Suppose everything goes just as you say," Jesus continued. "We walk into Jerusalem and everybody makes a big show with the palm leaves. And suppose the Romans let it all happen because it doesn't worry them what a bunch of colonial Jews do to let off steam. And let us even go so far as to suppose that the Sanhedrin decide to play along and not do the usual panic stricken act they do when anyone suggests anything that's not covered in the Talmud. What do we do about the Zealots and the other mountain gangs that we asked to support us and then left to kick their heels in the mountains? They want a great warrior warlord. What shall we do? Stuff straw up my robe, stand me on a platform and try to persuade them I am the greatest swordsman since Hercules?"

Jesus coughed a controlled hack and sunk back on the bed.

James waved his hand irritable at the weak man.

"It will work. Let's get the support of the city. Take one step at a time," he snapped.

Jesus shook his head sadly.

"James. I love you. No one could have a better brother; especially an undersized cripple like me. It was your understanding and protection that made me appreciate what a beautiful world we could live in, if everybody treated everybody else the way you treat me." Jesus controlled a coughing fit and went on in a husky voice which underlined his words. "But I'm sick and I don't think I have long to live. If I were stronger I wouldn't have let you spread the stories that have weakened our position. What are you going to say when the people question my immortality after I'm dead? They aren't going to listen to anything you say in future. All your stories are going to backfire. The great healer who can't heal himself. The Warrior King who can't stand up!"

Again Jesus went into a paroxysm of coughing.

He snatched the cloth that James handed him and spat into it. A deep red stain darkened the light material. Jesus looked at it and grimaced.

"How do you explain as glorious my death on a heap of sacks coughing my lungs up? Within a year nobody will remember us except a few half-crazed people who believed I healed them and the outlaws still waiting in the hills for my clarion call."

James looked defeated by his brother's pessimism.

"You'll be alright," he ventured lamely. "Once we get to Jerusalem you can rest." Jesus snorted with frustration.

"You aren't listening to me. It's too late. It's over. I'm dying! I'd do anything to make it not so but I can't help it. You shouldn't have built me up into something I'm not. Now there is no way out!"

Jesus closed his eyes and lay very still.

James picked up the pitcher of water and held it to his brother's lips. What Jesus said was true but James couldn't accept it. When the young Jesus told stories of a bigger and better world, James would sit and listen. The two were opposites. James: popular, tough and a great favourite with his parents. Jesus: small, deformed, constantly ill and a source of irritation to his mother who guiltily blamed herself for his withered leg. But Jesus's bodily weakness strengthened his mind. Sitting alone at the back of his father's workshop he watched the artisans and slaves work and dreamed of a world where there were no masters and servants. A world of Love where everybody helped each other and shared what they earned. Where there were no poor or diseased. A place where everyone could live in harmony, one big happy family.

James listened and thought about it.

What to Jesus was no more than an exercise in philosophy became for James a practical ambition. He was going to fulfil, through Jesus, the prophesies of the Testaments.

No matter what it cost or who it hurt!

Looking at Jesus breathing with difficulty in the dingy room James had to admit that he had made a miscalculation. If Jesus had been stronger! The idea of surrounding him, weak and crippled, by a band of the tallest, strongest, handsomest men in the country had been sound. People listened to them praising Jesus and then looked at the shrivelled body of the leader and thought: 'If these men think Jesus is so fantastic, he really MUST be!' It sold Jesus and his philosophy to them. James admitted mistakes. He shouldn't have tried to rouse the guerrillas for one. Then it seemed right. Now it looked like they were going to be a millstone around his neck. Neither the man with the money, Joseph, nor the man with the philosophy, Jesus, wanted blood. James just wanted results but hadn't the support to risk the generally inferior guerrillas taking on the disciplined troops of the Romans.

Jesus was right.

If he died before they had a chance to test their support in Jerusalem, James, Peter and the rest would be doomed to annihilation.

James couldn't have that.

He stood up to go.

"I know you don't agree with some of my methods. I'm sorry. I wish we could do it the way you want. But you have to be practical. The world wants excitement and spectacle. Without a sense of awe they won't listen to the words. We have to give them something to rivet their attention. So that they can go off and discuss it, embellish the facts with their own concepts. We have come this far and I don't intend to back down now."

He gave Jesus an encouraging smile.

"Just you rest until we leave. We will take it easy and see you don't come under too much stress. I intend to see that we get what we started out to get. I refuse to be just another set of footsteps in the sand, blown away forever by the first breeze. You undersell yourself and underestimate me if you think we can be so easily put aside. People have been cured by touching you. Whether you believe it or not. You ARE a healer! Just because you don't understand it doesn't mean it isn't so. You taught me the difference between strength and force. We have strength. Maybe we won't need force!"

James spoke loudly and without pausing. He was trying to convince himself as much as Jesus.

"James, our strength is an idea," Jesus reminded him patiently. "And you have publicly attached the idea to me. In a few days - weeks at the most - I will be dead. Each day I cough more blood. Each night I sleep less and sweat more. I can hardly walk. Get out now, James, while there is still a chance." Jesus urged his brother. James crouched down by the side of Jesus, his face hard and angry.

"You're the teacher. You tell me how. If I falter now I will be over-run. Joseph isn't in this for his health. He doesn't mind risking his money but if he feels I have taken his patronage under false pretences I will only live as long as it takes to get one of his *sicarii* here. But it's more than that. I don't want to get out if there is still a chance of support in Jerusalem."

Jesus could feel another coughing fit coming on. He wanted to spare his brother the distress of seeing him dying.

"Alright James. We go on. Make your impact in Jerusalem. I'll try not to die at an inconvenient moment."

James smiled and patted him on the shoulder.

"You'll be alright. Just you wait and see!"

The banality of the reassurance made them both smile.

Later, when Jesus lay awake through the long night, after a coughing fit that was the worst he had so far experienced, his words came back to him.

I'll try not to die at an inconvenient time...

Chapter 21

The two days journey from the house of Joseph of Arimathea to the arranged meeting place with the young Canaanite, Judas Iscariot, was accomplished on mental strength and the unstinting encouragement of Isaac and his daughter Naomi. For Robin it was two days of fear and pain. He still hadn't fully recovered from the fit he had at the house of Joseph. At first he tried to ignore the dull ache in his left arm and the tendency to cramp in his leg. He put this down to the after-effects of the attack. Joseph tried to convince him that it would be better to stay as his guest for a few days until he was stronger, but Robin couldn't wait. The pressure on him to be in Jerusalem was building hour-by-hour and the thought of inactivity was worse than the pain of movement. The servants carried him out and sat him on a donkey and Naomi took up position next to him – a position that she had not deserted for the entire journey. Pain robbed him of all energy for the first day on the road. That night Naomi slept by his side in case he wanted anything.

He woke early in the morning from an untroubled sleep. For a few moments he couldn't orientate to the surroundings and his familiar feeling of total vexation taunted him. Naomi put her hand on his and he stiffly turned his head. She was not wearing her cloak, just the brightly dyed cotton garments that she wore about the house when only her family would see her.

Robin felt flattered.

He tried to smile at her but couldn't get the side of his mouth to work. He prodded the waxen flesh with his hand. It was numb and cold to the touch. Frightened he looked at the young girl for comfort. She took his shaking hand and laid it gently on the blanket and went for her father.

Isaac had seen the condition before. It was the aftermath of a seizure. There was nothing he could do but try and comfort Robin and suggest they call off the venture. The sick man wouldn't hear of that.

As they rode along the hot dusty trail on the second day Robin's mind stayed crystal clear. In a way he was grateful for the pain, it took his mind off the awful truth that could no longer be denied. The effect of sudden physical and mental activity on the Haddaq body was accelerating its break-down. The constant headache was the product of the deterioration of the motor centre and of the body. Lesions in the brain were gradually cutting off areas of activity and the net result would be total paralysis. How long that was likely to take Robin couldn't know. There was always the chance of a massive haemorrhage settling the issue of his mission once and for all. The thing that surprised him was the feeling of freedom. He no longer felt threatened by the maniac Haddaq.

Without the constant battle to submerge the madman a new sense of identity burgeoned. He still couldn't quite grasp who he was, but he could now face the certainty that he wasn't a sane facet of Haddaq without feeling vulnerable. He associated himself with the man in his dreams – the man in the flooding light who had his face and seemed to be trying to tell him something. Now that Haddaq was locked out he was also finding a new sense of strangeness about the language. There had always been the feeling that he thought in an entirely different language to the one he spoke. Now he was certain of it. The peculiar aspect was that instead of reducing his vocabulary it increased it and he was able to deal with concepts that were beyond the mental and audio processes of the host brain. It was this rapid expansion of mental activity that was accelerating the mental collapse. Haddaq's poor, underdeveloped brain was being subjected to an intensified learning process that it could not sustain.

That evening, when they made camp a few miles short of their destination, Robin found sleep elusive. The dull ache down his left side and the pain of the bruises caused by his uncoordinated lolling on the back of the swift footed little donkey, made it impossible to settle in a comfortable position. He looked at the childish figure of Naomi, wrapped in a blanket, sleeping at his side, and felt tears of gratitude spring to his eyes. As he thought of the child's devotion the images became entangled with other, more violent scenes. Recurring were the terrible deaths of men nailed to giant crosses.

It was not an unusual scene.

Even in his restricted travels he had seen many executed men hanging at the side of the road. Always the scene triggered off panic and refired his need to get to Jesus. Each evening, when he was in a habit of discussing the impressions he had picked up during the day, the conviction hardened that unless he got to Jerusalem before the Passover Jesus would be executed.

Isaac agreed that all the evidence, if Robin's fevered fancy could be so described, pointed to that conclusion. Isaac still could not understand why he was so certain that what he was doing was right. To take up with a madman and treat his ravings as fact was more like madness complementing madness.

But then Joseph came into it.

If the trade lord had taken him aside and suggested he should keep out of the sun he would have reconsidered his position. That hadn't happened. Joseph listened attentively, asked the right questions and offered help. All because the body known as Haddaq had taken on a new personality and talked about events and named people that he shouldn't have known. Joseph's interest reinforced Isaac's and made him determined to follow the action through to the end.

Which might be the following morning.

Robin's reaction to the name of Judas had been a revelation, and a reaffirmation that the whole operation was more than a farcical charade.

Through the night, while Robin drifted through his dreams of strange but familiar concepts and the more frequently recurring flash of recognition of the man in the chair, Isaac tossed and turned in frustration.

He was used to being a motivator and this new role of being swept along by motivations not his own did not sit easily with him.

The sense of foreboding stayed with him as they set out next morning.

The sun was an inflamed sore in a dirty, sand-clogged sky, ironing out perspective and bleeding out colour. Even the indecisive, unsettling wind seemed worried by the ominously darkening horizon. Isaac, bad tempered from lack of sleep and the oppressive atmosphere, inspected his small train of donkeys to make sure that everything was secure. Before midday there was going to be a sandstorm and from the way it was building up it had all the earmarks of a big one. If a storm develops in the early dawn, in the fluctuation of temperatures brought about by the rising sun, it invariably loses power as the temperatures steady. The same in the evening after the strong, late afternoon wind. A building pressure ridge will be cooled by the night air. Neither of these rules of the thumb apply to a storm delayed until midday. This will join up with the desert wind and affect a larger area and the frenetic, rising winds gradually build up into a self-energising maelstrom of titanic energy. When this happens there is nothing for man to do but huddle in whatever shelter he can find and wait for nature's spleen to be vented.

The prospect of twenty or thirty hours huddled under a blanket with sand forcing its own abrasive entry into mouth, nose, eyes and matting hair, caking sweated clothes and making every movement painful, was not a happy one.

Isaac didn't tell Robin his fears. With only two days left before Passover, time was getting short and Isaac didn't think the sick man could handle more pressure. Experience told him that there was a good chance that the full fury of the sand might not be felt until after the noon meridian. That gave them a race against time to make the house that had been arranged as the meeting place with Judas.

Unmercifully, Isaac drove his donkeys and servants, giving them no respite even when the swirling, sand-laden wind attacked them with demonic force head on. Naomi, fighting to stay on her feet, stuck with Robin, urging on his donkey, holding him in place when he seemed to be about to be torn from his mount's back by the fury of the wind. Robin's lack of resistance worried her. He perched on the narrow back of the animal without attempting to hold on or direct it in any way. At one time the wind tore open his cloak but he made no attempt to close it. Naomi reached up to close it for him. She saw his face and a cold thrill of shock went through her. His head was sunk forward on his chest, the left side of his face slack and heavy. From his open mouth a sheen of sand-encrusted saliva covered his beard. The lax heaviness of his dragging cheeks pulled open his left eye and the inside of the lid was lined with the inflaming sand. Carefully Naomi wrapped the voluminous travelling robe around the semi-conscious man and tried to protect his suffering face from the scything fury of the wind. She would have liked to share her fears with her father but in the present circumstances there was nothing he could do. They had to get to some sort of shelter or she was afraid Robin would die.

As the wind became stronger and more persistent, sand formed in soft energy sapping drifts across their path. Isaac could still identify the extremity markers of the trail but doubted that even this small comfort could last much longer. Once they were obscured there was nothing to do but huddle down and try to ride out the storm.

All sense of time vanished.

There was just the wind and the trail beneath his feet, made unsteady and uncertain by the sand that covered his ankles in a constantly moving carpet.

Unexpectedly the wind began to abate. For the first time in what seemed like hours Isaac was able to look back over the length of his small train. All the donkeys were still tied together in a string and the packs appeared secure. He stood to one side and let them file past him as he made a physical check on the thongs criss-crossing the loads.

As Naomi led Robin past, he asked him if everything was alright. Getting no reply he fell in beside the donkey and put the question again. Naomi reassured him quickly. She was worried about Robin's condition but could see no point in worrying her father now. In spite of the drop in the force of the wind the sand still clogged the air and fell with a persistent hiss to the ground around them. The feeble light that located the position of the sun did nothing to restore Isaac's optimism. It was directly overhead. It meant that the drop in wind heralded a renewed onslaught that would be more terrible than anything they had so far encountered that morning.

They were at the eye of the storm.

Satisfied with the state of his small caravan, Isaac run quickly to the front again and exhorted his drivers to even greater efforts. The sudden dip in the road that crossed a dried out, primary irrigation canal took him by surprise. They hit it just as Isaac decided it was foolhardy to continue further. Already he had over-ridden the prime dictate of the desert. For half an hour he had driven on through the raging storm with no aid to navigation but instinct. And he wasn't fooled into thinking that his instinct was any better than that which left the bleaching bones of lost travellers all over the featureless desert.

The irrigation ditch meant that he was in the vicinity of some form of habitation. Isaac stopped and studied the situation. The size of the ditch and the absence of cultivation on the side they were approaching from indicated that it was one of the drain off channels that picked up the water from the main irrigation systems and fed it back into the river. He knelt down and dug into the soft surface sand. Beneath was hardening mud. The fact that it hadn't dried out completely meant that the sluice had been diverted during the last few hours. The problem was to figure out which way would bring them to the sluice gate and the prospect of meeting someone who could direct them to shelter. If they turned the wrong way it could mean a diversion around the periphery of the whole cultivated area.

How far that could be he had no way of judging - anything from a mile to twenty.

Isaac tried to guess where they were. He had travelled the path before but in a life of ceaseless plodding from town to town on tracks indistinguishable from each other, it was hard to pull this particular one out of his memory. His inclination was to turn to his right. He tried to define the reason but it eluded him. It might be something to do with the slope of the river bed, imperceptible to the eye but acting as an indicator to his subconscious. But he couldn't be sure and he wanted more than a fanciful guess before submitting his exhausted crew on a path to nowhere.

The donkey he was holding also seemed to want to go to the right. That way it would be walking more or less into the full force of the driving sand. It was not a natural direction for the animal to want to take. Unless there was something else out there that overcame his natural aversion to walking into the wind. Isaac looked at the donkey's sand-covered mouth and then quickly looked at the beast behind him. He couldn't see the others; they were lost behind the boiling curtain of sand that brought almost total darkness to the early afternoon. Both donkeys had their ears perked to the right and were champing impatiently at their restraining handlers to be on their way. There was only one reason they could be so positive about the direction they wanted to take.

They could smell water.

The sand had smothered the smell of water from the irrigation channels and localised it at the river. The river meant shelter. There was bound to be settlements all along the bank. With renewed strength Isaac urged his team on.

They didn't have far to go. Before they had gone a couple of hundred yards they could see frenzied, wind-torn citrus trees close to the bank of the ditch they were following.

Further on, high palm trees bowed and snapped, shedding dark fronds like shrouded spears. Dark stains of mud marked their footsteps briefly before being erased by the jealous sand. The bank on either side began to heighten and Isaac could see the ridges where water had eroded the soil at knee height. It was time to leave the comforting directness of the channel and look for some form of habitation.

He led his donkey up the slippery slope and waited for the others to follow. The first three made it without a problem but as the donkey carrying Robin tried to find traction in the mud the semi-conscious man fell to the ground before Naomi could save him. The donkey, free of its burden, scampered to the top of the slope and stood docilely waiting for direction.

Isaac called sharply for two of his men to go and help his daughter while he held the donkeys now becoming restless so close to the source of water.

Robin could offer no help as the two servants dragged him up the slope and tried to sit him back on his mount. He couldn't sit up and they draped him forward over the stout-hearted animal's back like a sagging bundle of rags. Isaac told one of the men to stay with Robin and keep him from falling off.

Once more they trudged forward, leaning at an incredible angle to maintain their balance against the savage onslaught of the wind. Isaac was beginning to wonder if, in spite of the near certainty of shelter close at hand, it wouldn't be wiser to wait until the storm blew itself out, when he stumbled over a sand-sledge, partly filled with field produce, half buried in a sand drift.

It gave him hope.

He peered around. In the eddying sand he thought he could see the dark outline of a building. Without hesitation he turned towards it. It was his last stroke. If it turned out to be a figment of his imagination it didn't matter. Neither he, his companions or the animals, could go a step further. A sob of relief broke the seal of sand on his lips as the dark, tenuous shape solidified into a comforting, hard lined silhouette.

It was a small barn lined with trays for storing fruit before being shipped into Jerusalem for sale. There was nothing on the shelves at that moment but the sweet tang of citrus fruit permeated the sand caked nostrils of men and animals seeking shelter. Isaac and two of his men battled the heavy door shut and propped a plank against the cross beam to secure it.

The noise in the barn as the wind tore at the roof and whistled through the cracks and holes in the eaves and doors was worse than out in the open but the calm after the constant buffeting of the wind had a soporific effect.

All Isaac wanted to do was sleep. His legs trembled and buckled under him and he sank to the hard packed sand, his back braced against the wind assaulted door. Through dulled eyes he watched his servants unpack the donkeys and spread blankets on the floor. One of them came and offered him wine that he drank greedily but he couldn't face food. Naomi made Robin a warm bed of straw and covered him with blankets. Robin's condition had worsened. His wrists curled inward and his elbows were locked into a clenched position across his chest. The stricture extended to his left leg. The foot strained to bend upwards from the ankle while the knee was a rigid right angle. Naomi looked across at the exhausted figure of her father slumped against the door. She couldn't burden him with the news of his friend's deteriorating health. There was nothing he could do while the storm lasted. There was nothing anyone could do. She had seen the results of seizures before and knew that the cramping muscles could sometimes be eased by application of hot towels and massage. There was no way of procuring hot water. Outside the wind would scatter a fire before it got started and inside, with the dry timber and piercing draughts it was too dangerous. Naomi carefully poured water on Robin's sand caked face and gently cleaned it up. His good eye was closed and it was comparatively easy to wipe the sand from his lashes, but his left eye, unwinking and permanently open, had suffered and was swollen and inflamed. She closed the lid as best she could and tied a damp cloth over it. The best she could do for his cramped limbs was to massage them. As she fell into an exhausted sleep she felt, for the first time in her life, the weight of depression and despair.

It seemed that only a minute later Naomi heard a faint sound and opened her eyes. It was daylight outside and what light managed to get in wasn't particularly cheering. Dust had settled on livestock and humans alike giving them a drab, equalising blanket of dirty tan. Only Naomi's super-sensitive alarm system, attuned to detect the slightest movement of her patient, was triggered. The rest of the party sprawled amongst the biers and racks in exhausted disarray. The girl quickly checked to see that Robin hadn't moved. He was still asleep but the feverish panting of his breath had calmed to almost normal respiratory rate. The pad on his eye had slipped sideways. It was dry so Naomi gently eased it from under the loosened retaining bandage and freshened it up with water from the chatty. Again she heard a noise, she could see the door move slightly.

Silence again!

She considered waking her father but fatigue hit her, and as the disturbance passed she sank down and went back to sleep.

The next disturbance wasn't so easily ignored.

There was a bang on the door and it was shaken in an attempt to open it that was stopped by the bar Isaac had put in place the night before. The noise awoke all of them, even Robin and they peered fearfully at the threatening door. From the light it was well into the day and Naomi felt a little guilty that she hadn't got up the first time she was awoken and started to get some food ready.

The door rattled again. It was more a device for making noise than a serious attempt to break in. A young, enthusiastic voice called loudly:

"Hello in there! Is anyone awake?"

Isaac climbed ponderously to his feet and walked over to the door. He didn't attempt to take the brace away.

"Who is it?" he croaked, with as much authority as sand paper throat and sleep-fogged wits could muster.

"Judas. Judas Iscariot! Is that you, Isaac?" came the enthusiastic reply.

"Judas!" Isaac repeated and shot an anxious look towards Robin, awake but still fighting to gather his tortured personality.

Without hesitation Isaac knocked the bar aside and threw open the door. The handsome young man, smiling with satisfaction, gave a mocking bow. He jerked a thumb at a scruffy, dirty faced urchin peering, with huge black eyes, at the collection of strangers sleeping in the barn.

"The boy came and got me. He guessed it was you. I put the word around that you would be coming this way after I heard from Joseph."

He walked confidently forward and clasped hands with the older man.

"I must admit I doubted if you would make it before I left. I should have been away by now. Another five minutes and the boy would have missed me. I'm due to meet James and Jesus at the house of Nicodemus today," Judas told him importantly.

He took in the stirring scene and stepped aside to allow the servants to take the donkeys outside.

Judas looked interested when he saw Robin lying in the bed of straw with Naomi bending over him.

"Joseph said you needed help. You have someone who needs to see Jesus desperately. Is that him?"

Judas strolled across to Robin without waiting for an answer. He saw the slack face and seized arm and turned quickly back to Isaac.

"I don't understand. Joseph said he was a man of great importance who knew things outside the sphere of other men." He frowned and jerked his head towards Robin. "But surely... it can't be him. He looks...," Judas searched for a polite way of saying what he thought.

Isaac helped him out.

"Like a madman?"

Judas gave a nervous smile. The last thing he wanted to do was upset the intimate friend of his powerful patron, Joseph of Arimathea.

Isaac gave a bitter laugh.

"Friend. If you had to put up with the torment in that poor fellow's mind you would be mad." Isaac looked over at Robin and saw the loose mouth twitch in the attempt at a smile.

The fever still burning in the ravaged face made him sad. He took Judas's arm and led him over to where Robin lay and hunkered down beside him, urging the young man to do the same.

"Robin. This is Judas Iscariot. He is going to arrange for you to see Jesus." Isaac said. He watched Robin's face for a sign of the emotion that the name usually provoked. The sick man didn't move.

Isaac leaned forward and peered, in the uncertain light, at his face. He was surprised to see the dull mindlessness in his friend's eyes. Only a few moments earlier he had tried to smile at him but now he seemed to have retreated into unconsciousness. As he pushed back the movement attracted the empty eyes. The thick-lipped mouth twisted into a grotesque smile.

"Haddaq hungry...!"

Chapter 22

James stood in the shadows of a little alley, leading off one of the less busy streets, watching a lime painted house on the other side of the narrow thoroughfare. The small roads and passageways were already beginning to get crowded as the people from the country filed into the city to celebrate the Passover with their friends and family but so far the small residential backwater remained relatively quiet A figure appeared on the flat roof opposite. James moved into a better position to see who it was. He nodded to himself as he recognised his sister, Miriam. Miriam picked up a small wooden cask and disappeared through the trap door into the house.

Still James hesitated.

He knew that the house was the one that Nicodemus had set aside for his family for the holiday but he was still not sure if he wanted to get involved with his family at that moment in time, especially his mother.

He had hoped that he could get through the holiday without having to face the family. His relationship with them had deteriorated since he had set off on his campaign to secure Israel for the Jews.

Mary, his mother, now approaching her fifties, had been particularly vociferous in her condemnation of his efforts to upset the status quo. His brothers, Simon and Judas, had been interested at first but had cooled off when James had expected them to undertake the hardships of the open road and become teachers revealing the good life that he, James, through the teachings of his brother Jesus, was going to bestow on everyone who listened to them.

His younger sister, Salome, was the only one who was interested and would have happily embarked on the journey with them if his mother hadn't made it quite clear that no daughter of hers was going to roam around the country with a bunch of men who should be at home looking after their families.

That hadn't bothered James. He agreed with her that the open road was no way for a fourteen year old to prepare for married life.

He was about to step out of the shadows when a man leading a couple of donkeys stopped in front of him and looked into the alleyway. James made no attempt to move and the older man looked at the tall figure blocking his way and decided there were probably easier billets further on. James watched him go. He was leading two sad looking donkeys and was followed by three black shrouded women and half a dozen kids of various ages. The donkeys were piled high with bedding, clothes, food and everything needed to support them for their stay in the city. James envied them their freedom to do what they wanted. He felt that he had so many burdens they were grinding him down.

He looked back at the building harbouring his family. The only sign of light came from a small, square aperture high in the blank wall. It was a ventilation hole. The flickering light was caused by the candle that illuminated the room beyond.

The blank, featureless wall reminded James of the house his father, Joseph, had built in faraway Nazareth. Not because the houses looked similar but because in design they were absolutely opposed.

Joseph had been one of the top overseers for King Herod. Through hard work and diligence he had been able to build a house that complemented his standing in the community. Herod was not the easiest man to work for but he had a passion for design and building. Although Joseph had never reached the stage where he could directly influence the tempestuous king, the architects and advisors he worked for knew that they could count on him to bring any plans Herod had to fruition without causing them any problems. It was a situation that suited Joseph, a kind, honourable man, only interested in his work and family. A more ambitious man might have gone further. Maybe even got into Herod's inner circle of developers. It was a mistake many made and paid the price when something upset the King and he subjected them to harsh punishment and, if they survived, banishment.

The home that Joseph built to house his growing family was large and comfortable. A canopy of palm fronds ran all the way around the walls ensuring that the summer heat was reduced as much as possible. The large open windows were each fitted with a tight fitting shutter that could be closed to keep the warmth in or the sand out. The roof was a wide-open terrace, covered by another free standing palm fronded canopy and it was where the family spent most of its time when the weather and work permitted.

The death of Herod and the crowning of his son Herod Antipas had benefited Joseph in the beginning. Although Herod Antipas was subject to fits of rage and could not be relied upon, Joseph's acknowledged expertise in design, together with his determination to keep a low profile socially, meant that there were few who envied him his wealth and those that did were in no position to do anything about it.

When Mary told Joseph she was pregnant he was ecstatic. He tried to cosset her in every way. He brought a woman in to do the fetching and carrying for her, made sure she ate the very best food and had plenty of rest. It didn't suit Mary. By nature she was a bustler, someone who wanted to get on with things. When Joseph wasn't there she still carried on doing the chores.

One day she took the family linen to the river. It was something she enjoyed and could see no reason to give it up. It was gentle work and a great chance to gossip with the other women gathered there.

All went well until one day when she was in a bit of a hurry. Joseph was expected home shortly and she didn't want to be found out.

In her hurry, as she was lifting the basket of freshly washed clothes to her head, her foot slipped on the muddy riverbank. To save the washing falling onto the mud she hugged the basket to her midriff. Everything would have been all right if she could have retained her balance. As the basket hit her stomach she fell forward across its hard rim.

The other women ran to help her. She pushed them away. She assured them that she was unhurt, but allowed one of them to carry the basket back to the house.

Joseph found her in bed. She tried to tell him it was nothing but he insisted the village midwife came to see her. Mary was able to bribe the nurse not to tell her husband about her accident. She knew that if he found out her secret he would keep a closer eye on her activities in the future.

James had only heard the story after the death of his father. The woman who had come to lay him out took great delight in telling the secret that had been hidden for over twenty years. She had delivered the baby and had seen the anguish on Mary's face when she saw the baby's deformed leg. She felt that she was to blame. If she hadn't deceived her husband and gone to the river that day, the baby would have been perfect. Jesus was beautiful. Big black eyes, a riot of curly hair and, from an early age, a wonderful, engaging smile.

Mary loved the baby fiercely.

She spent hours oiling, massaging and tending his shrivelled leg. For the first four years of his life Jesus was always with his mother. Even when James and then Miriam were born he was with her in the same room throughout her labour.

Then Simon was born.

There were complications.

Mary was in labour for more than a day. To save Jesus the distress of seeing his mother in pain Joseph took him to stay with some friends.

It was there that he caught the smallpox that nearly killed him.

James straightened up and stepped out of his hiding place. Before he could cross the road a youth came up dragging a struggling goat on a piece of rope. He stopped outside the door and banged on it with his fist. James kept on walking, determined to get out of sight of whoever answered the door. He heard the bolts drawn back and a voice he recognised as that of his sister greeted the youth.

The Sacrificial Lamb.

He was surprised to find that it made him feel a little guilty. He should be there with his family. As head of the household now that his father was dead it was up to him to conduct the sacrificial ceremony. He pushed the thought aside. Jesus was the head of the family and he was in no condition to make the onerous journey just to carve up a goat. It was a long time since he or Jesus had been around for Passover.

The door in the roof of the house opposite opened again. This time it was the woman who was preoccupying his thought that came out and started rearranging the furniture. Obviously the family were about to sit down to dinner. James tried to figure out if that was a good time to arrive or a bad. He walked back along the road to the small wooden door set in the wall. He was about to knock when some youths came out of the next house and walked past him. Among them he recognised his younger brother Judas. He turned away quickly. Not wishing to be seen. He watched them walk off down the road, laughing, talking, jostling each other in a friendly way.

James leaned on the wall beside the door and looked at it. All he had to do was knock on it. Probably Salome would open the door. She would be happy to see him and drag him into the kitchen where the rest of them would be getting ready to eat.

He knew how it would go then. His mother would pretend she hadn't noticed him. Simon would say hello and then probably go up onto the roof. Miriam would make some remark about his "turning up unannounced and just when they were about to eat" but would make a place at the table for him.

Once they were all seated his mother would start questioning him. Criticising everything he said; pointing out the error of his ways. He gave it ten minutes before he lost his cool and they had yet another ill-founded argument. It was ever thus.

He still found it hard to believe when others told him stories about his mother in her younger days. The happy child - the beautiful and engaging wife and the caring, loving mother. Most of what he had learned had been from the obliging midwife but he had no reason to disbelieve it.

The change came after the birth of Simon and the near death of her first born, Jesus. She blamed herself for his deformity and for his exposure to smallpox. If only she had controlled herself. Not screamed and carried on like a demented fury as her labour stretched out over the hours.

Her whole world had changed. Before, it had been full of sunshine and love. Now it was a place of hate, deformity and pain.

Before, she had doted on the infant Jesus. Now she couldn't bear to be near him. Joseph tried to reason with her, tried to point out that Jesus was innocent of any wrong doing. That only incensed her more. From that she saw only criticism of herself. It was her fault that Jesus had a gammy leg, it was her fault his face and body were hideously scarred by the dreadful illness he had suffered. Every time she looked at him she was reminded of her guilt. She saw only the ugly deformities that she had brought on him. She didn't see the beautiful smile and wide, friendly eyes.

The adoration Jesus showed for his mother was one of the reasons that James found it so hard to get along with her. In spite of everything Jesus had suffered she mostly ignored him or, at best, tolerated him in an off-hand, bad tempered way.

Again James stretched out his hand to knock on the door and again he lost the will to carry it through.

His assurance to Jesus that he would see their mother and the promise he had made that he would bring her to see him weighed heavily on his conscience.

For the first time in years James wished his father was still around to broker the relationship between Jesus and his mother. He had always been able to understand why Mary reacted the way she did but could do nothing to make her accept Jesus the way she had when he was a baby.

Joseph died when Jesus was about twenty. He was working on a project for one of Herod's Counsellors. It was a man that Joseph had worked with many times over the years and he was happy to get the private contract to design and oversee the building of his Summer Palace.

The work went well and was nearly completed. Joseph took his friend on a tour of inspection. Everything was exactly as it should be. As they were leaving, Joseph stumbled on a step. His head hit the wall. It didn't seem much of an injury and Joseph rubbed his head ruefully as he escorted the owner to his horse.

He hung around the site for a while talking to the workers and just making sure nothing was amiss. By the time he reached his house he was beginning to feel sick. Mary fussed over him but he refused to take any notice. It would all be right in the morning.

When Mary tried to wake him he was unresponsive. She screamed for James. Jesus came. He examined his father and then tried to take his mother is his arms. She pushed him away. Refused to believe that Joseph was dead. When Jesus tried to comfort her she wouldn't listen. James arrived on the scene while Jesus was still trying to get her to believe that Joseph was dead. She threw herself into his arms and insisted that James woke his father up. He looked at Jesus who slowly shook his head, near to tears himself.

James led her from the room. Jesus stayed with his father, gently laying him out in the Jewish tradition.

Mary's attitude to Jesus became even more distant after that. Although she didn't really think that her eldest son had anything to do with his father's death she, illogically, blamed Jesus for not being able to save him. On more than one occasion she voiced the opinion that if James had been there quicker her husband would still be alive.

The shrill voice of his mother coming from behind the stout door decided James. It was not the time to broach the subject of visiting Jesus a couple of miles outside the city.

He looked around and was glad that nobody was there to witness his act of cowardice.

He nodded towards the door, turned and walked rapidly away.

Chapter 23

Aliph pulled his goatskin robe tighter across his face and cursed himself for a fool. It wasn't the first time he had muttered that particular curse but it had more venom than the time before and he could look forward to even greater satisfaction next time he tried it. The storm was like a warning - a sign that said return to the security of the mountain cave, high above the shifting, wind-borne sands of the desert. Aliph carefully lowered the cloak and spat the sand from his mouth and cursed again when the wind tore the spittle from his lips and splashed it back into his face. He looked with sore, belligerent eyes at the other huddled shapes about him under the ledge. Hatred filled his heart and he wanted to jump up and run, berserk, through the still figures, striking at them with his heavy sword until they were nothing more than ragged bundles staining the sand with their leaking blood. Even that was too much effort.

Through the gloom he saw the giant outline of Seph picking his way towards him. The Negro seemed impervious to the vile weather conditions. Aliph buried himself deeper into his cloak and hoped that he would not be noticed. Instinctively he guessed that some mad proposition was going to be put to him that would provide maximum danger and discomfort.

He didn't want to know.

Aliph had already decided that his search for glory and social recognition was a mistake. As soon as the sand storm died away he intended to lead his men back to the hills and return to their simple life of banditry. Anything was better than facing the scything, sand-honed winds of the Bethy-Horon Pass. It meant breaking up into smaller units and diversifying their activities over a greater area but he was prepared for that. He now realised that the course he had missed when he was in the Roman army was the one that explained how you kept several hundred men happy. How you got food and shelter for them. A small group he could handle, but the continuous strain of thinking for everyone and making decisions was too much. He wanted the security of someone making a few decisions for him. Aliph didn't particularly care who it was as long as it wasn't him.

Seph's bulky figure settling down beside him hastily revised his mental decision. He didn't mind who made the decisions as long as it wasn't Seph! The mutilating whip had scored deep into the Negro's brain. He took no notice of the difficulty or consequence of any mad action he thought up as long as it promised a minimal chance of hurting the Romans. Aliph didn't care that much about the Romans. In fact, at that moment he didn't care about anything except the misery of the moment. Seph's soft voice reached him in spite of the wind roaring along the ledge.

"I've been thinking," he said.

Aliph's heart sank.

"Now would be a good time to move into the city," Seph continued. "Everybody will be indoors. Even the guards on the gates are not going to be too thorough in their checks. We could probably get a hundred men in there before the curfew. They could take up strategic positions before dawn and we could go in with the travellers arriving for the feast and take over the whole city before nightfall. What do you think?"

Aliph closed his eyes and wished he could disassociate himself from the whole crazy affair.

But he couldn't.

Seph wouldn't let him.

He would push and needle and threaten until in exasperation Aliph would make a decision that he instantly regretted but couldn't deny. Seph's fingers bit into his arm with the solid strength of a carpenter's vice, calling attention to his unanswered question.

Aliph carefully turned to look into the torn face of his tormentor.

"I think you are mad," he said, simply and succinctly.

The Negro gave an ugly laugh but relaxed the grip on his arm. "You are scared, little man," he pronounced with a sneer.

Aliph nodded acknowledgement of the condemnation and hoped his tormentor would leave him alone to continue his silent cursing.

Seph had other ideas.

He gripped the hood of Aliph's cloak and wrenched it off his head. Angered by the unprovoked assault Aliph's hand flew to his sword but before he could draw it, Seph's hand clamped down making it impossible to draw. Masked by the cloak he took his dagger out with his left hand. Seph sensed the danger and gripped his bicep in a crippling grip that robbed his finger of power. The knife fell into the sand between his knees.

Seph's deformed mouth twisted into the sickening grimace that had replaced his smile.

"I'm tired of your cowardice. You expect me to listen to you but you have nothing to say. I say we move now. What do you say?"Seph demanded.

Out of the corner of his eye Aliph was aware that menacing figures were looming up through the driving sand. He didn't need to be told that they were Seph's support if he didn't get the right answer. With his men mobilised and in strategic positions he would be more than a match for Aliph's superior numbers. Aliph wasn't expecting to be a hero. He just wanted to survive, against the odds, as long as possible.

He nodded.

"Alright. If that's what you want. What do you suggest?"

He tried to make his voice as conciliatory as possible through the muffling cloak he had pulled back over his face.

Seph stood and pulled him, reluctantly, to his feet.

"You take a hundred of your men and move into the city before nightfall. I will come in with mine in the morning. As soon as the streets are clogged with pilgrims we take over all the military posts and signal for the rest of the men to move in. With the barracks and guardrooms under our control it will be easy to take the men in the streets. With the garrison here secure everyone will flock to join us and we can march on Hebron and Masada. Then nothing can stand in our way!"

Seph looked stonily at Aliph to see if he agreed, his one eye burning bright at the thought of the Roman blood he would spill.

Aliph acted enthused although he had no intention of being drawn into the wild scheme.

"Shouldn't we wait for Barabbas? He should be back in the morning with his report on the situation in the town - what support we can expect from the civilian population, things like that," he temporised.

Seph brushed his suggestion aside without consideration.

"We can't wait. Once this storm blows out we will be exposed. If the Romans get wind of our presence they will be out here before we can move. And we can't possibly expect to fight the legionaries in the open," Seph warned.

Aliph agreed enthusiastically with that.

"Right then," he said, his mind made up. "Let's get started. If this storm dies away we will be out in the open and visible for miles."

Aliph left Seph and went to wake his lieutenants.

Within the hour he had mustered the men he was going to take with him. Seph called a conference to co-ordinate their attack on the military installations and brief the leaders of both groups on their responsibility once they were in the city. Aliph listened to Seph's scheme without interruption. With his lieutenants he dutifully nodded at the right time and made the right sounds. He supposed that there was even an outside chance that Seph's tactic might work. Assuming that he did get the support of the people, at least for a few brief hours Jerusalem might be considered a truly Jewish city.

But it would only be for a few brief hours.

Aliph was well aware of the contingency plans that were standing orders with the military. They wouldn't put up more than a token resistance in the streets. This would give them time to reform outside the confining rattrap of the city. A messenger would be sent to the other garrisons in the area and before nightfall there would be so many cohorts surrounding Jerusalem that the most Romanised mouse with the least Jewish connection wouldn't get more than five paces outside the walls without being nailed to a gibbet. Only the massive civilian support throughout Judaea that James had promised would have been pressure enough to keep the Romans behind their defences. That hadn't materialised and with nothing more than a handful of half trained guerrillas caught in a trap of their own making, Rome would squash the spot of local bother and consider it nothing more than a useful exercise for their raw recruits. So Aliph went through the motions and swore to support Seph when he made his bid.

The road into Jerusalem had been paved by the sweat of slaves and the expertise of the Roman engineers. Even in the most blinding sandstorm the arrow straight road was easy to follow.

Aliph and his men joined the road just before the marker for three miles to the city. Stumbling and cursing the men pushed on into the teeth of the storm for another mile. Aliph wanted to make sure that his suspicious partner hadn't sent someone to follow him to see that he really was going to the city. Blinded by his own hatred of the Romans, Seph believed that Aliph was as willing as he to be given the chance to strike at the oppressors. It was a mistake he was to regret.

Once Aliph was sure that he was not being followed he led his men off the cobbled road and followed the rising ground into the foothills. With the storm closing in and the night drawing near he wanted to be hidden from the road by the morning. Then he was going to go back to the safety of his mountain hideout as swiftly as his legs and caution could get him there. Uncharitably he hoped that Seph would be killed when he tried to take over from the Romans. That way he wouldn't be able to add Aliph's name to his list of hates and come into the hills looking for him.

The thought of the gargoyle-featured Negro appearing out of the night was to cause the cautious guerrilla leader many sleepless nights when he finally reached the comfort of his high cave.

Chapter 24

Jesus lay in the dark solitude of his cell-like room and listened to the wind. A lot of the force had died from it now and he could see the faint pinpoints of light from the delayed dawn as it filtered through holes enlarged by the storm. The dust had given him a bad night. Continuous coughing had weakened him but now, as the wind dropped, he found a serenity he hadn't known before. It was as if a difficult journey had ended in a quiet, safe harbour. There was no sense of urgency. He waited calmly for James to wake and come to see him. Jesus had no intention of telling him the difficult conclusion he had arrived at or involve him in its outcome. James had said there must be a way to bring about a successful end to their campaign and he had found it. Maybe not the end either of them foresaw or wanted but never-the-less, a climax that could crystallise their aims and focus the attention of the sensation hungry populace of Jerusalem. If the climax was handled right it was to be the rallying point for the whole country.

And James would know how to handle it.

That was one thing Jesus was sure about.

James came in to see him an hour later. He was surprised to see his brother looking so much better.

"Feeling better?" he asked.

Jesus's smile widened.

"Today I feel ready to go anywhere. Tomorrow - who knows..."

He slid his legs out from under the covers and with James's help stood up. He was a little shaky but his brother's firm arm steadied him.

"What's the weather like?" he asked.

James shrugged.

"The wind died down but there's still a lot of dust in the air and it's quite cold."

Jesus urged James towards the door.

"Let's go outside for a moment. I want to smell some fresh air."

James started to protest but the happiness on his brother's face silenced him. Instead he picked up a blanket and draped it around the thin shoulders of the frail man.

"It's cold outside," he repeated huskily.

Supported on his brother's arm Jesus limped out into the pale sunlight and sunk down on a bench beside the door. Even that short walk exhausted him but he was careful not to let James see just how weak he really was. He breathed in carefully, enjoying the cool air on the inflamed membrane of his nostrils but frightened of provoking another coughing fit. James sat down beside him. Neither spoke for a few minutes.

"Everything ready now?" Jesus broke the comfortable silence.

"Don't worry," James assured him. "If there are any problems we will know soon enough. If it looks like there might be a chance of disaster I intend to pull out. Philip should be reporting on the situation in Jerusalem sometime this morning now that the storm has died away."

Jesus mused on this for a few moments before asking another question.

"And mother? Has she arrived?"

James looked at him sharply.

He didn't want to lie but he couldn't bring himself to tell his brother that he had gone into Jerusalem with the intention of seeing their Mother and then funked it at the last moment. Jesus wouldn't understand. He wasn't sure that he understood himself. He had intended to tell Jesus that he had seen Mary and she had been happy to see him, had asked after him and promised to come and see him over the holiday if he wasn't able to come and see her. Why was it he found it almost impossible to lie to his elder brother? He lived a life mostly built on lies, misrepresentations and distortions of the truth without batting an eyelid. If people doubted his word they rarely, never, had the courage to challenge him. Yet Jesus…?

James realised that his brother was still waiting expectantly for an answer.

"Yes, mother's in Jerusalem," he said.

Jesus wanted more.

"Have you seen her?" he asked.

"Yes briefly," he admitted "You know how she is. Told me I was in the way and complained that we never came to see her."

"And Salome and the others?"

"You know Salome. Happy as a puppy to see me. Wanted to know what we had been up to and how you are." James said without a lot of conviction. "Saw Judas for a moment. He was on his way out with some friends."

Jesus looked at him without speaking for a few seconds. James hastily got up and made a show of stretching his legs.

"Good. I'm looking forward to seeing her." Jesus finally broke the silence and laid back against the wall

He meant it and James wished he could understand what his brother saw in their cantankerous old mother.

"And Nicodemus?" Jesus asked, "Was he there?"

James shook his head.

Jesus thought for a few seconds.

"Talking of Judas, where's that young boy you were so taken with? Is he staying here?" he asked casually.

"Judas Iscariot? Yes, he is in Jerusalem. Why?" James asked, more than happy to change the subject.

Jesus shrugged.

"No reason. It's just that he is such a bright lad. I get tired of the conversation of that lot in there. They still have a secret admiration for anyone that can drink a couple of wineskins dry and still stand on their feet."

James laughed shortly.

"They're all right. They impress the people and can be relied on to do their bit. Joseph's money helps but it's more a matter of prestige. They feel important striding around the country assuring their followers that they have direct communication with God."

Jesus smiled sadly.

"The funny thing is that they have, if they would just let themselves believe it."

He fell silent, morbid thoughts crowded in.

James watched him covertly. He suspected more in his brother's seemingly idle talk than he was admitting.

Jesus became aware of James scrutiny and shook away his black thoughts with a laugh.

"Perhaps something will happen to give them some real, old fashioned faith," he said.

Again there was silence broken eventually by Jesus.

"I would like to have a talk with Judas. How does he stand on our philosophy?" James thought for a second.

"He's still sold on the idea of a Champion on a fiery steed delivering his people with well-directed bolts of lightning. Sometimes I think he just humours us when we preach brotherly love because he thinks we are trying to hide what we are really doing from the Romans. But he is intelligent and he'll learn."

"I hope so," Jesus said with a touch of sadness in his voice. "It's the young ones we have to appeal to - the young, intelligent ones who will teach the next generation. Peter, Matthew, John and the rest are fine for the moment. They are like quarry-men cutting huge boulders from the hillside. What we need now are artists who can shape the rough stone into shape." He thought for a moment before continuing.

"You know already what I say is distorted and changed out of all recognition. I'm sure it's not deliberate but I find it very sad."

James defended his followers quickly.

"It's very hard for them. They listen to what you have to say but then they have to put it over to ignorant peasants who only understand the concepts they work in. So our boys throw in a little agony and fear mixed with the threat of a brimstone future and the yokels accept it."

Jesus looked at him, a faint, sad smile on his lips.

"But that's not what it's all about. That's the old way. If the people are to move forward they have to think positive thoughts. They need to want to help each other to shed the hatred and poverty of this world and prepare the way for another."

"That's what we tell them." James was hasty to try and convince Jesus.

Jesus shook his head. "You don't. Or at least you tell them in such a way that they think you mean something entirely different. You talk of preparing for another world and you let them think you mean in some milk and honey heaven. You tell them of the goodness and love that is all around them but then you couple it with a pagan image of a savage old Rabbi sitting on a cloud and handing down laws and judgements that satisfy only the cruelty and darkness that oppression, greed and poverty breed in man."

James tried to protest but Jesus cut in again.

"Don't tell me it's the only way to get the Word across. If that's a fact I don't know that we are using the right word! The stories that are circulating now make me some sort of a wizard, a magician who can heal bodies and shrive souls. We are peddling a mixture of Greek legend and barbaric superstition."

Jesus started to cough.

The excitement drained his energy. He had wanted to talk to James about his fear and disappointment for a long while but hadn't had the opportunity.

James put a comforting arm around his brother's heaving shoulders as he coughed and gasped for breath. He spat a globule of blood into the sand and rested his head on the big man's accommodating shoulder. James looked with concern at Jesus's bright eyes and flushed cheeks.

"Are you sure you can make it into the city?" he asked anxiously.

Jesus nodded slowly and forced a smile.

"I can make it. At least to the city."

He sat up and faced James. His excitement had abated and he looked tired and drawn.

"I guess I will be finding out whether there is anything in your promise of a paradise after death pretty soon. I don't know whether I will be delighted or annoyed if you turn out to be right."

He let James help him up and back to the straw paillasse in the dingy room. His brother settled the rugs and furs around him and turned to go but was stopped by Jesus as he reached the door.

"Thank you James. I'm not blaming you or the men. If I were stronger I could do my own teaching without having to have my words interpreted." He paused to make sure he had James's attention.

"This Judas, you say he is a bright boy?" James nodded agreement. "I want to see him. Tomorrow. I have to convince him that I am not a magician or a legendary warrior. It's important to me. Will you arrange it for me, James?"

James came back and gently pressed him back on the bed.

"Of course I will, Jesus. Now get some rest. As soon as Philip arrives I'll let you know what's happening. In the meantime I'll see if I can get a donkey for you to ride. I don't think you will be able to manage the walk, do you?"

Jesus shook his head, his good humour restored.

"Perhaps you could at least find a fiery donkey!"

Chapter 25

Robin Firth no longer looked the cool, immaculate executive that was his worldwide image in the past. Hours of sitting in front of the transmitter console desperately trying to make sense of the jumble of impressions that nagged at the corners of his consciousness had frayed his suave facade. An aura of disaster settled over him. He felt ill and uneasy, his usually cool analytical mind darted and pecked in a frenzied search for stability. Only thirty-six hours were left of the time allotted for the experiment but it was more than just the proximity of an unsatisfactory conclusion to an exercise that he had started with such high hopes. If he wanted to carry on there was no reason why he should close down the transmission. Mayer and Sanderstead might object, they had experiments of their own they wanted to try out, but the Firth Foundation was footing the bill and Robin was, in the final analysis, *the* Firth Foundation. Now it was the sense of impending disaster that kept him chained to the hot, airless room drugged by the almost inaudible drone of the transmitter.

Those remaining thirty-six hours were vital. Regardless of whether the switches were thrown the drama being enacted nearly two thousand years in the past would go ahead!

Certain of that, he should have been satisfied.

The pictures in his mind, and the unsettling metabolic change that had overtaken him, were nothing more than a psychosomatic reaction that would hopefully disappear with the end of the experiment.

But it was more than that.

Mayer and Sanderstead arrived just after twelve o'clock. Not having Firth's pristine image their state of exhaustion was not so easy to notice. Maybe Mayer's hair was a little less sleek and Sanderstead's pouchy eyes more pendulous. Tired as they were they looked at each other in open surprise when they saw the state of their boss. He impatiently waved them to chairs and then limped across to collapse uncoordinatedly into his usual low armchair.

"Something wrong with your leg, Robin?" the mathematician asked with genuine concern.

Firth waved the question aside.

"It's nothing, a little cramp, that's all."

Unconsciously he kneaded the bicep of his left arm, trying to release the muscle seizure that had become perceptibly worse in the last twenty-four hours.

"Now - what have you come up with?" he asked in a voice not devoid of a certain amount of worry.

Mayer let Sanderstead start off but Firth noticed that the little engineer had dropped his usual pose of bored disinterest.

"Well, to be absolutely honest, we have not been able to come up with anything concrete. However...." Sanderstead hesitated.

"Come on, Korky," Firth snapped. "I'm not interested in a tried and proven experiment. We are out on a limb with the branch sawn practically through. I want anything that might help."

Sanderstead looked to his fellow scientist for support. Mayer nodded encouragement. "There does appear to be a possibility of some sort of feed-back. You understand we haven't got the figures to prove it beyond a reasonable doubt, there are too many unknown factors. Given more time we could check…"

Again Firth cut him off. This time the desperation in his voice was unmistakable.

"For God's sake, man, get to the point!"

Confused by Firth's uncharacteristic behaviour Sanderstead again looked to his companion for support. Mayer, in his thin, cold voice, took over.

"If I may use an analogy," he started in a condescending voice. "If you direct a jet of water under pressure into a body of static water the impact of the jet causes a reciprocal movement of water in the opposite direction. This has neither the force nor focal direction of the jet and is dissipated through the whole of the body of water. The effect diminishes the farther it gets from the main stream."

Mayer gave Firth a supercilious look as if expecting the businessman not to be able to follow even the most simple explanation.

Firth nodded for him to continue.

"Close in, the feed-back is most concentrated and rapid. Now. What we are doing here is sending the equivalent of a pressurised jet of electrons through the standard speed of space, which is the speed of light roughly three hundred million metres a second!"

Having stated what he saw as the obvious, Mayer retired from the fray. Firth could see what he was getting at but was no nearer a practical solution to the problem. Before he could speak Korky Sanderstead broke in. He had recovered his poise and his voice was slow and placatory.

"Yes, you see Robin, my figures only prove there is a back-flow. At the moment the flow seems to be only of short duration and distance. It would not account for any relay of information of any type."

Firth drew in a deep breath but before he could speak Sanderstead held up his hand and plunged on.

"It's okay, Robin. I didn't leave it there - I went up to Lancaster University and talked to Professor Sharland. He is a leading authority on ESP. I had a theory and I wanted to test it out on him."

Sanderstead's speech was interrupted by the practical engineer, Mayer, expelling air noisily from his nostrils and crossing his arms to show that he had nothing to do with his associate's crackpot theory. Sanderstead reddened a little but plunged on.

"Sharland could see no practical reason why Extra Sensory Perception should not operate over vast distances on some sort of modulated carrier wave. It would mean that the frequency would have to be stable and uninterrupted. Even if the transmissions were individual and short lived - as long as they were in touch with other harmonic frequencies - if there was a sufficiently powerful medium in contact with that frequency, ESP impressions should be possible. If the conditions are right, maybe even stronger than the impressions a medium gets from handling inanimate objects! That only works on the frequency of the object the medium is touching." Sanderstead looked at Firth to make sure he was following the argument.

Robin rubbed the stiffening side of his face with the tips of his fingers.

"I understand what you are getting at but you have the wrong horse if you think I'm some sort of a clairvoyant. I don't even get intuition about the weather."

Sanderstead shook his head vigorously.

"I think that's covered," he blurted out excitedly.

Another snort from his companion cooled him down.

"Assuming you agree with this theory, which of course is purely conjecture with no scientific basis," Sanderstead cautioned.

Firth absolved him for his unscientific thought with a weary wave of the hand.

"Professor Sharland stipulated a receptor at this end with the necessary resonant frequency. As the transmission only acts as a carrier wave for your thought module, a pattern unique in the universe, it is reasonable to assume that you would act as the perfect receiver."

Sanderstead slowed to a halt and snatched a guilty look at Mayer. The engineer seemed to have dropped off to sleep. A worried look flitted across Sanderstead's face as he sensed tacit disapproval of his unsubstantiated theory. Mayer was making sure that he couldn't be held responsible if it collapsed around the mathematician's head and snuffed him out of academic existence.

Firth was less cautious.

For Sanderstead to make such a statement he must have gone beyond the solid mathematical theory and made an intuitive leap that never-the-less was not totally inconsistent with what he could prove. A sense of weakness reminded Robin Firth that he couldn't remember the last time he had eaten. While he thought through Sanderstead's report he pressed a button on the intercom and ordered a utilitarian lunch of a steak sandwich and a pot of coffee. Neither of his advisors cared to join him.

"Right! So there is an outside chance that my brain has not gone soft and I am receiving impressions. Have you any practical suggestions of how I could improve the quality? At least, to a state where I could understand what they mean?"

Both men were silent.

Sanderstead felt that he had stuck his neck out enough. He put Mayer on the spot.

"Leo has a suggestion."

The big man spoke with a trace of satisfaction. Mayer gave him a filthy look but didn't try to back out.

"Yes, well... It seems to me that if a situation existed such has been extrapolated here, reception could be improved in two ways. One: by blocking extraneous transmissions by means of a lead shielding and two: directing reception by isolating the receiver." Mayer stopped and showed no signs of elucidating further.

"Yes...," Firth prompted flatly.

With a hint of menace in his voice, hastily Mayer continued. "Quite simple really. We could line the transmitter room with lead on the outside leaving only a small directional opening. You would sit in direct contact with the transmitter surrounded by a reflector of highly reflective silver foil. It is a principle used in ESP experiments.

A Fairchild cabinet I think they call it. This will not give you perfect reception by any means. If I had to guess a percentage I would say an improvement of not more than two percent, but in the time available that's all we can do."

"Okay - get on with it," Firth ordered him.

Mayer looked startled for a moment but a look at his employer's white, twitching face and burning eyes told him that now was not the time to show his independence. At the door he passed a security man with Firth's tray of food so he vented his feelings by making an exhibition of his frustration at not being able to get out the door to get on with his top priority job.

With his prickly assistant out of the way, Korky Sanderstead relaxed and accepted a cup of coffee from Firth's shaky hand. Firth bit into the steak sandwich. Mouth full he asked Korky what he had found out about the concept of time engineering.

Without hesitation Sanderstead brought him up to date.

"While I was at Lancaster I also dropped in to see an old mate from Oxford, Doctor Grayson. I put the problem to him as an interesting hypothesis brought home from school by the kids. *'What would be the effects on subsequent history of any alteration in the story of Christ?'* He took it seriously. It seems that the focal point of Christianity is the death of Jesus on the cross. This is the fulcrum that counter-weighs actions post-dating this point with those pre-dating. In other words, without the crucifixion the stories leading up to and leading from it would not have existed! They are historically unsubstantiated by any agency independent of the Bible."

Surprised, Robin interjected.

"What about the actual crucifixion? That's a historical fact, surely?"

Sanderstead spread his hands as if appealing for clemency.

"Not if you use the arbiter of independent corroboration. The first mention, said to be by Paul, is claimed to be written at least sixty years after the death of Jesus and even this is denied by a lot of historians. The trouble is it has gone through so many interpreters. If you have ever played 'Chinese Whispers' when you were a kid, you know how fallible re-telling a message can be. You know the game I mean? You all sit in a circle and someone starts off with a sentence *like 'Johnny Smith's mother makes mince pies for breakfast on Sundays but his father has kippers.* ' By the time it's gone the rounds it comes back something completely different like: *'Johnny's mother spies on his father's slippers on Sundays'* or something like that." He looked worriedly at Robin who was sitting with his eyes closed, the half-eaten sandwich in his hand and his mouth full.

"For instance it has been proven that Joseph was not a carpenter as has always been believed. It seems that the word was misinterpreted and it is now believed he was a builder. One of Herod's architects."

There was still no reaction from Firth. Sanderstead was about to leave when Robin's eyes snapped open.

"Go on," he said, proving he was listening.

He remembered his sandwich in his hand and started to chew.

"Well, Jesus came from the north of Judaea and would have spoken in Aramaic. Paul, being an official, wrote down his memoirs in Greek with strong Latin influences. When Constantine decided that the whole world should be Christian -or dead- a translation into Latin made sure that the Roman way of life was well reflected. Later, more romantic than Roman editions were commissioned, each taking into account the social *mores* of the time. But always the focal point was the cross. Grayson's theory is that without the crucifixion, without the martyr's death that his followers could exploit to their advantage afterwards, there would have been no Christianity! It is even doubtful if the name of Jesus would have survived his time."

Robin Firth looked at his old friend open-mouthed.

"That can't be!"

Sanderstead shrugged.

"I'm sorry, Robin. It's not my line but Grayson is one of the best alternative society historians in the country."

Robin's mind raced desperately.

"But what if Jesus had survived for another ten, twenty years? Surely that would have given him a chance to make sure that those around him understood what he wanted to achieve and be more capable of carrying on after him."

Robin pleaded for comfort but Korky was unable to offer any.

"I don't know. It does seem to me that if you take away Christ's execution you take away his divinity confirmed by his resurrection. As I say, it's not my subject, but it seems a reasonable premise that without his martyrdom and the example and prestige it gave to those around him, at best his teaching would have been looked back on as that of a minor prophet with delusions of grandeur."

Sanderstead's words bit into Firth like the whip that was said to have scourged Jesus at Calvary. He pushed himself to his feet and staggered towards the door of the transmitter room. Before he could reach it he slumped to his knees and buried his face in his hands.

"What have I done? What have I done?" he asked in torment.

Sanderstead helped him to his feet and back to his desk. In one of the drawers he found a bottle of Valium tablets that Firth was using to calm himself down. Sanderstead gave him two with a glass of water and waited while his employer regained control of himself.

"Feeling better?" he asked.

Firth nodded.

Sanderstead put his hand on his friend's shoulder and gripped it comfortingly.

"It'll probably be alright," he offered.

Miserably Firth shook his head.

"I don't think so! You said that when the carrier beam holding the thought-module in place decayed that module would return to this time although not necessarily to me. Is that right?"

There was a plea for denial in Firth's voice that Sanderstead could not satisfy.

"That's right," he agreed.

"But the implanted thought in the host mind would continue to be active - yes?" Again Sanderstead could not satisfy his patron's latent demand for denial.

"We think so. Of course we are not a hundred percent certain, but it seems obvious that after a time the thought pattern will be imposed on the host mind and even after the cessation of direct transmission the contact will continue to act in accordance with a thought process which will now be his."

Firth gripped his hand. "Don't you see? I've sent an instruction back in time to stop Jesus's execution! I don't know if or how it can be done but if I'm successful I will have destroyed Christianity and all Jesus worked for!"

To Sanderstead's horror Firth burst into tears.

The phlegmatic mathematician didn't know what to do. He looked longingly at the door but couldn't bring himself to desert the weeping man.

Suddenly Firth straightened up, a new look of determination on his face. He was almost his old self as he pushed himself stiffly up from the desk.

"I'm sorry, Korky, but we're in desperate trouble. I need to know what's going on, to see if there is anything I can do about it. Chase Mayer up, will you, Korky? I need information now!"

Sanderstead nodded understanding and silently left the room.

Firth went back to the lonely chair in front of the space-time regressor.

Chapter 26

Nicodemus was nervous. He wasn't a brave man or the sort that you would expect to be a revolutionary. If someone had even suggested that what he was doing could have been construed as sedition he would have laughed. He was a laughing man. But the laughter would have stopped when he realised his accuser was serious and would have gone to great lengths to explain that he was only trying to bring an easier interpretation to the laws of Moses. After all, wasn't he a respected priest in the Sanhedrin?

And were not priests of the temple there to see that the laws were obeyed?

That didn't mean that the law should be obeyed in its literal sense or in blind terror of God's wrath. They weren't all Essenes.

God had given the law to his servant Moses in plain, unequivocal language. It was a pity *He* had taken a negative attitude primarily. It coloured the context and put connotations into the law that Nicodemus was sure God hadn't meant. Nicodemus didn't want a revolution about it. He just wanted to point out to a few well-meaning friends that there were other interpretations. Few bothered to listen, and those that did warned him of the dangers of trying to tamper with tradition. Minds greater than his had put the laws in their respected place, and it was not his job to question what the Elders said. With difficulty Nicodemus stopped himself from commenting that the only advantage the Sages had was that they were dead. And

Nicodemus was alive and happy and wanted to spread his wonder to the world.

Like most of the more advanced thinkers he had adapted many of the Roman influences to his own needs. He had a small but effective hypocaust and he had built his house with two-layer walls and roof to give insulation against the climactic conditions. Soon he was hoping to run in some form of ducted plumbing so that his water supply, dependant on an ample rainfall in the mountains maintaining the water-table at a usable level, would be more reliable.

About the house he had taken to wearing the informal Roman toga and encouraged his household staff to wear the simpler, shorter shift. His priestly ethics might call for a display of elevated ideals but there was no harm in a man enjoying the fresh, smooth limbs of his servants. They provided him with spurs to goad his imagination into flights of fancy centred round Homeric times. Interest in Homer and the increasing demand for fine Grecian statuary and tableware brought with it the liberal thoughts that had struggled for existence for the last couple of generations. The soft, lifelike Greek statues had replaced the hard martial Roman ones, even in the homes of the resident military officers. As long as he kept them out of view of the general public and particularly the older, more entrenched, colleagues from the Temple, it wouldn't do any harm.

Nicodemus got on well with the occupiers. He admitted to himself that the absurdities in their character gave him a good deal of private mirth. They were the greatest thing since Alexander but were quite prepared to pray to pieces of wood and stone or have their movements directed by a handful of entrails torn from a living animal. They were far worse than the most bigoted Jew. At least the Jews put it all down to something that couldn't be seen and had made them in his image.

It was these cosmopolitan influences that made Nicodemus ripe for the blasphemous proselytising of the Nazarene, Jesus.

Nicodemus had been up country a couple of years earlier and heard tales of the scandalous conduct of a wandering Rabbi. Although the priest had his own unorthodox ideas about religion he wasn't happy to hear that someone else was undercutting him. Next time Jesus held a teaching session Nicodemus sneaked in disguised as a tradesman and, whatever his motives were for going, there was no doubt about his agreement with what he heard Jesus say. Afterwards he tried to see Jesus but was intercepted by the burly Peter. The fisherman was adamant that no one could see Jesus without his permission. James heard the ruckus and came to see what was going on. Shrewdly, from the way the stranger spoke, James guessed that he was more than he seemed. Instead of barring the way James welcomed Nicodemus and took him to see his brother. While they talked James studied the disguised priest. Gradually the Nazarene began to relax. Whatever Nicodemus's original intention was, Jesus, with his calm reasoned arguments and all-engulfing humanitarianism, had won him over.

Before he left Nicodemus confessed his deception and promised support for their campaign as long as it didn't bring either the priesthood or the temple into disrepute. Nicodemus became a major cog in the complicated machinery of intrigue that James built up. With free access to the council of the elders, an 'advisor on Jewish affairs' to the military and a minor shareholder, a position only granted to very few, well connected people, in Joseph's monopolistic trading empire, Nicodemus commanded a lot of respect. At the beginning of their relationship Nicodemus backed James. The Hebrew nation needed a strong military leader. A man that peasant and priest alike could follow with pride. A growing fear of James's ambition and a discreet instruction from Joseph swung him towards a non-aggressive campaign.

Nicodemus could never understand his dislike of James. The man was friendly, strong-minded, fanatically devoted to his brother and fearless. But it was his cynical misinterpretation of Jesus's words and his own freer, more easily assimilated, code that frightened the priest. The men surrounding Jesus were schooled to respond to his words with an interpretation supplied by James.

While Jesus believed that gentle example would triumph, James's message was more graphic: *Do as we say or we stomp all over you!*

If trouble came, Jesus could turn it aside with a word. James would meet it head on and wrestle for the best hold.

One of Nicodemus's tasks was to find influential positions for the followers that occasionally turned up with a token from James. When Judas knocked on his door he was impressed. The boy was already a prolific writer. Before coming to Jerusalem he had been in Qumran helping to write the history of the Jews and their religious philosophy. Nicodemus had no hesitation about getting him a job in the temple as a scribe/theology student.

Later he wasn't so sure it was a good idea. There was nothing he could fault in the boy's behaviour, his manners and deportment were a credit to his patron, but he had absorbed a good many of James's unorthodox principles and came dangerously near to heresy at times. His wide, clear eyes and ready smile had so far kept him out of trouble but Nicodemus looked on him as a volcano that could erupt at any moment and jeopardise their plans.

All morning, following the sandstorm, the priest paced nervously about his courtyard. The little walled house was just outside the city. A place he could retire to and relax after the hurly-burly of council meetings. The highly fanciful tales that circulated about the wild parties and colourful guests that filtered continually through his little wicket gate were not entirely without foundation although they slandered the host's refined taste. Nicodemus didn't try in any way to discourage the tales. It did him no harm, titillated the palates of his associates and provided cover for visitors such as he was expecting at that time.

His servant had already returned to tell him that the party was on its way. The delay worried him. They should have been there earlier.

There was always the chance that a random patrol had picked them up for no other reason than they were not a group of men easily overlooked in a land populated by slightly built men. The occupying forces were, per capita, hardly any bigger and this could be a cause of jealousy. If Nicodemus had known the real reason for the delay he would have been even more worried.

Jesus had gone less than a hundred yards before having a coughing fit and collapsing. The men were taking it in turns to carry him but progress was slow with frequent stops to accommodate his consumptive fits.

Judas arrived in the early afternoon and was full of the story of the strange man Joseph had told him to see.

The priest listened with only one ear; the other was cocked for news of his friend Jesus and his party. The sun was sinking towards the craggy mountaintops when a servant came to tell him that the party had been sighted. He was annoyed when the energetic Judas outpaced him and greeted his guests before him.

When Nicodemus saw the state of Jesus his heart sank. The tiny figure, supported by the tall Thomas and the rotund John, looked devoid of life. He was relieved when he saw Jesus stir in reaction to a whispered advice of his arrival. Judas was excitedly darting around the group asking a stream of banal questions but a harsh word from James quietened him down. Judas eyed Jesus furtively, unable to believe the deterioration in the state of the leader in the few weeks since he last saw him. Nicodemus was more practical. After a brief greeting he hurried back to the house to organise a bed for the invalid and hot food for his companions. That evening, what should have been a joyous reunion, was overshadowed by the absence of the man that they relied upon to confirm their standing with the people and set them on the road to a glorious future.

Judas, younger and less worldly than his fellow teachers, was more depressed than any of them. His self-generated conception of the exalted standing of Jesus had taken a hard knock. Judas had not seen the slow degeneration of Jesus's body or been properly instructed in the new doctrine. His young mind was still populated with altruistic missions, heroic tableaux and a famous victory at the right hand of a fearsome and all conquering God. Try as he might the dying man in the next room didn't fit into the picture.

Nicodemus, who had been sitting with Jesus for most of the evening, came into the room. He whispered to James and looked across to Judas. James nodded assent without looking up and the priest went across to the boy.

"Judas, dear boy, Jesus wants to see you. Don't stay too long, or you will tire him."

Startled Judas scrambled to his feet.

"What does he want?" He couldn't stop a certain amount of anxiety creeping into his voice.

Nicodemus didn't know but he wasn't going to let the lad think he wasn't privy to Jesus' thoughts.

"You'll find out soon enough." Nicodemus told him enigmatically and walked past and out into the courtyard where he could sit and think undisturbed.

Judas was wearing a long galabia as befitted his status as an intimate of the controversial Rabbi. He ran suddenly moist palms over the cloth to iron out the creases before entering the sick room.

Jesus lay on a couch of packed wool. Sheer willpower had expedited his recovery and in the dim light he looked a different man from the frail figure that had been carried in earlier.

"Hello Judas. Come in and sit down," Jesus told him, indicating the piled sheepskins beside him.

Judas did as he was bid and anxiously waited for the Rabbi to speak.

"James tells me that you are intelligent. Is he right or wrong?" Jesus asked without beating about the bush.

He didn't know how long his nervous energy would last and didn't want to collapse before he had the chance to convince the boy of what he should do.

Jesus carried on quickly.

"I'm going to ask you to do something that will seem strange to you. I don't expect you to understand it but it is essential! I have picked you rather than Peter or John or Thomas or any of the others, including my brother James, because I think I can trust you. You are young and have ideals. That is good. You are intelligent enough to know that sometimes it is necessary to do things that seem wrong, ultimately to get the right result."

Jesus was panting a little with the exertion of talking, with a colossal physical effort he checked a cough that tore at the back of his throat. He studied Judas while he calmed himself. Jesus realised he had to be careful. He must not insult the boy's intelligence by telling him too much, nor leave him in doubt about where his duty lay by telling him too little.

"Do I have your unquestioning co-operation, Judas?" he asked.

Dumbly the young Canaanite nodded his allegiance.

Chapter 27

Jerusalem had never seen so many strangers thronging the narrow streets. For three days friends and relatives crowded through the main city gates to be greeted by sons, daughters, mothers, fathers, brothers, sisters, aunts, uncles, grand-parents, second cousins or anyone else who could be pressed into service for cheap accommodation. In their wake came the beggars, traders, whores and entertainers and all the hangers-on that moved with only the motivation of their victims to give them direction. Even the growing population around the outside of the walls, ranging from the shanty towns of the garbage-pickers to the little pied-a-terre of the wealthy beyond the olive groves, felt the compulsion to move into the city for the Passover. The old hands who came yearly disregarded the delights of the sweetmeat sellers, the men with their lemonade jugs, the soothsayers and the acrobats and concentrated on settling in. Those who couldn't be accommodated with friends found whatever shelter they could and dug in. The few inns the city boasted had been crammed tight for days. Once some sort of accommodation, however crude, was secured, it was time to help with the preparations for the feast.

Traditionally the weather was good. The sandstorm was considered a good omen. It meant that God was pleased. He let them see what he could have in store for them and made a tacit promise of fine weather. Throughout the city cakes were baked and wine brought out of the cellars under the floor and poured into jugs to mellow for the great day. The eldest sons were given the responsibility of making the extra special candles and they stood solemnly by the bubbling vats of wax, dipping the growing stalks. Daughters helped their mother clean the house from top to bottom and made sure that all the clothes and house linen were spotlessly clean. The men folk had an equally traditional role. They drifted together in groups and gossiped and drank while they affirmed old friendships and sponsored new enemies. This year, as most, the stories were of the guerrillas poised to strike just a few miles outside the city gates. That their intention was more serious than a little casual robbery was confirmed by the almost total lack of incidents as the travellers moved across the open space in front of their gathering place. Rumours bounced around the walls of the ancient city fuelled by lies, facts and wishful thinking. Men solemnly told others drunken stories that they in turn heard later in the day and didn't recognise as their own invention.

In this atmosphere James's agents were able to spread the word. It was easy to connect Jesus with the men in the hills.

Why deny the stories of Jesus arriving on a white stallion flanked by knights with mystical powers?

The agents listened to tales of magic that travellers, with drunken conviction, claimed to have seen with their own eyes. The agents accepted their drinks and plagiarised their stories. Added weight was given to the promise of a Holy war by the capture of one of the guerrillas.

Barabbas had become caught up in the excitement. He lifted a few purses and spent the money on trying to taste all the products of the proliferating whore-houses. When he found himself short of cash he went back into the streets and tried to replenish his coffers by manual dexterity. Sober he could lift a diamond from a belly-dancers navel without even the closest student of the dance noticing. Drunk he couldn't lift the coins off a corpse's eyes without calling him back from the other side. Caught red-handed he was too drunk to notice and was captured by a mob looking for a bit of excitement, casually beaten and then handed over to a Roman squad that happened to be on its way back to the barracks.

The Centurion ordered the legionaries to take the thief back to the garrison dungeons with them.

Barabbas talked!

Nobody wanted him to. Nobody even thought he had anything to say.

At first his solemn, self-important stories of forces about to invade the city were taken for nothing more than the imagination of an alcohol pickled brain. The soldiers had heard it all before. He quietened after they threw him down the steps of the dungeon and slammed the door leaving him in total darkness.

It sobered him up.

Around him he could hear moans and whispers of others incarcerated with him. Terrified, he huddled against the wall. He kicked out at a stab of pain on his ankle and felt the fat, furry body of a rat. He blundered to the door whimpering and crying. Nails split and broke as he desperately tried to force a way through the cracks in the heavy woodwork. Exhausted he sunk down and stared, sightless, into the dark, convulsively kicking out every few seconds as he felt the presence of the rodent hordes pressing in.

Barabbas might still have gotten away with nothing more painful than a public flogging if Seph had not arrived in the city to join up, as arranged, with the forces of Aliph. As his men filtered through the city gates Aliph and his men were already well on their way to their mountain retreat, but the black giant had no way of knowing that. The bustling normality of the streets gave him false assurance - Aliph had been able to overcome the soldiers without raising the alarm and alerting the main garrison. Seph wasn't fool enough to think that his spectacular size and hideously distorted features were going to be overlooked even in a city bustling with oddities.

He had no way of hiding.

The crowd covered his men and made it hard for the Romans to seek them out when the fighting started. Seph's men would not have the same problem. Each Roman uniform would be a prime target. Once Aliph showed himself master of the guard-houses and control-posts throughout the city and Seph's men started the slaughter of the patrols on the streets, the citizens would join them on the march to the garrison.

It was time for action!

The bandit picked his way through the small, poorly-constructed houses squashed between the expanding city centre and the unyielding wall.

The guard-post was backed up against the wall with an open, lightly barricaded fence ensuring that the space-hungry civilians didn't encroach on military property. Running along, close-to and following the contours of the wall, was a cobbled road used exclusively by the Romans for rapid communication between the guard-posts. Just under the top of the wall was a timber constructed lookout post from which a sentry could survey the city. Each sentry post was in visual contact with the one on either side and there was also a mechanical alarm that could be operated after dark or if the weather conditions were bad enough to obscure visibility. The alarm was simple but effective. Supported by brackets built out from the wall a light chain ringed the city. At each post, and from these to the garrison, bells were connected to the chain. In an attack the sentry or guard-commander had only to pull the chain to alert the entire military force of the city. The system functioned efficiently but it was so long since it had been used the soldiers had almost forgotten its existence.

As Seph surveyed the scene he began to worry. If Aliph had done his work properly the guardhouse should be in the hands of his men. If it was, Aliph was cleverer than Seph gave him credit for. The guard-post looked absolutely normal. The sentry lounging in the box on the wall even had Roman features. Seph sat against the wall of one of the crude huts and thought.

His thoughts were not therapeutic.

Aliph had obviously not done what he promised. The city was still in the hands of the hated Romans. And now, in the light of day, it wouldn't be easy to surprise them. Seph's mutilated face writhed as he cursed the bandit leader and his own stupidity. He should have known that Aliph had no intention of getting caught in an open stand-up fight. Aliph was only interested when he thought he could use the civilian population as a buffer. A surging, amorphous mass that would engage the swords of the oppressors with their naked bodies while Aliph and his men pranced on the periphery, urging them on but only joining in when there was a high degree of certainty that they could carry the day.

Seph's bitter hatred of the Romans and his need to let Latin blood, had blinded him to the fact that Aliph's motivation was purely professional. And that meant that he only moved if the chances for survival out-weighed those against by a healthy majority. The Negro guerrilla forced himself to be calm.

It was no good railing against Aliph. That was for another day. Now the problem was more imminent. Was there still the possibility of taking over the city? He eased his good eye around the edge of the building. To take the guard-post would be relatively simple. But to do it in broad daylight without the sentry on the wall pulling the alarm or the sentries on adjacent boxes seeing the disturbance was impossible. The only chance was to wait until after dark.

But the problem was that he had no way of telling his men the new plan. They were spread throughout the city, edgy and spoiling for the fight. If they didn't get an outlet for their adrenalin-tuned nerves they would burst out in individual actions that would alert the military and abort any chance they had of taking over. He had to try to find them, or at least as many as he could, and tell them of the new plans. Suddenly he wished his appearance wasn't so remarkable.

The most simple-minded legionnaire only had to catch sight of him to recognise the description of the maniacal Seph - the Nubian. The reward on his head was large enough to put steel into a soldier's arm. Seph pulled his hood close across his face and bowed his shoulders in an effort to disguise his size. All it did was make him an even more grotesque figure.

It took ten legionaries to arrest him. Three of them were killed instantly by his outsized sword, and even when his sword arm was hacked off he managed to break a neck and rip off a nose before his gaping wounds disgorged enough blood to weaken him sufficiently to be seized. The Centurion who had arrested Barabbas earlier, looked down at the hideous, bloodied corpse at his feet, and began to wonder if there was more to the drunken thief's story than he thought. Seph was known to have a savage band of killers at his command and was hardly likely to risk coming into a Roman stronghold alone. The rising excitement amongst the Jews and the fanciful tales running rife might be more than religious fervour.

The Centurion dispatched a couple of soldiers to bring the frightened and subdued Barabbas to the guardroom.

The bandit's riotous living of the last couple of days had caught up with him and he was wallowing in an alcoholic depression. The soldiers slammed him against the guardroom wall, laced leather manacles around his wrists and hauled him up so that his toes were just clear of the ground. A piece of wood with notches cut in either end to accommodate the wrists, was jammed roughly into place, spreading his arms about four feet apart and effectively stopping the prisoner from using his muscles to support his body. With his full weight a pendulum from his dislocated shoulders, circulation inhibited, lungs cramped by the distorted rib cage and creeping suffocation as the lungs filled with unaspirated water, all the interrogator had to do was wait until the initial defiance was subdued by the unrelenting agony, put his questions and take a drink while the victim babbled out everything he knew, thought or could invent.

After that there were a number of choices. They could either leave him where he was for a couple of hours to suffocate to death, sling him off the city wall and if he survived - forget him, put him in with the quota that were to be crucified immediately after the Passover, to remind the Jews that they were now dealing with the Romans and not the Egyptians or, in the case of almost unbelievable leniency, send him to the galleys.

The Centurion looked the screaming Barabbas over and put him down for a fall from the wall or being nailed up somewhere outside the city where his noise and smell wouldn't matter. The Roman dismissed the possibilities of the galleys and being left on the guardroom wall. The prisoner was already smelling up the guardroom were he had defecated all over himself and the whimpering and whining was getting on The Centurion's nerves. The Centurion shook the amulet of spices he wore under his shirt in a vain effort to combat the stink and stood well off while he put his questions.

As befitted an officer of the Roman Legion his interrogation was conducted with subtle decorum.

"Now Barabbas…" He started in a friendly voice and waited until he had the hanged man's attention.

"We have just picked up a man we have wanted for some time. His name is Seph. Unfortunately he resisted arrest and was killed before we could talk to him."

The Centurion frowned as if Seph had not quite played the game.

"This morning, Barabbas, you were trying to tell me about an uprising that was going to sweep me and my homosexual cohorts into the sea. Stupidly I neglected to take any notice of what you were saying. Now you can tell me again and I will believe you."

He sat on the table and waited.

He didn't expect to have to ask a second time. Already Barabbas's lips were turning blue as his circulation began to fail, and he was having to make a tremendous effort to suck in air.

"Please please. I'll tell you anything. Cut me down. Please, I'm dying. Cut me down!" Barabbas screamed.

The Centurion said nothing.

Barabbas sucked in air with another tremendous effort.

"It's true! It's true. There is going to be an uprising! It's scheduled for tonight before the festival of the Passover... Please, cut me down. Please!" Barabbas sobbed.

Still the Centurion made no move. Frenetic, gabbling, at times incoherent, the tortured man rushed on.

"Tonight Aliph! Aliph is my chief. He is probably already here. If Seph's here - he will have come with Aliph. There are - maybe - two hundred..."

A scream tore from his lips as with an audible snap the ligament broke in his elbow. He tried to lift his head to plead for relief from the guard commander but slumped unconscious.

Irritably the Centurion gestured for the guards to revive him with a bucket of water and waited while Barabbas tasted once again the horror of his situation.

"Thank you, Barabbas," the Centurion said in his calm, friendly voice when he was sure he had the thief's undivided attention.

"You were saying that you thought there were about two hundred of your comrades in the city? Well, that's no problem. They won't get far. Now, you say that there are two groups, one controlled by the late Seph, the Nubian and the other, your gang, who are under Aliph. We know him too. But what is it all about? Why this futile attempt to take on Rome?"

Barabbas didn't reply. He welcomed unconsciousness and let the black waves crowd in. Pain came flooding back as he was shocked into consciousness by another bucket of cold water.

The Centurion patiently asked his question again. Before he had finished Barabbas was trying to answer.

"It's the Messiah! He's coming into the city today! It's the Day of Deliverance! The country will rise and throw out all the foreign invaders!"

Barabbas was skirting the borders of delirium. He was no longer conscious of what he said. Only what, in his innermost soul, he would like to believe.

"When Jesus walks through the city gates the prophecies will be fulfilled! Israel will rise again!!" Barabbas gasped, struggled to pull himself up and without warning, collapsed.

The Centurion sat looking at the unconscious man without seeing him.

"Jesus eh? The new prophet?!" He looked at his two assistants inquiringly.

"You know him?"

They shook their heads and waited for further instructions. The Centurion pondered his next move.

"These bloody Jews have more prophets than they have fleas. Well, I suppose it won't hurt to take precautions."

The Centurion pushed himself up from the table and looked with disgust at the contorted wall decoration.

"Put him in the pit with the others for execution. Let the word get around. It might draw some of his friends from their holes."

Chapter 28

Since early morning Robin Firth had been aware of a sense of isolation. The impressions that played tag with his mind over the preceding days no longer taunted him. In accordance with the specifications of the engineer Mayer, men worked through the night isolating the transmitter room from random transmissions that might interfere with the reception that he insisted he was picking up. He avoided contact with Mayer and Sanderstead. They might have guessed that he was having trouble and been convinced that his claim of receiving impressions from the past was nothing more than they had at first suggested - the imaginings of a deranged mind.

While his insulated retreat was being built he remained in his little sitting room. It now had a bed and a refrigerator full of comestibles suitable for cooking in the microwave oven that had been installed.

He tried sleeping.

It didn't work out.

Every time he almost dropped off the nightmare of what he might have unwittingly launched on the world came back to poke at his eyelids. He gave the sleep thing up as an unreachable goal and tried to feed his brain with some of the ready-meals packed into the fridge. It wasted some time but did nothing to restore tranquillity to his fevered mind.

Of course the thought that he might be completely changing the course of history had been with him right from the start. But he was sure that the change would be for the good of mankind. That the life of the Saviour Jesus Christ being lengthened, even by just a few years, would give his disciples the time to fully understand his teaching so that when they went out into the world to carry his message to the people it would be fully formed. No more misunderstandings. No more divergent cults and sects.

Just the plain words of Jesus.

That would save the world from the corruption of conflicting religions and ideologies.

Where could it possibly go wrong?

If Korky Sanderstead's friend, Dr.Grayson, was correct, and he had to accept the strong possibility that he was, without the death of Jesus the immense, civilising force of Christian doctrine would have been long forgotten. In his ignorance he had assumed that the fundamental block to civilised advancement was the misinterpretation of the teachings of Jesus by his immediate followers magnified by proceeding generations.

Robin Firth now doubted that.

But the damage was done.

His thought-module in the past had not taken with it the new knowledge. It did not see that Christianity hinged on the crucifixion. The subsequent stories of resurrection, true or folkloric inventions tacked on to substantiate the divinity of Jesus, were essential to the growth of the ideology.

If the body hosting his thought-module were able to stop the crucifixion, history would be changed at a stroke.

Christianity could well be obliterated and with it all the influences, good and bad, that it had made on history for two thousand years. There was no way of knowing what such a change would have on the world or even if such a momentous piece of history could be engineered in such a manner.

The risk was too great to dismiss.

Robin Firth had to do everything he could to try and avert the most monumental catastrophe in history.

If he could he had to make sure that Jesus of Nazareth died on the cross in the manner prescribed in the Bible and revered for two soul-searching millennia.

Without warning, for the first time in four hours, he felt a stir of foreign impressions invade his mind. With a sob of thanks he pushed aside his frustrations and let his mind fill with the impressions relayed from the past.

Pictures formed in his mind and the stiffness and cramp returned to his body.

Chapter 29

For hours Naomi crouched in the corner watching the contorting, slobbering figure of the madman strapped to the racks. Isaac instructed his servants to tie him there when he realised that the insane Haddaq had banished the reasoning influence of Robin and taken control of his body again.

Isaac didn't know what to do. It was obvious that there was no point in taking Haddaq into Jerusalem. Only the captive mind of Robin was aware of what needed to be done. Without him their whole journey was without objective. Isaac fell into a troubled sleep.

He was awakened by a hand shaking his shoulder.

Naomi stood by his side looking intently at the still body of Haddaq.

Isaac got to his feet and looked down at the ugly figure lying spread-eagled by the retaining ropes. Haddaq's face was covered in drying spittle and blood from his bitten lips. But he seemed to be sleeping calmly now. As father and daughter watched, the tortured eyes opened and gazed vacantly at the roof. Intelligence flooded back as the pupils focused. Slowly the malformed head turned to look at them and the flicker of a reassuring smile plucked at the torn lips.

Naomi started forward but Isaac held her back.

The recovering man swallowed noisily and worked his lips soundlessly as he tried to form words.

"What day is it?" he at last managed to croak in the careful, stilted voice that they associated with Robin.

Without waiting for instructions Naomi fetched the water jug and started to bathe his face while Isaac cut loose his bonds.

"We must get to Jerusalem!" Robin insisted. "It's getting late."

Isaac helped him into a sitting position. Robin looked around.

"How long have I been unconscious? Where is Judas?" he asked.

Isaac helped strip off Robin's soiled clothing.

"Judas had to leave. He promised to tell Jesus that you wanted to see him!" he answered, unsure of himself.

"When?" Robin wanted to know.

Isaac shrugged.

"I don't know. They should have already left Nicodemus's house by now I should think. They will be in the city soon."

Robin tried to stand up but the effort was too much.

"We must leave at once. There may still be time…"

Isaac looked at him sharply.

"Time for what?"

Robin grimaced.

"I don't know exactly but Jesus is in great danger. It's something to do with Judas!"

"Judas?" Isaac pressed.

Robin nodded.

"Yes. Quickly! We must not waste more time. Jesus will know what to do."

Robin managed to pull himself erect but when he tried to take a step his legs buckled and he would have crashed to the floor if Isaac hadn't leaped forward to save him. Robin gave him a strained smile as thanks and allowed the older man to lower him onto the storage rack. Isaac stood and looked at him. He wasn't encouraged by what he saw. Robin's left arm was clamped tightly to his chest, the wrist twisted inward. His leg was also drawn up and his foot cocked. Only the bright intelligence blazing from the wide eyes promised an inner strength. Whether the body could, in any way, match that strength was another matter.

Isaac crouched down beside Robin.

"We still have time to call this off," He offered. "You have done your best. More than anyone could expect considering your state of health. No one would blame you."

Before he had finished Robin was trying to sit up, shaking his head wildly.

"No! No! We can't give up. We must be in Jerusalem before the Passover," he pleaded, close to tears.

Isaac stood up and looked down at the man whose motivation for reaching the city was still not clear to him. What was even more worrying was that it was not clear to Robin either. Isaac didn't regret the decision to bring the sick man on the long and painful journey. If he hadn't he knew he would have spent the rest of his life wondering what it was all about. Besides, Robin was on his last legs. His condition had deteriorated so rapidly Isaac sometimes doubted that he would even be fit enough to reach their destination.

So what did it matter? In a matter of days his poor friend would be dead. So they might as well make the final effort and let him die, happy in the knowledge that he had done everything he could to play out the scenario he had set for himself.

Isaac came to a swift decision.

He had come so far on nothing more than intuition and curiosity. To turn back now would be pointless.

Isaac clapped his hands to get the attention of the crew. They didn't really need it. They had all been watching the interaction between their master and the poor wretch he had befriended, with interest.

"OK. We're moving into the city. I will only need two donkeys. Naomi will accompany us. The rest of you will stay here until I get back. If any of you want to go into the city you can but make sure there is a couple of you here to look after the animals." He thought for a moment. "I want you all back here ready to leave the afternoon of the day after tomorrow."

Isaac didn't have any reason for stipulating that time but he had a feeling that the impending drama, or anti-climax, would have played itself out by then.

It took them only a short while to get organised. They were nearer the gates than the house of Nicodemus and could still get to the city before the Nazarene's party. As they neared the city their progress slowed. On either side families sat amongst their possessions and stared at the endless stream of hopeful travellers pressing on towards the crowded city. Hours before the watchers had been a part of the endless stream of pedestrians, sure that they could find a resting place in the city. It was pointless telling the newcomers that every inch within the walls was already spoken for. Everybody demanded their own experience.

Confusion reigned at the gates. Orders had been promulgated to search any travellers that looked as if they might be carrying concealed weapons. The task was daunting. Most desert or mountain travellers carried some sort of weapon for protection, either against the wild animals or against the footpads that infested the main routes. As the backlog of people waiting to be searched grew, a crowd of impatient travellers spread out around the gates, jeering and cat-calling in a mistaken impression that ridicule would make the guards let them in.

It had the opposite effect.

The soldiers had started the day in good humour. Festival meant a chance to see some excitement. A time when the barriers between oppressed and oppressors were briefly lowered. By mid-afternoon their mood had changed. Falling back on their authority they became rude and obstructive. Isaac saw the surging mass and almost gave up. It looked impossible to get into the city.

Naomi possessed the optimism of youth.

Holding the head of Robin's donkey firmly by the halter she coolly walked into the throng, gently touching arms and bowing politely as she eased forward. Isaac just held on to Robin and let himself be drawn along. Barring the way was a small detachment of Roman guards, spears at the ready and tenseness in their hard-muscled bodies that suggested they were willing to use them.

Naomi walked straight towards them and stopped only inches from their spears. She bowed politely and then just stood and waited for them to let her through.

Surprised, the soldier in front of her looked at the slight black-enveloped figure and at the emaciated figure on the back of the donkey and didn't know what to do. Shrewdly Naomi judged his indecision, gave another deep bow as if thanking him for his help and walked forward. The guard snatched a quick look at his companions but they were too busy with their own problems. To save face he gestured with his spear for her to proceed and then repelled others who tried to follow with unnecessary savagery.

Inside the walls the conditions were hardly better than on the outside. Some attempt had been made to keep an area clear to provide a route for the flow of traffic but it was hardly adequate and eroded second by second by the spectators lining the sides. Isaac had no way of knowing, but a good many of the people lining the road were the supporters organised by James to orchestrate the welcome to Jesus.

The merchant moved up beside Robin and peered into his face. He was afraid that the obscene Haddaq personality might return at any moment. Robin recognised him and nodded his head reassuringly.

He looked terrible.

The tremendous energy he was directing to keep his mind free and active was draining what little strength remained in his body.

He couldn't go on!

Isaac tapped Naomi on the shoulder. There was too much noise to speak so he nodded towards the side of the road and pointed at Robin. Without hesitation Naomi agreed and helped take the weight as Isaac lowered the frail body to the ground. It wasn't easy. Those already installed resented being behind the new arrival and tried to push Robin's inert body aside. Isaac stopped them. With calculated force he brought his whip down on their arms and then stood over them daring defiance.

They got the message. They muttered bravely but ignored the huddled body amongst them. Satisfied that they accepted the situation Isaac knelt down beside Naomi, who was trying to make Robin more comfortable on his hard bed, and shouted close to her ear.

"I'll go on to the meeting place and see if I can get some assistance. You stay with Robin. I'll take the mule and get back as soon as I can."

Without looking up, Naomi nodded understanding and Isaac pushed off through the crowd.

Joseph had told him he had made available for Jesus a small house that he kept on the North side of the city near Herod's temple. The most immediate supporters of the Nazarene would meet there.

Naomi propped Robin up into a semi-sitting position, his head supported by her shoulder. Although small, her childish strength was built on a life of hard work and the fleshless body of the sick man was a minor weight compared to some she carried daily.

To Robin the noisy, constantly shifting scene passed unnoticed. The last attack, when Haddaq had completely taken control, and the subsequent weakness of his body, told Robin there was little time. Another personality struggle would be too much.

His host body could not possibly survive.

But his concentration on keeping the spark of consciousness alight was having a secondary and fascinating effect. The shadowy images that taunted his sleepless hours came back with renewed and more articulate force. The subconscious link he felt with his other self in some other, unimaginable world, was very strong. At times it seemed to be calling to him, urging him to do something important.

Something of which he should have been aware but couldn't quite grasp.

It was terribly confusing.

Jesus was the only thing that mattered. He must be warned of the danger!

Robin felt Naomi gently shake him to draw his attention. With an effort he dragged his thought from their limited merry-go-round and concentrated on what the girl was trying to point out to him. The noise level seemed to have risen and there was an agitation in the crowd that hadn't been there earlier. Everyone was pressing forward trying to see something. Hemmed in by the straining, imprisoning legs of the crowd, Robin looked to Naomi for an explanation. She shouted something to him but it was drowned in the rising chant of the people around them:

"JESUS! JESUS! JESUS!"

The chant orchestrated and reinforced by James's professional agitators picked up rhythm and became distinguishable from the general background hubbub of noise.

Robin felt excitement swell in his chest.

There was still a chance!

The proximity of his goal seemed to strengthen him. He scrabbled at the legs barring his way, pushing himself, serpent like, in the direction pointed by the feet of the straining crowd. Naomi helped as much as she could. She couldn't understand Robin's sudden, feverish activity but she did not question the necessity. Through the restlessly moving feet Robin could see the slim hooves of a donkey moving towards him.

'Riding on an ass!'

The words echoed in his mind. He didn't pause to analyse them. They were the confirmation that Jesus was real.

Robin tried to pull himself erect on the nearest person to him but he was knocked impatiently to the ground. Naomi tried to get her shoulder under him to give him support but the surge and ebb of the crowd kept her off-balance and she couldn't make it.

Robin was frantic now. His eyes bugged and his mouth writhed in futile agony as he tried to summon the last spark of energy that would fulfil his mission.

The donkey was only a few feet from him and in another second would pass from him in the crowd!

With his failing strength he knew that there would be no second chance.

Somehow he coiled his legs under him and drew iron from unplumbed sources. He drove down with his dying adrenalin conjured strength and dived through the intervening bodies. In the fraction of a second that he was face to face with Jesus of Nazareth he saw the noble features, the wide, magnetic eyes, compassionate mouth and tall compelling figure of the Italian Renaissance, regarding him with understanding and encouragement.

Robin crashed unconscious across the donkey's neck and was dragged away and cast to the ground by Peter stationed beside Jesus to see that he didn't disappoint his supporters by falling off. Hardly an incident likely to convince those, still expecting a Prince on a white charger, that the crippled figure clinging precariously to the narrow back of a sad looking ass was a passable alternative.

Jesus hardly noticed Robin.

Pain and the deadening effect of the constant ear-splitting roar had isolated him. He was aware that the crowd were partly hostile, contemptuous of the *Ersatz-King* they were being fobbed off with. Dust, rising from the stomping feet, hung thick in the air and threatened to bring another bout of coughing.

Another weakness hardly likely to appeal to the masses.

For the millisecond their eyes met Jesus read the mute appeal in his assailant's eyes. As he saw Peter push the crippled man aside Jesus put out a weak, futile hand and touched Robin's face.

The touch, fleeting and light as it was, hit the collapsing Robin like a high voltage shock. His whole body seemed to stretch and explode in fizzing, burning whirlpools of cleansing pain.

In his head the mewling Haddaq roared, convulsed and departed forever.

As Naomi cushioned Robin's fall and lowered him to the ground, the memories of his other life in the future flooded back. With them the memories that had been kept behind the barrier of physical restriction by the brain damaged Haddaq body. He tried to get to his feet and run after Jesus but the demands on his depleted metabolism had drained his last reserves of energy and as the braying, frenetic crowd surged after Jesus he drifted once more into unconsciousness.

Chapter 30

Two thousand years in the future Robin Firth reared up in his chair, eyes wild and staring, blood dribbling down his chin from where his teeth had bitten through his tongue. The last couple of hours had been almost as debilitating for Firth as they were for his virtual sibling physically suffering in the past.

Contact with the past had been better once it was re-established. The makeshift lead and tinfoil receptor that Mayer conjured up worked to a certain degree although with nothing like the efficiency Firth would have liked. Over the many days that he fumbled with the vague, melting concepts before Mayer came up with a partial solution, he had schooled his mind to utmost receptivity. The thoughts and perceptions that filtered through didn't quite form a cogent picture. Consciously he filled out the faint sketches and coloured them with his contemporary knowledge.

As his thought-module motivated host moved towards his meeting with Jesus he brought the scene into focus by recalling pictures from the Bible and films he had seen. They had no bearing on the actual scene and tended to confuse rather than clarify his perception. Regularly he tried to send out the message to his renegade thought-module that the mission should be aborted! That the pattern of history with regard to Jesus should not be altered!

He wasn't getting through.

Firth felt the backlash of the stultifying shock that the proximity of Jesus caused and felt the mind twisting response in the body of Haddaq.

But that was all!

It was like a movie when the projector breaks. One second he was involved in the cataclysmic scene and the next he was a confused spectator, divorced from the action and dazed by the abrupt disintegration of his pseudo world.

Firth slumped in the chair while he gathered his cartwheeling thoughts. Whatever had happened so far he thought there was still a chance. If he was right in his supposition, Jesus was still not aware of the proposed treachery of Judas.

That was good.

If things stayed that way there was nothing to fear. It might even be that the host body bearing the Robin thought-module was dead. In that case the danger was over.

For some reason Firth could not quite bring himself to accept that. The rapport between present and past had been severed completely but he was sure that it was not because of death. Contact had been possible through the undeveloped part of the host brain. When Jesus swamped the host personality, the unformed part, it opened the way for complete domination by the Robin thought-module.

The module still indelibly imprinted with the command to save Jesus at any cost.

The pattern was now set.

Turning off the space/time modulator would make no difference.

Firth ripped the shining silver foil from the door and ran into the outer office. His secretary looked up in surprise. She hardly recognised her debonair, slightly absentminded boss in the unkempt, frantic man who leaned across her desk and shouted instructions in a rush of ill-formed words.

"Get Mayer and Sanderstead here immediately. Do you know where they are?"

His secretary nodded, bewildered by his panic.

"Where, woman, where?" he shouted.

"At the aerial installation, I think..," she whimpered timorously.

Firth banged his hands on her desk in frustration.

"Well - get them! Tell them it's a matter of life and death!"

He rushed back into his own room and sloshed coffee into a cup from the ever-primed percolator.

Indecision was in the past.

He now knew what he must do.

When Mayer and Sanderstead arrived ten minutes later, he had washed his face and put on a clean shirt. He was calmer now and ran an electric razor over his chin while he told them what he wanted.

"We have to attempt another transmission."

Sanderstead looked at him in surprise.

"For the same setting?" he asked.

Firth put his razor away and sat down facing them. He was aware that time was running out but he needed prompt co-operation and his reasoning must not be questioned.

"For the same setting," he confirmed.

Before they could ask questions he told them why he wanted their co-operation. Or rather, he told them as much as he felt they needed to know and he had time to tell them.

"Everything points to the original transmission precipitating a major deviation in history. What the parallel history is likely to be we have no way of telling. We can't change it. I want you to transmit another thought-module with an overriding instruction to stop any interference with the destiny of Jesus."

The two scientists looked at each other, disturbed by the request, but not willing to face a showdown with their powerful patron.

“But you must understand that there is no guarantee that the module will be picked up by the same host-receiver,” Mayer protested.

Firth waved that aside.

“I know that but I must try. I’ve got a feeling that the same standard would apply to a transmission as you explained was happening to my reception here. The identical brain pattern at the receiving end would attract the new transmission.”

He made the statement and didn’t ask for their opinion.

“Now, how long will it take to set up a new fix?" Robin Firth asked, getting up and indicating that the time for talk was over.

Mayer lumbered to his feet and walked towards the transmitter room.
“

“Ten minutes or so. The co-ordinates are already in the computer. We haven’t got enough reserve energy to maintain two beams so we will have to cut off the original.”

Mayer explained with more compliance than usual.

Firth fought to control his impatience as the two men carefully checked the equipment and made the minute adjustments necessary. Ready, they helped him into the transmitter cubicle and fixed the bowl-like pick-up on his head.

Sanderstead stood in front of the timing consul and watched the green LED figures drain away the millisecond countdown to transmission.

“Thirty second mark coming up. Changing to automatic countdown - NOW!” Sanderstead pressed a button to bring transmission on to the exact schedule so that it coincided with the shutdown of the original transmission and didn’t overload the transformers.

Fascinated, Firth watched the numbers race in a writhing jumble of half seen figures, towards zero. He was not prepared for the shaft of pain that threatened to rupture his brain as the dying transmitter dragged with it, through the vacuum caused in the frequencies, a totally unexpected influx of new data. Firth gasped and tore the metal hood from his head and staggered from the seat.

Sanderstead rushed to his side fearing a malfunction in the equipment but Firth brushed him aside and stumbled into his private office and slammed the door in an unmistakable hint that he wanted to be left alone.

In the brief moment of pain he had received, distinct and clear, all the impressions that had registered in his thought-module while it had been trapped in the past. The new concepts were so dazzling that he needed to be left alone to let them invade his mind and bring him up to date on the possible consequences of his ill-advised attempt to improve history.

Chapter 31

Joseph Caiaphas, President and High Priest of the Sanhedrin, was not amused. The yearly humiliation of having to go to the military Procurator and ask for the ceremonial robes was not something he could stomach easily. It hadn't been too bad when his old friend, Valerius Gratus, had been Rome's man in Jerusalem but Pilate was another matter. He hated every moment he spent away from his luxurious villa on the outskirts of Hebron and intended to take it out on anyone who crossed his path. As Caiaphas followed the supercilious Albinus through the courtyard he kept his eyes fixed on his sandals. The busts of Roman Emperors and frescos of idyllic country scenes were an offence.

An offence that Pilate appreciated, and enjoyed giving.

"One moment." Albinus spoke in a voice that made no effort to mask the disdain he felt for the High Priest. "I'll see if the Praefectus is ready to see you now."

Hot words rose to Caiaphas's lips, but he bit them back. He had already waited the best part of the day but he knew Pilate. If he showed any sign of impatience the Roman would make everything doubly difficult just to see him sweat.

Albinus reappeared and held open the door.

"The Praefectus will see you now."

Caiaphas nodded and went into the room. At first he thought it was empty.

"Joseph, my old friend."

Caiaphas turned and peered into a bower that led out into the courtyard. Pilate was stretched out on a couch wearing only a short tunic. By his side, perched on a pillow was a young girl, still in her early teens. The High Priest wasn't fooled by the apparently friendly greeting. It didn't mean anything. In fact it was pretty offensive. He was the High Priest of the Temple of Jerusalem, religious leader of the Jews and this jumped up Roman officer dared to address him familiarly. Caiaphas was enough of a diplomat not to let the Roman know what he was thinking but he found the girl's presence hard to take.

"Grab a cushion and try some of this wine. Just in from Cyprus. Tell me what you think," Pilate said, still being ultra-friendly. "Dolly, be a nice girl and get your High Priest a goblet."

The girl got up to do his bidding but Caiaphas was determined to get his business done and get out of the pagan household as soon as he could.

"No. No, thank you," Caiaphas said quickly.

The girl settled down on the cushion again. Caiaphas gave her a hard look, but she felt safe with Pilate as her protector and ignored him. The High Priest made a mental note to discipline her at a later date and addressed Pilate.

"Sir. As you know tomorrow is the eve of Passover. It is usual to receive the ceremonial robes at least three days before Passover so that they can be cleaned and restored in time for the sacrifice. I did ask for them yesterday but…."

Pilate gently pushed Dolly aside and stood up.

"Is that a complaint, Joseph?" he asked in a deceptively amiable voice.

"No, of course not. It's just that when Praefectus Valerius was...," Caiaphas began.

Pilate had had enough play acting. He didn't like Jerusalem. He didn't like having to stay there for the couple of weeks that the Jewish feast of the Passover took - and he didn't like Caiaphas.

"Gratus isn't here now. Or hadn't you noticed? You'll get the robes in time for the festival. At the moment I'm busy." Pilate turned to go.

Caiaphas looked at him open-mouthed.

"You…you can't do that," he managed to stammer out.

Pilate turned to him with a thin smile.

"I can't?" he asked.

"The Temple. We must make sure everything is ready." Caiaphas said weakly. It had never occurred to him that Pilate would be so unreasonable.

Pilate signalled the girl to leave them. He went across and sat in a high-backed chair and looked Caiaphas over, contempt on his face.

"Tell me, High Priest, what would you do if I decided not to give you the robes?" he asked.

Caiaphas stepped forward angrily.

"It was agreed. You must hand the robes over to me in time for the important ceremonies. Tiberius made the agreement with Herod."

Pilate nodded.

"Do you know why the robes are kept in the fortress and not in the Temple?" he asked.

"So that...," Caiaphas started but Pilate ploughed on.

"So that the Roman Emperor, my Lord Tiberius, could keep a check on what you lot get up to. Basically to remind you that you are allowed to continue in your worship, unhindered, as long as you do nothing against your overlords. Do you understand?"

Caiaphas was ready to blow-up but he fought manfully to control his temper.

"I do," he grated out.

"Good. As far as you are concerned - I am your overlord. Do you agree?" Pilate pushed, he got a good deal of satisfaction out of seeing the old man eat crow.

"I shall appeal to Tiberius!" Caiaphas at last managed to get out.

"Good." Pilate got up and confronted Caiaphas. "That's your privilege. Say - six weeks - if you're lucky. Let's see, this is - what do you call it? *Pesach*? Should just about get a reply by - what's that other big feast I have to come back for - *Shavuot*?"

Pilate walked to the door but before he could leave Caiaphas clapped his hands together in frustration. It was always like this with Pilate but he never learned how to deal with him.

"If I'm forced to write to Caesar I will have to tell him about the aqueduct." Caiaphas blurted out and instantly regretted it.

But it had the required effect on Pilate. Pilate stopped, turned back and stood menacingly in front of the High Priest.

"The aqueduct?" he prompted.

Caiaphas looked wildly around the room as if looking for a way to escape. The aqueduct was a genuine grievance but a foolish subject to bring up in the circumstances. There was no way out. Now he had brought up the subject he had to press it home or back down.

And he had backed down enough.

"You know what I'm talking about," he said hotly. "You had no right to use the temple funds for the aqueduct."

Pilate absentmindedly tapped his teeth with his forefinger while he considered how best to handle the Priest's accusation.

"Your father, Annas, was happy to agree to let us use the funds. The aqueduct brought water right into the city centre. A benefit for all," Pilate claimed.

Caiaphas shook his head vigorously. Now the subject of the temple funds had been brought up he wanted to have his say.

"He had no say in the matter!" Caiaphas shouted. "You had no right to take the money from the temple!"

Pilate thrust his face close up to the older man. The money for the aqueduct was a delicate point. He had instructed his men to seize the money then congratulated Annas, joint High Priest of the Temple with Caiaphas, for his civic generosity. He didn't think he would have much trouble convincing Tiberius that it was for the good of Rome.

Problem was Tiberius had become increasingly despotic over the last few years and it was never safe to assume to be able to judge in advance which way he might jump.

"Right. You've had your say. I'm willing to overlook the insult to Imperial Rome for the moment," Pilate said grandly.

Caiaphas rushed in. The suggestion that he might have insulted Rome was not something that he wanted to have to defend in the future.

"I'm sorry. I had no intention of insulting Rome. I just meant..." he said, an edge of desperation in his voice.

Pilate gave a lordly wave of his hand.

"Of course, I understand. However, there are matters that will have to be looked into." He picked an orange from a bowl and started to peel it.

"But we'll let it go for the moment. Now - if you're ready - let's get those robes."

Chapter 32

Mary stood on the roof gazing blankly along the narrow lane that ran past the house that Nicodemus had loaned her for the Passover. She felt very alone. All her friends and extended family were back in Nazareth. Not that it made a lot of difference. She could no longer bear to be with any of them. She knew that the way in which she spurned her friends and family was foolish but she felt so vulnerable with everyone.

It was partly why she had agreed to make the long journey to Jerusalem. At home everyone knew who she was and what she had done. Not that anyone ever said anything but she was sure she knew what they were thinking. There was also the need to see James. She knew that she was nearing the end of her life. Every day the pain became more unbearable. James had told her he would be in the city for the Passover and when she had expressed a wish to spend the holiday with him he had arranged for her to have one of the houses Nicodemus had put at his disposal. When he had made the offer he didn't really think that his mother would take him up on it. When she did he didn't have the nerve to turn her down.

Mary was aware that she had turned into a shrew. A veritable virago, but she could do nothing about it. She understood the reason. Most of it was to do with Jesus and her neurosis that she was to blame for all the ills he suffered. Knowing didn't help. Deep down she still loved her eldest son but whenever they were together she felt ashamed. Often, if she knew in advance that he was coming to visit her, she schooled herself to be warm and friendly. To maybe expiate the sorrow and suffering he had suffered over the years. Then, as soon as she saw his pitiful pock marked face and wasted body the guilt returned and she couldn't let herself relax and enjoy his company. She was aware that Jesus in no way blamed her for his condition but it didn't help. In fact, in a way it made it worse.

Mary gave the long lane one more searching look, still hopeful that James, and, yes Jesus, would appear and come for a meal. It would also be nice if she had someone to kill the goat. It didn't matter that she was perfectly capable of dispatching the creature in the orthodox way, she had done it many times before; it would just be nice to have a man do it for her.

She was so tired. Every day she found it harder to do all the household chores. In spite of the fact that she grumbled non-stop it didn't mean that she wasn't happy running everything. Salome and Miriam were very helpful, especially Salome, but the boys were too idle to shift their feet. Usually it didn't bother her, just gave her a good excuse to let off steam. Lately it had become more than that. She tried to explain the pain away but didn't fool herself.

It was the tiredness! The journey from home to the city!

Of course for her it didn't stop when they unloaded the donkeys and moved into the house.

The house had to be made spotless for the Passover. In previous years it had never bothered her too much. She liked the thought of moving into a dusty house and then, through work and close supervision of the children, turn it into a home that God would be happy to visit. As she manoeuvred her stiffening body through the door she wondered briefly if this was going to be the last year she would be fit enough to make the journey. In the past she had always said, only half in jest, that when she couldn't get up the energy to make the trip to Jerusalem she would die. It looked like that time would soon be on her. She knew that it was just tiredness talking but she was worried that she was disposed to listen.

When she entered the main room Salome instantly came to her.

"Can I do anything for you," she asked.

Mary looked at her and shook her head.

"What have you been doing while I was upstairs," she asked, more harshly than she intended.

"I've been snaggling the wool." Salome told her gently, hoping not to upset her mother.

"You could do that anytime," Mary snapped. "Baking the bread for tomorrow is much more important."

Mary moved over to stand in front of Miriam.

Miriam nodded.

"Don't worry, Mother, everything will be ready for the feast."

Mary looked around, trying to find something to complain about.

"Where's Judas?," she asked.

"He's gone out," Miriam told her and slowly rose to her feet and went to the table and started laying out the plates.

"And Simon?" Mary wasn't really interested.

The 'boys' were young men now. Simon should be married but it was difficult to get a commitment with no authoritative male head of the household.

And Judas!

Talking to him was like talking to a blank wall. She sometimes wondered if, maybe, he wasn't all there.

"Why is it they're always missing when there is something to do?" she demanded of nobody in particular.

Salome put her arm around her mother's shoulders.

"Do you think James will come tomorrow?" she asked.

"And Jesus," Miriam chipped in.

"I hope not," Mary claimed. "There won't be enough to go round."

They all knew that wasn't the truth. The way it was, at that moment, there would be just the five of them to eat the goat. Of course there was always the chance that some distant relative might drop by but it wasn't very likely.

"Why don't you get some sleep?" Salome gently encouraged her mother. "We can look after things here."

Mary shrugged her off.

"I haven't got time for all that," she said in a brisk, no nonsense voice and instantly regretted it. She knew that they were ready for the next day. The things undone would all be needed to be done on the following day.

Mary picked up a large clay water jug and hoisted it onto the table. Miriam laid her hand on her mother's shoulder.

"We'll do all that. You will have plenty to do tomorrow," she said softly.

Miriam was worried about the state of her mother's health. The arthritis had been developing over the years but Mary had learned to deal with it. Recently she had developed other worrying symptoms - headaches, lapses of concentration and, most worrying of all, crippling pains in her abdomen. Most of the time she disguised these by rushing around, keeping on the move so that no one would know the agony she was experiencing. At other times she would hide out in one of the outhouses until the pain subsided.

In the close confines of the little house in Jerusalem there was nowhere to hide.

Miriam took her mother's arm and pulled her towards the curtained off area at the back of the house. Mary put up a show of resistance but let herself be led.

"I expect James will come tomorrow," Miriam told her soothingly.

Mary said nothing but allowed Miriam to help her into bed.

Miriam stood and looked down at her mother for a few moments. The fact that she had allowed herself to be put to bed was even more worrying.

"Good night," she said softly and pulled the curtains.

Mary laid in the darkness and thought about James. Why hadn't he come to see her like he promised? It wouldn't have taken him long. She knew he was only a couple of miles away. She wondered if it was her fault that he didn't come. She knew that she never showed any love when he visited. She wanted to, planned to – but then... She felt tears run down her face. She cried a lot lately. She tried to move into a more comfortable position. A pain shot through her stomach. She tried to massage it away but it made no difference. It was God's curse on her for being an evil woman.

It was a long time before Mary was able to drift off into an exhausted slumber. So many past events raced through her mind. Each one a pointer to what might have been if only she had let it. When she finally managed to doze off the images in her dreams were of her husband Joseph. At first they were happy dreams of when they were first married. Her excitement when she found out she was pregnant. The wonder of the birth of Jesus and the despair brought on by his crippled leg. Then her guilt had made her love fierce and unequivocal. His crippled leg made her love him more intensely. She dreamed of her infant son's dark curls, his brightly shining eyes and ready smile.

The scene changed abruptly. The smiling face was disrupted by huge bleeding pockmarks. She tried to staunch the flow of blood but the more she tried the more the blood flowed. Before her eyes Jesus changed from the beautiful, smiling baby to a bloodied, corrupted thing of horror. She cried out for her husband but before he could appear in her dream and soothe her distress away she was jerked awake by another searing pain in her stomach. Before she could control it a scream was torn from her lips. Instantly Salome was at her side.

Mary recovered quickly and turned away.

"What is it?" Salome asked in a small, frightened voice.

Mary made an effort to control her voice.

"Nothing. Just a nightmare. I'm all right. Just leave me alone."

Salome was joined by Miriam.

"Are you sure you are all right, Mother," Miriam pressed.

"Leave me alone. I told you. I had a nightmare. Now go. I want to sleep," Mary told them fiercely.

Mary heard the curtain fall back into place and the muted whispers of her daughters as they discussed her distress. She wished she could call them back and share her fright and pain with them but she had built such a barrier around her feelings that she knew it would never happen.

Mary spent a fitful night slipping in and out of a restless sleep. Always the image was the same.

Jesus, the son she loved but felt too much guilt to acknowledge.

Chapter 33

Robin opened his eyes and gazed uncomprehendingly at the beautiful smiling face looking down at him. Quickly he glanced around to orientate himself. He saw the tiny, black clad figure of Naomi standing at his feet and felt reassured. Robin gave her a welcoming smile and was warmed by a quick response in her beautiful black eyes. He struggled to sit up but was still not strong enough. Naomi ran forward to support him.

"Thank you," he said easily, without the effort that usually made his speech so painful to hear.

Everything was clear to him now.

He could remember his life as the head of the mighty Firth Foundation Conglomerate. His growing distaste for the materialistic, hedonistic world that he had helped create. The conviction that only a deeper understanding of, and obedience to, the Christian faith in its purest form would save the world from extinction by its own folly.

Mayer and Sanderstead had given him the tool to do something about it. To alter the cruel fate that Jesus suffered on the cross and give Him a chance to fulfil His ministry; to explain more fully his philosophy and by example ensure a better world. Robin remembered, too, the nightmare awakening in the ugly, maladjusted body and the mind-sapping fight he maintained to stop Haddaq ousting him from his unsure post. Most of all he remembered the brief confrontation with the Messiah, with Jesus Christ himself, and the spontaneous healing and cleansing of the body of the crippled Haddaq and the banishment of the defective mind for ever.

Robin tested his limbs under the watchful eye of the silent woman. He had a million questions he wanted to ask but first he wanted to taste the joy of being in command of himself once more. Satisfied, he examined the unknown woman beside him. She was taller than the usual Judean women and sure of herself. Compared with the childlike Naomi she looked an adult. She was wearing a light silk scarf around her braided, jet-black hair. Wound around her shapely body was a cloth of heavily embroidered Damask, held in position by thick gold pins at the shoulder and a linked, filigree gold chain at her waist. Her bare arms were encircled with bangles of gold and silver and precious stones flashed wealth from the rings on her fingers. She fitted the finely furnished room with its sybaritic Grecian ambience made personal by the finest Egyptian cotton and Abyssinian silk. Feeling more secure now, Robin looked back at his benefactress. She gave him a calculated smile and sat down beside him on the high Roman bed.

"Feeling better now, Robin?" she asked with warm familiarity.

"Thank you, yes. But I don't," he gestured to the room.

"I saw you try to get to Jesus and then collapse. So I got my servants to bring you here." She leaned across and patted Naomi on the arm affectionately.

"Naomi told me all about you. At least she told me about a half-crazy village madman who talked of wonderful things that no one else could understand."

She looked him over appraisingly.

"You don't look so hot physically but you seem to have your brain under control."

Robin stretched his arms with relish.

"Yes. It was Jesus," he said simply.

The woman nodded understanding although Robin fancied he sensed a slight derision in the wide smile she gave him.

"Yes. Of course," she agreed.

"But who are you? And why are you helping me?"

Robin thought he could guess the answer but wanted to hear from the beautiful stranger herself.

"Mary," she told him.

He nodded satisfaction.

"Of course. Mary Magdalene. It had to be."

Startled Mary jumped to her feet and looked at him with renewed interest. She had only half believed the tales told by the innocent Naomi but Robin's claim to know her came as a surprise.

"How do you know my name?" she demanded.

Robin waved her question aside.

"It doesn't matter. I know you are a friend of Jesus the Nazarene and that is all that is important."

He stopped her as she tried to break in and continued.

"I've been trying to find the key to unlock the secrets in my mind. In spite of everything I couldn't understand what was happening. Now I realised it was all fate. Divine fate! Right from the start. Isaac finding me, believing in me, bringing me here, leaving me on the streets where I would be able to meet Jesus. It all led to my miraculous cure. It was a sign. Now I'm sure that I'm right in what I'm doing. I'm guided by the hand of God!"

Mary Magdalene's interest quickened as Robin told her of his driving force but when he claimed divine guidance her interest fled.

"So! You are a prophet! What a bore. I thought you might be someone interesting."

Mary, genuinely disinterested, turned to go but Robin's next words stopped her.

"Jesus is in danger. Unless I can stop it, he will die tomorrow," he said in a menacing monotone.

Mary looked back at him.

"Do you really know something or is this all part of your act? Not just divine guidance, but Godly foresight as well?"

Robin shook his head vigorously.

"It's a fact. Unless he can be stopped Judas Iscariot will turn Jesus over to the Romans with enough evidence of sedition to merit Pilate sending him for execution. And the Sanhedrin won't lift a finger to save him!!"

Mary gave an unsure laugh.

"I believe the Sanhedrin would be more than happy to have the Romans get rid of Jesus for them but - Judas? Nicodemus's pretty young friend? Anyone else, but surely not Judas?" she came back and stood beside the bed again.

"How do you know this?" she demanded.

Frustrated Robin looked around as if searching for proof.

"You wouldn't understand. Please, believe me, I know what I'm talking about."

Robin had a sudden inspiration.

Excitedly he swung his legs off the bed. Mary's servants had stripped him before putting him to bed. Modestly he clutched a bed rug around his body and tried a tentative step. He swayed and felt dizzy but he was happy to realise that it was only the weakness of the convalescent.

He looked at Mary.

"Where are my clothes?" he demanded.

Mary sat back on the bed, a stubborn look on her face.

"You are not going anywhere until I am convinced you are either hopelessly mad or sane enough to make sense."

Robin searched the room with his eyes but could see no evidence of clothing. He needed the courtesan's help if he was going to save Jesus and time was running out.

"Where is Isaac?" he asked.

Mary looked at Naomi.

"I expect he is looking for us now," the girl said quietly. "He hadn't come back when you fainted and Lady Mary brought us here."

It was a problem.

Isaac could have convinced Mary Magdalene that she should help without any trouble.

Robin marshalled his argument.

"Look Mary. Please believe me. Jesus is in trouble. Isaac believes it. Ask Naomi." Mary glanced at Isaac's daughter and received a confirmatory nod.

"We knew that Judas Iscariot was somehow bound up with it but in exactly what capacity we weren't sure."

Robin deliberately included the absent Isaac in his story to add weight. It also made it sound as if they had conducted some sort of an investigation to get to the facts.

"In spite of my illness Isaac brought me here so that I could remember. Now I have total recall and I am sure of what I am saying. Before the night is out Judas will denounce Jesus to the Romans and receive thirty pieces of silver for his service. Why Judas will do this I don't know. It's a mystery. Once he is taken we can do nothing about it. He will be taken before Pontius Pilate and accused of being an *agent provocateur*. The Sanhedrin will encourage the Roman Governor to get rid of him and he will be nailed to a cross."

Robin looked at Mary, listening to him with a mixture of fear and disbelief on her face.

He laughed nervously.

"I'm sorry - I know it sounds far-fetched but I'm not mad. All that will happen - unless we do something to stop it. Now - do I get some clothes?"

Mary clapped her hands and sent the servant, who appeared from behind the drapes, to get Robin something to wear.

"I don't necessarily believe what you have said but I understand that my friend Joseph was convinced enough to pass you on to Judas and Isaac was willing to lay aside his business affairs to accompany you on what seems to me to be a completely mad undertaking."

Mary spoke with emphasis, choosing each word carefully.

"If they were convinced that the threat to Jesus was real I am prepared to help you. But I will not do anything that will cause trouble or irreversible damage to either Jesus or myself. Do you understand that?"

The servant brought Robin a thick woollen galabia and a cotton undershirt and left.

Robin spread his hands understandingly.

"Of course. But how can I convince you that time is critical. Once Judas contacted the guards there is nothing we can do!"

Mary stood up.

"Let's go straight to Jesus and tell him what you fear. He will be able to make whatever arrangements he thinks necessary," she suggested.

Robin let Naomi strap on his sandals.

"How near is the house where they are staying?" he asked. Mary waved her hands vaguely.

"The other side of the city. Behind the temple."

Robin dismissed the suggestion of going directly to see Jesus. He was afraid that they had wasted too much time already and while they were making the long, slow journey through the tortuous city streets at night, Judas would already have completed his terrible mission.

Robin had a sudden inspiration.

"Which guard post or camp is the nearest to where Jesus is staying?" he asked.

"We could cut Judas off between the house and the soldiers. That should convince you that he is a traitor."

Mary's interest quickened.

"The nearest military establishment of any type is the headquarters in the square opposite the temple. The Antonia Fortress. The Jewish temple guards also have a barracks there. It's the logical place for Judas to go if what you say is true. The Romans would know better than to try and arrest a popular teacher when the people are celebrating Passover. They would probably get the Temple guard to do it. It is usual for the local law enforcement agencies to make civil arrests. The Romans would probably let the Jews take the brunt of the unpopularity and work in the background."

Impulsively Mary caught hold of Robin's arm and urged him forward. Naomi quickly slid into position on the other side and steadied by the two women Robin walked slowly and with great deliberation from the gilded room.

The journey through the hilly streets was exhausting for the weak man. Swathed in a heavy, dark-hued cloak the sweat poured from his body and soaked his under-garments. Mary had insisted on bringing one of the big Etruscan slaves that guarded her door. It was a good idea. Strong as the two women were, they could not have supported the tottering Robin. The Etruscan had an arm around his waist and supported most of his light weight without apparent effort.

Although the streets were almost entirely empty of human life its overwhelming presence was evident in the piles of luggage and personal belongings jammed into the narrow spaces between the houses. Some of the passageways were entirely blocked by parties of pilgrims observing the Passover in the open. A number of times the small party had to retrace its footsteps and circle round. Another very real hazard was the number of hungry, frightened dogs abandoned on the streets by their celebrating masters. These rushed out from dark corners, barking and snapping and it was only the fearless action of Naomi rushing at them and laying about her with a stout stick that kept anyone from being bitten.

They reached the area at the back of the temple and Mary suggested that to avoid inquisitive guards wanting to know their business on the streets at the Passover, they should keep to the alleyways behind the shops. The shops were jammed together along each side of the temple and did a flourishing business with the devout and sycophantic that crowded the public courts in an attempt to buy favour. Hugging the shadows the four dark figures skirted the rush-lit barracks and moved up the slope, through the more residential area, on the road that would eventually lead to the house where Jesus and his followers were dining. But Robin had reached the end of his endurance. He called Mary back as she led the way along the steeply inclined path.

"It's no good. I can't go any further. If we are right and not too late he will have to come this way. We will wait for him here."

They were in an open space that hadn't yet fallen under the developer's hand because it was too uneven for easy construction. The weeds grew luxuriant between the scattered boulders and there wasn't a house within a hundred yards in any direction. Silently they pushed a few feet in from the path and sunk down out of sight to await the self-incriminating arrival of Judas Iscariot.

Chapter 34

Spread out on the floor on a dried reed mat was a proliferation of steaming dishes and raw vegetables and fruit. Sprawled on hessian sacks around the room the team of teachers, taken on to assist Jesus, ate, drank and chatted. They had a lot to mull over. The reception they had received could have been better.

A lot better!

The mocking laughter and cat-calls had punctured their pride, and caused them to fear for their safety. In the final analysis their only real protection was the goodwill of the people. It would make the civil and military powers think twice about attacking them if their popular support was unanimous. It hadn't been that by a long chalk so they argued and complained, trying to convince themselves that their reception hadn't been that bad. The alternative was to cut and run. All of them considered the alternative but so far pride and self-interest kept them in line.

And James!

He wasn't easy to hoodwink. Under his steely eye they went through the motions.

Adoration of Jesus!

Love everybody! Freedom for the people!

Even Peter, drinking increasing amounts of wine daily, becoming proportionately more bucolic and unstable, made an effort and impressed everyone with his handsome mien and imposing stature. In fact, he was so majestic that most of the people lining the streets mistook him for the vaunted Messiah without even noticing the little man limping along in his wake. It was a double-edged sword that worried Peter as he sat beside Jesus, cramming nuts into his mouth and washing them down with jugs of red wine. Spies had reported to him the sudden military interest in their arrival in the city after the arrest of Aliph's right hand man: Barabbas.

Peter had met Barabbas a couple of times and didn't think the bandit would prove too hard to break. If the bandit named Jesus, Peter, James or any of the others it would be highly dangerous. Peter wished he had taken the advice Jesus gave him not to aggravate the orthodox priests. The Nazarene wanted to persuade them to take a more liberal view of the teachings of the testament and view God in a less pagan light. Peter ignored all that and, secure in what he thought was going to be a popular uprising with himself as the strength and force of the party, attacked the established ecclesiasts with insolence and unrestrained hostility. Now, sitting in the walled city, a stone's throw from the temple, he wished he hadn't been so free with the invective. In the villages, surrounded by easily inspired peasants, he felt supreme. He cursed himself for a fool and looked at Jesus lying beside him, sick and frail, supported by cushions, too sick even to sip his wine. How could he ever have let himself be led into danger by this man?

But of course it wasn't him!

It was that brother of his - James!

Peter took another swig and looked blearily around the room.

James had arrived late and had hardly said a word to anyone. His food was still sitting untouched. Something was obviously disturbing him. Something that probably put them all in immediate danger. Something that should be shared. But the chances of James sharing anything were minimal.

Peter remembered the worry on Isaac's face when he had arrived earlier. Peter had tried to overhear what they were saying but they deliberately walked away as he approached. Isaac was still hanging around, obviously intent on talking to Jesus. As usual James was being difficult, taking decisions on himself without consulting anyone else.

James was like that; he did everything without consulting anyone else. Peter moved into a more comfortable position and nodded solemnly to himself.

"I've had enough," he agreed with himself. "I'm going to tell James that unless I am consulted I will pull out. That would show him."

Jesus watched the heroic figure at his side, subsiding under an overdose of alcohol, with sadness. He wished he could get through to him. Peter had the ability to do so much if he stopped drinking and began to believe in himself. The drinking was a result of his insecurity. As powerful and handsome as he was he still could not accept that people really liked him. He wanted to lead but was frightened of failure. At the first sign of a setback he crumbled and expected the worst. Even minor defeats could be turned into major catastrophes by his masochistic distrust of his own abilities. Jesus let his eyes roam around the room, taking in the serious faces and the furtive looks of the men as they talked in earnest whispers. He missed the laughter and assurance of earlier days and knew that the fault lay with himself.

The men were unsure.

They could see he was failing. James could no longer cover for him. His death, choking on his own blood-torn lungs, would kill the movement stone dead. And that could happen at any time. Realistically, without eating, and haemorrhaging constantly, he couldn't last out the coming week.

Death was not so bad!

It would free him from the fierce, exploding pain in his chest and the constant mind-freezing headaches that never seemed to abate. He had only kept going because the others had invested so much faith and time in supporting both James and himself. His death must add, not subtract, from their strength.

It seemed impossible at first.

When the solution occurred to him he was surprised by its simplicity. He wondered if James had ever had the same thought? It was the type of lateral thinking that his brother used to get the required results. The big man paying homage to the little man, denying rumours of miracles which nobody had heard of, strenuously denouncing kinship with God while pointing out that his family was directly descended from David and in line for fulfilling the prophecies, all the clever ploys that James used to enslave the hopes of the subjugated people.

Jesus smiled to himself.

Poor James! So sure of himself, yet so hampered by his love for his crippled brother that he shrunk from making the one decision that would recover the ground he was losing by protecting him.

Jesus looked across at James. The big man sat upright, legs crossed in front of him, forearms resting on his knees. It was unusual for James to seem so detached, he was usually the life and soul of the party. He tried to attract his brother's attention but got no response. James depression made Jesus even more determined to follow the course of action he had planned. He wished he could tell James but he didn't think he would get a lot of encouragement - just the opposite.

It was not too late!

"James," Jesus said quietly.

James didn't react.

Jesus broke off a piece of bread and threw it at him. Startled, James looked up. Jesus forced a smile.

"Wake up," Jesus said, jokingly, "I thought you were going to bring mother here tonight."

James shrugged.

"She wants to come in the morning,"

"Couldn't you go and get her?" Jesus suggested.

"Too late. Supper will be ready by now. She wouldn't want to leave the rest of them by themselves. Tonight of all nights."

Jesus nodded, appearing to accept the situation.

"I hate to think of her all by herself for Passover," was all he said.

James looked at him, sensing some criticism.

"OK," James said, a touch of anger in his voice. "What do you want me to do?"

Jesus shrugged but made no comment. This annoyed James even more.

"Would you like me to go and see her," he demanded.

Jesus smiled.

"I think that would be what she would want, don't you? Why don't you stay the night and bring her here in the morning?"

James rose angrily to his feet. Deep down he was glad of an excuse to get away for a few hours.

"Give her my love," Jesus said, ignoring his brother's annoyance.

Jesus was glad to get rid of James so easily. It would be hard on him to see Jesus taken without putting up a fight to protect him. Once it was over Jesus counted on James's pragmatism to assert itself and see that his brother hadn't died in vain.

He watched James leave the room. At the door he was accosted by Isaac. James tried to push past him but Isaac was not an easy man to shake off.

Jesus looked along the table to where Judas sat.

The boy was not happy.

He was sitting next to Thomas and the tall man was talking to him but not getting any response. Jesus touched Peter's arm. The fisherman blinked and concentrated on focusing his eyes on him.

"Pour some wine and pass it along to Judas. Some bread too. He hasn't touched a thing all evening," Jesus instructed him.

With difficulty Peter poured a liberal tot of wine into a wooden goblet from the table in front of him. He picked up one of the rounds of flat, unleavened bread and handed the food and drink to Philip before collapsing back into his cushion.

Philip passed them to John and John to Matthew who reached across and placed the bread and wine in front of Judas. Surprised, Judas looked up and Philip jerked an explanatory thumb towards Jesus. When Jesus saw he had the young Canaanite's attention he gave an imperceptible nod and smiled encouragement to the still uncertain youth. Mechanically Judas broke off a piece of bread and chewed it slowly. Suddenly he made up his mind. He washed the bread down with a draught from the wooden goblet and stood up. No one took any notice. He looked again at Jesus and again got a reassuring smile. Without looking back he turned and left the house.

Chapter 35

Robin Firth sat in the chair in front of the high-powered transmitters and concentrated on the spinning numbers with bugging eyes, leaning tautly forward in his effort to break through the barrier that barred him from the past.

He was receiving nothing.

Not the vaguest impression of what was taking place two thousand years in the past. The dial on the console in front of him told that the transmission was still taking place. His faculties told him that the new instructions that he had sent along the pipeline of space and time were not being received. On his knees, open at the page describing the crucifixion, was a Bible.

Firth knew that as long as the New Testament remained, there was time!

Time to undo the stupidity of the plan he had put into action across the centuries. But time was running out and unless he could make contact within the next few hours, civilisation as he knew it could be wiped out - an alternative society that had been stillborn. Desperately he willed his mind to find the tenuous web of other consciousness. Tiredness and longing at times played tricks on him only to be revealed for what they were when they conveyed no new information. Three times he demanded that Mayer checked the space/time regressor to see that it was functioning correctly. Each time Mayer irritably assured him that everything was in working order. Firth probed the memories that the Robin/Haddaq thought-module had brought back to him for an indication of what might be happening. It gave him comfort. At first he had considered the idea that the sick man had died, burned out by the cataclysmic meeting with Jesus.

He wanted to believe that.

It would mean that Jesus would fulfil his destiny on the cross and history would move ahead without interruption. Cruel, apartheid, the excuse for conflict and dissention. But gradually and inexorably bringing Man to an awareness of himself and his environment.

The schisms and factions that chaffed and rubbed against each other were man-made. Christianity was used as a weapon, as an excuse for Man to commit bloody atrocities and subjugate his fellows. It was the nature of man that had misled him, not the true basic theme that had jelled by Jesus hanging on the cross. It didn't matter if Jesus was the Son of God or the Messiah promised by the prophets or just a simple builder's son who had been at a certain place at a certain time.

Man needed a symbol to cling to - to lead him - to follow.

Maybe by accident, maybe by some basic universal law or maybe by the hand of God, an action had taken place at a time and a place and in certain circumstances that it suited Man to follow. The cruelty and injustice would have happened anyway. The Inquisition would have flourished, if not in the name of Christ - then in some equally high-flown ideal. Europe would have found another excuse to commit bloody war on the rapidly expanding and consolidating people of the Holy Lands without the easily adapted Crusade concept. Missionaries would still have forced their own inhibited views on the natives and spread their diseases and mistaken doctrine amongst the simple savages...

The one thing that the cross had contributed was a sense of guilt! It flayed the slave owners as they whipped their slaves. Politicians resorted to guilty bombast as they sent their troops to bomb civilian populations or annihilate the armies of other nations. Over the centuries that guilt had paid off. People were beginning to care about each other, they now wanted to preserve the goodness of the earth for future generations. The bloody conflicts and cold, calculating cynicism for human endeavour still persisted but a start had been made. And Robin Firth, in his ignorance, had unleashed a power that could make the pain and suffering of generations count for nothing! His awareness of the atrocity he had committed battered at him with uncompromising violence.

Chapter 36

Isaac's impatience grew as the evening wore on. James had promised him an audience with Jesus but insisted that he must wait until after supper. Isaac fretted against the delay but mollified his growing irritation with the bromide that Jesus was still alive and well and so far Robin's dire warnings of imminent disaster had not happened. Isaac was a thorough man and wanted to make sure that he had done everything he could. He was not happy that James had so far not allowed him to see Jesus and had kept him kicking his heels in the garden.

He rose to his feet, thought for a moment, came to a decision and headed for the door leading into the house. Before he could open the door James stormed out, almost bumping into him.

Isaac recovered quickly and grabbed the big man's arm. James tried to shrug him off but Isaac was not in the mood to be marginalised. The big man swung around to face him, his fist clenched. Isaac didn't budge. For a moment the two men stared eye to eye. Suddenly James relaxed.

"I'm sorry," he said in a controlled voice. "What can I do for you?"

"You know what you can do for me," Isaac retorted angrily. "You've left me hanging around here for hours when I told you that it was imperative I saw your brother immediately."

James nodded.

"Sorry about that. I'm afraid I forget. I've got a lot on my mind at the moment," James explained.

"So much that you can afford to dismiss a threat to your brother's life?" Isaac grated out, still not appeased by James apparent mood swing.

James was in danger of losing his temper with the insistent merchant but at that moment Judas threw open the door from the house and slammed it shut violently.

James turned around angrily.

"What's your problem?" he enquired menacingly.

"I have to do something Jesus has ordered me to do," Judas said stentoriously, hoping that James would stop him from carrying out his mission.

James had more on his mind than having an argument with his inferior.

"Well don't hang around gabbing. Go and do it," James told him.

Still Judas hesitated.

"But...."

"Go" James commanded him angrily.

Judas glared at him, trying to summon up the courage to argue but the look on James's face advised him that it would be better to do as he was told. He turned abruptly and hurried away without looking back.

When James turned back to Isaac he was in a more conciliatory mood.

"Look, I have to go across town to see my mother. Jesus wants to see her," he explained. "I'm sure Jesus would love to have a chat with you. Don't keep him up too late. He gets tired easily," James said.

"But what about the danger..." Isaac said, trying to grab his attention.

James patted him on the arm and gave him a reassuring smile.

"Don't worry about that. Peter is more than capable of dealing with any trouble." James nodded and walked briskly away.

Isaac stood and watched him until he was out of sight. He couldn't believe that James was being so cavalier with his brother's life.

Isaac turned and opened the door into the room beyond.

Matthew and Philip jumped instantly to their feet and barred his way into the room. They recognised Isaac but didn't give way.

"I must talk to Jesus," Isaac explained soothingly.

They both nodded and smiled. They didn't want to be accused later of acting offensively to the powerful merchant baron.

Isaac decided that actions not words were going to bring the best results.

"I can't wait. I came from the other side of Jericho to see him!" he insisted.

"I'm sorry," Matthew said but didn't make much of an attempt to stop him when he pushed past.

The activity by the door attracted the attention of Peter. At first he thought it might be the guards but when he recognised Isaac he hauled himself to his feet and joined the others at the door. By now everyone was watching. Including Jesus.

"Problem?" Peter asked.

Matthew hurriedly explained why Isaac was there.

Peter turned importantly to Isaac.

"I'm afraid Jesus is seeing no one until after the Passover," he said.

Before Isaac could protest Jesus spoke, his voice a hoarse whisper.

"It's all right Peter. Let him in."

Thomas helped Jesus to his feet.

"Shall we walk in the garden? I could do with some fresh air," Jesus suggested.

Isaac hurried forward and helped to support the frail body of the man he had come all the way from his distant home to see.

"Thank you. I'm Isaac. I come from Arimethea, from Joseph," he started to explain.

Jesus nodded and smiled a welcome.

"I know who you are," he said.

Isaac looked around at the others who had joined them.

"I need to speak to you. In private," he told him.

Jesus looked at his friends and gently nodded his head, indicating that they should leave. Reluctantly they moved away. Jesus, supported on Isaac's arm, moved further into the garden.

Peter watched them go. 'Typical," he thought. 'I'm not good enough to talk with the great Isaac.'

He stood and looked blearily around.

He wished he could enjoy the scene: the huge moon, high above the horizon, the dark shadows that gave a clean, clear definition to the bushes and trees that covered most of the area. The warm night air was heavy with the scent of the herbs and flowers massed along the perimeter of the little garden.

All Peter was aware of was the frightening possibility that the Romans or the Sanhedrin might decide that now, while the people were preparing for the Festival of the Passover, would be the best time for them to terminate the call to insurrection broadcast by the followers of Jesus and, no doubt, recounted to them by the captured bandit, Barrabas.

Morosely Peter wandered back into the house and breached another keg of wine.

Isaac was distressed by the deterioration in the health of Jesus since their last meeting..

The cruel, hard light of the moon etched the illness and suffering into Jesus's thin face like scars made with a sharp chisel. It was only a few months since Isaac last met him and he had not expected to see the physical deterioration written so callously on the sick man's features.

"Sorry to be so insistent but…"

Jesus gave him a reassuring smile.

"Don't take any notice of Peter. He can be over-protective at times."

Jesus sunk carefully back into the shadows and beckoned Isaac to join him.

"Perhaps we should go back into the house. The night air.." Isaac began.

Jesus silenced him with a chuckle.

"Even you're doing it now?"

Isaac looked around at the other men, still trying to act as if they hadn't a care in the world but fixing their undivided attention on Jesus. They were used to seeing the distress of Jesus after a long walk in the desert and could understand it. What they weren't prepared for was his apparent collapse since they arrived in Jerusalem. And in spite of the overtly overwhelming reception they received on their arrival in the city, they were conscious of an undercurrent of hostility. The fact that no one from the temple had been there to welcome them hadn't gone unnoticed. Jesus was well known in Jerusalem and in spite of resistance from some of the older, more religiously entrenched, members of the Sanhedrin they had expected some sort of acknowledgement. They were beginning to have doubts about the advisability of allowing themselves to be virtually trapped in the city if anything should go wrong.

"How's Joseph?" Jesus asked, changing the subject. Weighing Isaac up, trying to gauge how he would take the preposterous idea that he was about to lay on him.

"Fine. He's in Jerusalem, I believe." Isaac answered slowly, trying to figure out how he was going to put over his story without sounding too ridiculous.

"So I heard," Jesus said absently.

He had to be careful. What he was about to ask of a man he hardly knew wasn't something to bring up casually in polite conversation. But he had to convince the hard-headed merchant that what he wanted was not only important but the only way out.
Jesus began cautiously, "I'm going to tell you something, something you'd probably rather not know but you're the only one here that can make a difference now."

Isaac leaned forward urgently.

"I'm sorry but I have to tell you something important." he said.

Jesus held up his hand to silence him.

"Please, I'm not sure how long I can go on. You must listen ..." he said with a great effort.

"But…." Isaac tried to speak but Jesus ignored him.

"At any moment the temple guard will arrive with instructions to take me prisoner," Jesus stated flatly.

It was enough to keep Isaac's attention focused.

"I want you to promise me something!"

Isaac looked around, tried to get Peter's attention but Jesus didn't want the big man in on the conversation.

"Judas..." he began and Isaac swung around to face him.

"So Robin was right!" Isaac said loudly.

A couple of the men nearby looked across but Jesus smiled reassuringly at them and they lost interest.

"Who's Robin?" Jesus asked.

"Someone I found in the desert. He's the reason I'm here. He said there was danger for you here and thought it was something to do with Judas," Isaac explained excitedly.

"I don't see how he could know what I planned to do. I only told Judas earlier today," Jesus said in a puzzled voice.

"Robin has known about Judas going to the authorities for about thirty days. At first he wasn't sure exactly what was going to happen. Just that it was going to happen during the run up to the Passover and that Judas would betray you to Pilate."

Quickly Isaac filled in the gaps of how he had been persuaded to make the journey to Jerusalem. How Joseph had been persuaded to back the venture.

Jesus was amazed but accepted the situation pragmatically.

"He was only half right. I told Judas to bring the guards," Jesus said simply.

Isaac looked at him in amazement.

"But why?"

As if in answer Jesus coughed and sunk further back into the shadows.

"I can't last much more than a couple of days..." The voice from the shadows was thick and congested. "If I die now our cause is lost! If I'm executed I will be remembered as a martyr. It's as simple as that."

"I'm sure something can be...," Isaac tried to offer hope but was cut short.

"Nothing can be done. Accept that and what I want you to do will be easier," Jesus told him.

Isaac sat in silence.

Jesus accepted it as acquiescence.

"Most people mistake James for me," Jesus chuckled. "Though once they know us they soon recognise their mistake. But that's all to the good. When I die I want you to get Joseph to bury me in his cemetery at Gethsemane."

He stopped and thought about what he was going to say for a few seconds. When he spoke again it was in a whisper.

"When I am dead I want you to go to James. Convince him that the only way to save himself and our ideals is to do exactly what I say."

Again Jesus lapsed into silence.

Isaac was about to speak when Jesus leaned forward and grabbed his hand.

"Tell him to let a few days elapse and then to take my body from the grave and say that the prophesies of Ezekiel have been fulfilled. That I have risen from the dead and that I am the true Messiah."

Jesus sank back into the shadows.

It was Isaac's turn for silence.

"But... how will...?" he stammered, overwhelmed by what was being asked of him.

"Only this lot here and a few others know what I look like. And it's not in their interest to talk," Jesus said, faintly, almost at the end of his tether.

"You mean...?" Isaac whispered.

Jesus nodded.

"James will take my place!"

Chapter 37

Robin lay in the thick bushes and tried to ignore the discomfort of the chill night air on his sweat-covered body. Compared with the excruciating pain he had known over the last few weeks, the present discomfort was almost welcome but it did have a depressing effect. He looked at his companions. They were an assorted lot. Little Naomi, kneeling beside him, silent, unmoving, a black outline in the waxing moonlight.

Naomi's stillness was counter-pointed by Mary Magdalene. The energetic courtesan found it difficult to just sit and wait. She regretted the stupidity that had led her into the uncomfortable, nocturnal adventure.

"Judas!" she told herself mockingly. "Judas! Of course it's all untrue!"

Mary looked across at Robin and caught him watching her. She was about to tell him that she didn't believe him any longer and wanted to cut out when her servant, who was hidden on the edge of the track, hissed a warning. Instinctively the little party crouched down. There was a rattle of a kicked pebble skittering across the rocky path. A slap of leather sandals and the rustle of garments told them that someone was approaching from the direction of Joseph's house, now the headquarters of Jesus. If it was Judas the nervous waiting was over and Robin's insane insistence on intercepting him, justified.

Mary moved forward stealthily so that she was beside her manservant. She was the only one who could make a positive identification. Robin's brief glimpse of the young Canaanite had been confused by the sudden upsurge in the ego of Haddaq that resulted in the mental cripple taking over for a while. The traveller was opposite their hiding place before Mary laid a restraining hand on the man beside her and relaxed. The stranger was just someone on his way home, whistling softly between clenched teeth to ward off the fear that travel at night in a city filled with strangers evoked.

Mary slid back and pulled the extra cloak she had taken from her manservant, around her shoulders, and shivered noisily. When Robin didn't take any notice she dragged herself to her knees in front of him.

"Look. This is pointless," she said. "You are probably just upset and it makes you imagine things." Fussily she pulled the front of her robe together. "Now let's go home and get a good night's sleep. In the morning we can go up to the house and talk it over with Jesus and James. If there is anything in what you fear they will sort it out," she coaxed.

Slowly Robin shook his head.

"I'm right. Tomorrow will be too late. Believe me - if we leave now, Jesus will die and the world will go into a future of terror and genocide the like of which has never before been seen!"

Robin delivered the words heavily, a world of terror and torment thickening and blunting his voice.

It convinced Mary that further argument was useless.

Depressed and frightened she pulled the cloak close and settled back. Silence descended on the surrounding area, even the night noises of the insects stilled by the presence of the waiting humans.

Robin sat and relished his new found lucidity. Since he had met Jesus and lost the mental block that gave the Haddaq personality a hold on Robin's reasoning mind, he had not had a moment to sit and let his old personality fully catch up with him. His present position he accepted. He remembered his reason for wanting to alter Christ's destiny and how he insisted on using the time/space regressor to try and do it. Something they hadn't counted on was the fact that the thought-module, finding a home in a brain without the strength to fight against its influence, would become independent of the transmitted brain-pattern. The brain in the new host would have its own survival instinct. It would grow without regard for but with the knowledge and ambitions of the originator, in the environment it inhabited. Robin found it rather surprising that he had no wish to become part of the prime Robin Firth personality. And that was in spite of the fact that the body that housed him was weak and ugly and unable to come near to fulfilling the demands he would put on it.

It was a matter of survival.

The Haddaq body was the only tangible evidence of his actual existence. His memories of another life, as vivid and practical as they appeared, were only a mental process that he was privy to but could not prove to be actual.

What did remain was his unassailable knowledge of what he wanted to do.

A touch on his arm brought him back to the present.

The moon had cleared the dull horizon and was climbing rapidly into the cloud-scudded sky. The cloud shadows raced with furtive speed, hugging the contours and outlines of the undulating ground. Naomi put her finger to her lips for silence and pointed up the trail. Clearly coming down the hill towards them was the white-robed figure of a man. He was in a hurry. A flowing galabia flopped about his hurrying feet in nervous agitation. Again Mary slid forward for a better view but now the light was so good that she was able to recognise the lithe build and the tight curled hair of Judas long before he approached their hiding place. Keeping low she slid back to Robin.

"It's him - Judas! What do we do now?"

Adrenalin pumped into Robin's veins giving him an unaccustomed strength. He pushed Mary brusquely aside and crawled forward to where her servant sat waiting for orders. Robin watched the approaching figure and tried to decide what he should do. He didn't think that a reasoned argument would carry the day. Whatever motive was guiding Judas on to betray his master wasn't going to crumble under the pressure of a few castigating words in the moonlight. Robin wished he had given this part of the operation more thought before. The trouble was that everything was so new to him. He had been too subverted by the miracles happening to him to give serious thought to the way to obtain a satisfactory outcome for their present operation.

Mary solved the problem for him.

As Judas approached she stepped out onto the path and waited. Seeing the sudden appearance of the cloaked figure, Judas hesitated.

Mary pushed back her hood and smiled. The white moonlight enhanced her beauty. The perfect white oval of her face was highlighted and embellished by her wide perfectly shaped lips and almond eyes.

"Hello Judas," she said, her voice a low purr. In spite of his depression, caused by what he was about to do, Judas's smile was instantaneous and ingenuous.

"Mary!" he laughed. "What are you doing out here at this time of night? You nearly scared me to death."

He came forward and greeted her enthusiastically. Judas was aware of the friendship between Jesus and Mary Magdalene.

There might be a way to avoid thc tasteless mission that Jesus had sent him on.

"Where are *you* going - I would have thought was more to the point?" Mary answered coolly. "It's a funny time to be heading into town on your own."

There was something in Mary's voice that warned Judas that the meeting wasn't the coincidence it seemed.

He frowned.

"I have to deliver a message for Jesus," he offered by way of explanation.

Mary walked farther into the road turning the youth's back to where Robin was hiding.

"To the guard commander?" Mary suggested.

Surprised Judas blurted out, "Yes!"

Mary nodded solemnly.

"And what message could Jesus possibly want delivered to the guard commander at this time of night?" she asked in a reasonable tone.

Judas shrugged his shoulders.

"I can't tell you that. He made me promise to tell no-one!"

"Not even James, Judas?" Mary persisted.

"No. He said only I was to know what was happening!"

Judas was beginning to get angry.

"Look, I have to go or it will be too late."

Before he could move, Robin stepped out of the bushes. Startled by the new arrival Judas peered at him closely.

"I know you. You are the friend of Isaac's that's been making all the strange predictions. What are you doing here?" Robin walked over to stand by Mary.

"It's all over, Judas!" Robin told him. "We know what you are about to do."

Angry now, Judas was looking to justify the feeling of guilt he was trying to hide.

"What of it? It's nothing to do with you. Who are you - anyway - eh? The last time I saw you, you were frothing at the mouth and babbling like a madman. Not like a madman you ARE a madman. Now get out of my way. I'm in a hurry!"

Judas tried to push Robin aside but Mary held on to his arm. Before he could break away Mary's servant got into the action. The big Nubian rose from the shrubs and looped a forearm like a steel hawser over the young man's head and picked him up by the neck. Judas tried to lash out with his feet but his assailant didn't flinch. Blows to the ribs with his elbows had no effect. He could feel himself weakening as the hard muscle across his throat cut off the air to his heaving lungs. In front of him he could see the figures of his three tormentors, the diminutive, black clad Naomi, Mary, white and wanton in the aphrodisiac moon - and the madman! In frustration he lashed out with his feet in a vain effort to hurt one of them in payment for what they were doing to him. The effort of kicking drove his head back and it thudded with a sickening squelch into the face of the man behind him. For the first time he felt the arm relax. Judas didn't wait for an invitation. He again drove his head back and felt it make jarring contact. Success spurred him on.

In mad convulsions he crashed his head backwards, driven to greater efforts as he felt the restraining arms shift and move to protect the vandalised face. Judas expedited his escape with a hard smash to the manservant's solar plexus with his elbow. Robin moved forward to restrain the panicking boy but was easily felled with a blow to the head. Mary tried to block his way but also got a punch in the face for her trouble. Judas looked quickly at the three moaning bodies on the ground. For a second he was tempted to stop and explain that what he was doing was on the expressed instruction of Jesus. But his temper got the better of him. Reluctantly he told himself that he would do just what he was told. He didn't care what people said. Jesus told him to do something that he didn't understand. He wasn't trusted with an explanation. Now these people appeared out of the night with accusations and recriminations and half killed him without giving him a chance to explain.

All right!

He would deliver Jesus's message to the guards and then leave. If they really wanted him back they could come and get him. If they didn't, he wouldn't care. He could do without them all.

Judas's moment of indecision was his undoing. He had disregarded the slight figure of Naomi. As he turned to continue his journey down the trail she hit him, hard, in the back of the legs with the full force of her body. Judas staggered, wind-milling wildly in an effort to stay upright. Naomi had her arm wrapped around the youth's legs in a grip that she did not intend to loosen without a struggle. Inevitably Judas lost the battle to keep his balance and crashed heavily into the bushes at the side of the path. Naomi went down with him, her head buried in the backs of his thighs, her arms and legs restricting his movement. Judas tried to knock Naomi from her position of vantage with blows to the head. It wasn't easy. Because of her position behind him he couldn't get enough force in his punches to have effect. He rolled over so that his legs were across the lightweight girl. Judas was now beyond reason, fear, guilt, temper and the nightmarish attack under the moon had driven his mind beyond reason. All he wanted to be was free. Free from the devils in human form attacking him without cause. He pulled his feet up, easily pulling the girl forward, and then crashed them down with all his force on her defenceless body.

Judas felt her grip break.

He scrambled free and aimed a kick at Naomi's rising body. It caught her full in the stomach and with a thin scream she crashed backwards onto the path. As Judas turned to run he caught a movement out of the corner of his eye but before he could move a solid weight hit him full in the chest, driving him backwards. He looked down at the battered face glaring up at him with hate clenched teeth and wanted to cry. It wasn't what he wanted. Not this animal action of hurting each other. He wished he had time to explain. The white moon slashed across the heavens in a wild arch as he was carried backwards by the weight of the charge. A savage blow struck him in the back as he crashed down on one of the boulders thrusting from the ground. Instinctively he tried to turn sideways so that he could bend away from the weight bearing down with terrible force on his spine. He tried to push the man off, to explain the mind-ripping pain. All that came from his throat was a blood-chilling gurgle.

Slowly the victor stood up and looked down at the broken body. Frightened by what he had done he bent down and eased the lifeless body of Judas off the fatal anvil. Mary, the first to recover, bent down beside the grotesquely sprawling figure. She knew instinctively that Judas was dead but listened to his chest for silent confirmation. She looked around for Robin.

Robin was kneeling down beside the unconscious Naomi. Gently he pulled aside her cloak so that she could breathe. In the bright overhead light she looked even younger than her thirteen years. Tenderly he touched the livid mark on the side of her face where she had taken the force of Judas's fist. She seemed to be breathing, a little fast and noisily, but strongly enough to assume her injuries, though extensive and painful, were not likely to be fatal. He placed his cloak under her head and went across to where Mary Magdalene was still kneeling beside the dead Judas.

Robin sank down beside her.

"What do we do now?" she asked in a hopeless voice.

Robin shook his head, his wits scattered by the mindless violence of the last few seconds.

It was Mary, conditioned by her life on the edge of raw passion, who made the decision.

"Take the body and hide it in the bushes," she ordered her servant.

Somehow that didn't seem right to Robin. He started to protest as the Nubian bent down and picked up the body of Judas and walked into the area covered with shrub. Mary waved him impatiently to silence.

"How's the girl?" she asked.

Robin looked towards where Naomi lay. She was still unconscious.

"I think she is alright. At least she will be. Judas knocked her out," he said. Mary gave a wry look towards the bushes.

"I'd say he got at least as good as he gave. I just hope you were right. When the Romans find him there is going to be a hell of a stink. Judas was well in with the Sanhedrin and the priests are not going to let his death go without complaining to the Romans about the break-down of law and order."

Her servant re-joined them.

"Did you hide him?" she asked.

He ducked his head.

"As well as I could, my Lady," he affirmed.

"Alright! Well - let's get away from here before someone sees us and starts poking their nose in where it's not wanted."

Mary Magdalene went and knelt beside Naomi and checked her condition briefly.

She nodded her head as she stood up.

"She'll be alright. A few bruises and maybe a broken rib or two but I've seen worse after the soldiers have been on leave."

She signalled to the servant.

"Pick her up. I have a friend on this side of the city. We can stay there for the night and sort everything out in the morning. It will be better if we stay out of the way until we see what happens and we also won't run the risk of being seen by a patrol who might be curious about someone running around in the night with an unconscious girl."

Robin shook his head gravely. He saw the sense of what Mary proposed. But he wasn't thinking a lot about the possible repercussions of their night's work. The feeling of elation growing in him ousted all other emotions.

He had saved Jesus!

By his action that night, no matter how crude or violent, he had saved the Messiah! Now Jesus could work on for many years, teaching, healing and consolidating!

It would mean that in the future there would be no possibility of wrong concepts distorting the ideology. There would be no factions or schisms based on different interpretations of inaccurately remembered facts only written down hundreds of years after Christ's death. Now the Epistles of St. James, Jesus's younger brother, could be written with authority and perception under the influence and intellectual superiority of Jesus.

When they neared the safe house of Mary's friend, she went ahead to prepare the way. Robin was only vaguely aware of helping to put Naomi, now conscious and in pain, to bed. Mary saw him settled down and then went off to bathe the wounds of her servant.

Robin lay on his back staring at the ceiling above him. Sleep eluded him as he thought of the exciting events of the night. Several times he almost dozed off but was jerked awake by the feeling that someone was calling him. Each time he listened he could hear nothing and decided it was just his taunt nerves playing tricks with his idling brain.

It was dawn when he finally dropped off. Far away he heard a cock crow to the lightening sky. He was amused by the thought that the cock would now no longer take its place in history. It no longer announced the first cock crow that would have accused Peter of denying Jesus thrice. As he slipped further into the bank of sleep he again became aware of the figure sitting in the room countless millions of miles away in space and thousands of years in time. He let the strength of the image grow. It no longer threatened him. He was master of his own soul and body. Robin studied Robin Firth sitting in the transmitter room of the future. He could see the taut concentration of his body and the dishevelled state of his clothes. Behind him the walls shimmered with reflected light. It puzzled him.

It wasn't a part of his Robin Firth memory.

Suddenly he wanted to tell the figure sitting silently in the future that everything was all right.

That Jesus would live!

He opened his mind but instead of imparting information his mind was engulfed with a tide of new facts. The new, updated thought-module that Robin Firth had transmitted had at last found a home. Too late Robin picked up the thought that had hung in the ether waiting for him to let his mind relax enough to receive it.

As the Robin Firth updated information filled his mind Robin began to cry.

Clearly he saw the futility, the criminality of killing Judas!

He saw the meaning of the cross, and its binding, grinding and chastising effect on succeeding generations. As he scooped the thoughts into his mind he also saw that from that moment on history would not be the same. Different religions with other ethics and ideology would rise and dominate. Whatever happened in the future it would be a world completely unknown to the world of Christian influence.

Even as the realisation of the enormity of what he had done hit him, history changed.

Chapter 38

Jesus waited out the evening with growing foreboding. As the hours crept by the realisation that Judas had not played his part in the scheme became apparent. The willpower that sustained him and buoyed him up for the final dramatic act drained slowly away with the hours. Matthew put him to bed. He made no attempt to discuss the plans for the morning. He could see Jesus was exhausted. He smiled and shut his eyes. Through half-closed lids he watched Matthew go quietly from the room. Tears forced a way through his lashes and dripped onto the cushion under his head.

It was all over!

His last chance to redress the disaster caused by his illness had faded. For some reason Judas hadn't brought the guards and given Jesus the satisfaction of a meaningful death!

Jesus could feel life dropping from him but he didn't care. He was paying for the strength that he had mustered for the last dramatic act of wilful self-destruction.

Now it was out of his hands.

He tasted the familiar salt of blood in his throat.

A pressure built up in his chest and seemed to spread in a cold pain to his head. A great, barking cough crashed from his throat to be smothered in the blanket. Terrified, Jesus felt the hot blood spew from his mouth and nostrils and spread across his chest. He tried to cry out but the only sound was the gurgle of blood in his throat. The terror passed immediately and was replaced with the calm serenity of death.

James, arriving in the early hours with their mother Mary, who had only come to see Jesus because of James's insistence, found Jesus lying on his cot of lamb skins, black congealing blood from his ruptured lungs spreading through the wool and covering his galabia. Mary, going in before James, took one look at the terrible scene and fell to the floor in a dead faint. The movement disturbed the thousands of flies feeding on the blood. They arose in a black angrily buzzing cloud soon to resettle on the white face. James swore and dragged his mother out of the room before returning and driving off the flies.

Tears streamed down his face as he sank down beside the still body of his dead brother.

Now there would be no bright future. They would try to repair the gap; to regroup and re-educate the peasants. But it would only be a limited success.

Timing was everything.

Now was the time for the big push: the consolidating effort that would carry them into the future.

They had based everything on Jesus.

And Jesus was dead!

Epilogue

As James stood in the small, fly-infested room in Jerusalem looking down at the bloodied mortal remains of his brother, Jesus the Nazarene, the future world of Christianity vanished. The world of Roman Catholicism, Protestantism, Seventh Day Eventists, Jehovah's Witness, Jeanne d'Arc, Billy Graham, Albert Schweitzer, Father Hullahan, the Reverend Paisley, Christian Constantine, Elizabeth and Mary, Pope John Paul II, Cliff Richard, General Gordon and Father Christmas - vanished.

And with it Robin Firth.

All that remained of the world shaped by the pressure of the guilt-laden cross was a tiny gossamer of electrons stranded in time.

But the thought-module was only sustained by the immense power radiating from the space/time modulator. When the future of technology vanished to be replaced by the religious conservatism of Islam in the alternative world brought about by the ignominious death of Jesus, the thought-module originated by Robin Firth and supplemented by the memories and actions of Haddaq/Robin in the time of Jesus, was catapulted through time and space to take its rightful place in the complicated frequency structure of its natural time.

It took Robin a while to realise that he had been returned to his own, but radically changed, time.

At first he was afraid that the weak body of Haddaq had relapsed and had another break down. He prodded in the recesses of his awareness to try and find a trace of his dark host.

Nothing!

He was without tactile sensation. It was as if he were only a thought adrift in the universe.

The idea sobered him.

Of course!

The full flood of realisation crashed over him. What the thought-module originator, Robin Firth, had managed to relay to him in those last few seconds, had happened. His interference in the skein of time had knitted together a new future.

And somehow he was still a part of it.

Robin was aware of a jumble of thoughts, fear, pain, confusion, dashing with growing strength at the secured stockade of his own identity. He wasn't frightened or confused. It was nothing like the awakening in the crippled body of Haddaq. Now he seemed to be omniscient. To understand exactly what was going on and able to meet the challenge without emotion. He let his thought reach out and touch the other mind. The shock to Cassio was tremendous and Robin felt his mind reel and skirt the borders of insanity. Almost apologetically Robin withdrew. The last thing he wanted was to find himself trapped again in a Haddaq-like body. He needed at least partial control over his new host's mind so that he could communicate with the world about him.

It should be easier now.

Even if the world of Christianity had vanished, the two thousand years of progress would have produced a degree of sophistication that would be able to cope with the evidence of the possibility of time warping that he would produce.

Again Robin reached out but this time with circumspection, touching his host's mind gently, stroking it with soothing thoughts. Gradually impressions flowed into his awareness.

He saw the hard, technically immature world of Islam.

It was a shock that had him searching with frantic haste through the memory of the comatose Cassio for some comfort; for maybe a concept, an idea that had survived his temporal interference.

There was nothing!

Just the implacable native-hatred of the Pict police, and the fear of falling into the merciless hands of the Islamic Inquisitors.

Robin needed to gather other information to corroborate the disturbing facts that he received from Cassio. His experiences in the Haddaq body came to his aid. The motor centres of his new host were inactive, cut off by the heavily concussed brain. Robin could see no chance of the Cassio personality reactivating the body for a long time to come. The head injury he had received was too severe. Although the injury had not damaged the brain to any crippling extent, it had scrambled the nerve system. Robin forced his way past the neural barriers. Shock-waves of pain hit him and he hastily withdrew. He needed control without having to suffer the pain that his host-brain was subject to. Robin reached out and tried again. Gradually, searching, probing he found a way past the tender nerves and took a restricted control of the Cassio body.

Robin was still hampered by the random stirring of the host personality. He could have short-circuited it entirely but he needed a link up with the Cassio memory to orientate him in the strange mad world he had seen there. Satisfied with his control he forced open his eyes.

Pain hit him again but he reacted quickly and cut it off.

He cut out his surroundings as he carefully took control of the motor centres of his host's body once more.

Now there were more areas of pain and less of control. One leg was completely useless and the arms moved uncertainly and only with the greatest difficulty. At last he managed the complicated business of sitting up. He propped his back against the bottom of the stone steps and looked around. In the dim light it was difficult to see. Robin suddenly was aware of the dead silence. For a moment he thought it was the absence of sound in the underground dungeon. Then he realised that in his effort to master the mobility controls of his host body he had short-circuited the audio. He found the brain area that he required and tapped in.

Instant sound!

For a moment he thought there was some malfunction. The only sound he was picking up was low frequency, a blend of deep guttural noises that were meaningless. He tried again to make some sense out of his surroundings. All he could see was a jumble of bodies, some dormant, some restless, strewn across the cold stone floor.

A shriek crashed across the low pitched drum of sound.

Startled Robin forced his head slowly around to local the source of the sound.

Sitting at the side of the room a man stared at the frantically waving stumps of his arms and screamed with mindless intensity.

The meaning of the words of the man in the mortuary came to Robin. He had been placed in a room full of men sentenced to death. But first they were being made to suffer for their crimes. A terrible suffering which only the sweet release of death could soothe.

All the men in the room had suffered some form of amputation at the sword of the fanatical religious executioner. Now they were being made to wait out the night in agony until the final part of the sentence was completed in the early morning. Knowledge fed form into the unbelievable scene.

Lying around were bodies with arms and legs roughly amputated. The stumps dipped into vats of hot tar to stop the bleeding. Infection wasn't a problem. They would all be dead before it could be. Some of the lucky ones had already died, their bodies unable to take the shock. A few had gone out of their minds and were mercifully separated from the pain and horror of their surroundings.

Robin looked them over.

Initial shock had been replaced with nothing more than curiosity. He accepted that he must die!

It was his punishment!

But before he died he wanted to know what had happened. He wanted to know more than was available to him in the restricted area of action of his host's mind. Cassio had been living a life of subterfuge and self-effacement for so long that outside the stark dangers of his own profession he was ignorant - especially of the past. And Robin needed this knowledge. He looked once more around the cellar. He saw several men propped up against the wall who appeared to be conscious. Awkwardly and with great difficulty he manoeuvred his host body across to the nearest man.

Before he spoke he could see that it was pointless. The tortured man had withdrawn into a serene world of his own making. The smile on his face belied the horror of the blackened stumps were his arms had been cut off above his elbows. Impervious to the shrieks and moans Robin slowly circled the room. Nowhere could he find anyone lucid enough to tell him what he had to know. The thought that he would die in ignorance shocked him. It seemed impossible that he, who had engineered the most enormous crime in history, should die without knowing exactly what he had done.

He sank down by the steps.

A cool, firm voice startled him.

"Is there any water, do you think?"

Robin looked quickly around.

Lying a few feet from him was the truncated body of what had been a powerfully built man. His head, appearing unnaturally large on his limbless body, was twisted around towards Robin. Robin slid towards him and looked into the wide controlled eyes in the strong bearded face.

"No - I'm sorry. There isn't any water I'm afraid." Robin apologised for their gaoler.

The man nodded.

"Pity. I'd given up the idea but when I saw you moving about with arms and legs intact I thought there might be a chance."

His control was utter and complete. In spite of the dreadful mutilations he managed to maintain control of his mind and exorcise the pain. Robin looked down at him. He wanted to ask if there was anything he could do but hated the banality of the question.

The man gave him a comforting smile.

"Perhaps I should introduce myself. I'm Michael Kleinberg. Last of the British Rabbis. I should have left when I lost my congregation. I stayed and now it's too late. It doesn't matter..."

For the first time his face betrayed emotion. Angrily he wiped it aside, afraid to admit anything that might erode his iron control.

Robin sat beside him and pushed the hair from his eyes.

It was fate!

Without thinking it through Robin was convinced that this meeting, in the dark dungeon on the eve of a horrible death, was pre-ordained.

"My name was Robin Firth," he said carefully.

The Rabbi looked worried. For a moment he thought that the comforting stranger was insane. As Robin began to tell his story the Rabbi forgot their surroundings and listened with a gratifying attention.

Kleinberg kept silent until the end when Robin finished telling him about his return to the present, a present totally alien to the present that he had left as Robin Firth.

Kleinberg nodded.

"From what you say you brought it on yourself, in the fullest meaning of the phrase."

Robin agreed.

"Yes. But what I want to know is why and how it happened. Why the teachings, the ideals of Jesus vanished without a trace."

Kleinberg shook his head slowly in denial.

"No. Not without a trace," he said.

Robin looked at him stone-faced, his inadequate control of his host body concealing the excitement the Rabbi's words produced.

"Not completely?" he asked. "What do you mean? Are there places where Christianity exists?"

Kleinberg sadly shook his head.

"No. I'm afraid not. From what you say we could do with it. But no!"

Kleinberg frowned in an effort to drag from his memory the few surviving stories that involved the man Jesus that had been handed down. In the dark, evil smelling room, lit by the feeble flame of guttering tar flares and made hellish by the bizarre orchestration of suffering men, the doomed Rabbi, the last remnant of a once dominant people, spoke softly to the spark frozen in another time continuum trapped in the broken body of an inadequate spy.

"In the testaments there is a minor book written by James the Just. The main reason that it has survived is that it gives contemporary account of Simon Peter."

Kleinberg looked at the expressionless face beside him but got no response. It didn't matter. His people had always been great storytellers. With or without an audience, it made no difference. It diverted his mind from the horror of his situation and if it helped the tortured soul beside him it was an added bonus that God might take into account. Kleinberg smiled to himself in silent derision. After all this he still believed in God. He realised that it was this madness that was sustaining him. Making him live; a filthy, obscene remnant of a man, glorifying his Creator by clinging to obtuse standards of human behaviour when he should be following the example of the poor demented creatures around him. He hoped the man who had been Robin Firth could hear him.

"When Peter rallied the crowds and marched them north after the Passover, Pontius Pilate, the Governor at the time, decided to make an example of him. A squad was dispatched to arrest him and bring him back for trial. But Pilate left it too late.

"By the time they caught up with Peter and his followers they had reached the mountainous country where the avenging forces of Aliph were waiting. An Angel had appeared to him as he waited outside Jerusalem ready to take the city in the name of the Prophet Jesus. The Angel told him that Jesus had offended in the eyes of God and was through and done. Aliph was told to go to the mountains and there Peter would come with the Children of Israel and a great victory would be won over the Romans.

"The battle was recorded by James the Just who later became one of the leaders of Peter's council of Twelve."

Again Kleinberg stopped and looked anxiously at the slumped figure beside him. Slowly the head turned, in small uncoordinated jerks, as Robin forced Cassio's failing body to respond to his commands.

"Jesus?" he asked. "What happened to Jesus?"

Kleinberg shook his head.

"I don't know. Nothing else is known about him other than he was a part of Peter's movement and was sometimes referred to simply as '*The Healer*'."

Robin let his head droop.

Kleinberg stayed silent for a while. He was experiencing a feeling of exaltation that spread through his body like a strengthening spirit. He was at the centre of the universe. About him crashed and soared sounds and chords not of the ordinary mundane world. He welcomed them, let them take over his body and make it whole and strong. Deliciously, like a gourmet savouring his favourite dish, Kleinberg held the beckoning infinity at bay while he fulfilled his obligation to the man at his side.

"But Peter upset God. He was not content to dwell in the land of his fathers, to fulfil the prophets of Israel. He declared himself Moses re-incarnate and led the people, without the word of God, to Rome. God, in his anger, smote Peter as he stood on the bow of his ship, throwing him into the water where he drowned. With the Forces of

Peter decimated by the wrath of God the desert tribes were able to move in and take over the Holy Land. God's anger was awful in its intensity and he ordained that his chosen people would wander on the face of the earth for eternity, reviled and hated by all humanity, until the crystal thought of salvation was once more amongst us on the day of the Death of Israel."

Kleinberg had to fight harder to resist the enticement of the music now. He watched the swirling colours pulse and race to the rhythm of the universe. He saw Robin's eyes, bright and filled with wild hope, fixed upon him and he let the music lift him up and take him.

Robin looked down at the remains of his last friend. There was nothing he could do for him. He lay back against the steps and withdrew his connection with the dying host body. In the silent, unfeeling depths he was able to think about what the Rabbi had told him without distraction.

When the executioner took him from the cell in the early hours of a cool summer morning he neither felt the sun nor heard the crowd gathered to watch the execution. When the axe flashed in the morning sun it dismembered only the insentient body of Cassio Dio.

But while it destroyed with the callous imprecision of the sword it also created with the inviolable perfection of the cosmos.

Into the brutal world was released the intangible web of neutrons that in their precise juxtaposition gave promise of a better world.

-THE END-

About the Author: Ingrid Pitt

Ingrid Pitt was born in Poland on 21 November 1937 to Jewish parents. During World War II she was imprisoned with her mother in a Nazi concentration camp, reuniting with her father after the war's end.

Following a spell with the Berliner Ensemble, Ingrid settled in London at the end of the 1960s, becoming a familiar face in film and television including parts in *Doctor Zhivago*, *Where Eagles Dare*, *Ironside*, *Jason King*, *The Vampire Lovers*, *Countess Dracula*, *The Wicker Man*, *Doctor Who* and *Sea of Dust*.

During that time she became an international sex symbol and earned the informal accolade as 'Queen of Horror' for her appearances for the likes of Hammer Films.

In the 1980s Ingrid turned her hand to writing, publishing ten books in her lifetime including fiction (*Cuckoo Run*, *The Perons*), children's fiction (*Bertie the Bus*) a series of acclaimed non-fiction books (the *Beside Companion* series) and her autobiography, *Life's A Scream.*

With her husband, Tony Rudlin, Ingrid developed a number of screenplays, and a *Doctor Who* serial, *'The Macros'* – which was released on CD in 2010 by Big Finish.

At the time of her death on 23 November 2010 she had just completed work on a second volume of memoirs, entitled *The Hammer Xperience.*

Annul Domini is the first of several previously unpublished books by Ingrid Pitt to be released by Avalard Publishing.

Her official website is at www.pittofhorror.com, and a website containing much of her work as a columnist is at www.ingridpitt.net.

Avalard Publishing Presents

THE INGRID PITT COLLECTION

ANNUL DOMINI
DRACULA WHO...?
CUCKOO RUN
PIGEON TANGO
ICE PHOENIX

Original novels from Ingrid Pitt

www.avalardpublishing.com
www.ingridpitt.net

Coming soon from Avalard Publishing

SHANE BRIANT
THE WEBBER AGENDA

In the tradition of, le Carré, Forsyth and Follett, Avalard Publishing is proud to present for the first time in the United Kingdom, Shane Briant's best-selling espionage novel, *The Webber Agenda.*

Set in post-Cold War Europe, *The Webber Agenda* is an iconic spy thriller, posing the question *'What happened to the billions that funded the East German Secret Service, the Stasi, when the Berlin wall came down and East Germany collapsed?'*

In a relentless chase across Europe from Spain to Germany to England to France, to the breathtaking finale in Poland, the most powerful criminals in Europe know they must silence the one man who has the power to destroy them. Guy Cooper is a man that must be silenced.

The Webber Agenda was Shane Briant's debut novel, first published by Harper Collins (Australia) in 1995 where it became a best-seller. Not previously available outside Australia, Avalard Publishing are delighted to be bringing this exciting espionage thriller to the international audience it deserves. *The Webber Agenda* is sure to ensnare and delight thriller fans everywhere.

www.ingramcontent.com/pod-product-compliance
Lightning Source LLC
Chambersburg PA
CBHW081127300726
48982CB00005B/879

* 9 7 8 1 9 0 8 5 6 6 1 6 4 *